TABOO

Yoshe

www.urbanbooks.net

Urban Books
1199 Straight Path
West Babylon, NY 11704

ISBN- 13: 978-1-933967-80-6
ISBN- 10: 1-933967-80-3

First Printing January 2009
Printed in the United States of America

10 9 8 7 6 5 4 3

Distributed by Kensington Publishing Corp.
Submit Wholesale Orders to:
Kensington Publishing Corp.
C/O Penguin Group (USA) Inc.
Attention: Order Processing
405 Murray Hill Parkway
East Rutherford, NJ 07073-2316
Phone: 1-800-526-0275
Fax: 1-800-227-9604

Acknowledgments

First, I would like to dedicate this book to my beautiful man-child, Paul Anthony Miller, Jr., my loving mother, Mary A. Thomas. Thank you, Mommy, you are my strength and to my sis, Monica Turner, who knows me better than anyone else in the world.

I would like to thank God because without Him or His blessings, this would not have been possible. I would definitely like to give a shout-out to my mentor, Mark Anthony (M. Spark) for giving me the guidance, the support. I love you, cuz. You're my IDOL!! Kiss Sabine and the kids 4 me. My li'l big brother, Jay, for shelter from the storms. To my brother-in-law, Anthony, thanks for the support, Bruh and being a great uncle. To Daddy and Ada, see I told you so!! Duwanna and Yanni, love y'all! My Auntie, Delois Leary, thanks for spoiling me! To J. Shipman of HDM fame, thanks, Cap!! To my BFF, Raquel, thanks for keepin' me sane! To Brigitte, you always comes through for me. To my goddaughter, Breezy, you're the best! To Paul Sr., thanks for holdin' me down! To my soul sister, Teri, they hatin'!! To Crystal, you rollin' with me, right? To my special friend, D. Jones, it was fate that brought us together. To Bill Blast, my dude, for life. My BMF, Pooka, thanks for the shoulder! To Kim Marcell, for keepin' me laughin'! To T. Speights, you inspired me!! Last but not least, Y. Green, Jasmin, I will never forget y'all, love is love!! To Mr. Adams, may God touch your soul. To the CO's at OBCC and CPSU, hold y'all heads! To the female correction officers who fell victim, my heart goes out to you. Just remember those who judge don't matter and those who matter don't judge. Anyone else I didn't shout-out it was because I wrote too much already but you know who you are!!

Chapter One

SIERRA

Sierra hurriedly exited the female locker room. She didn't want to be late for roll call, which was located in the front of the facility's main control room, a large area that was protected by thick, glass partitions. An eight-year veteran of the New York City Department of Corrections, Corrections Officer Sierra Howell was rarely late for work, let alone roll call.

Sierra stood in formation with the ten officers that were reporting to work for the 5:00 AM to 1:00 PM tour. When a tall, handsome captain wearing a white uniform shirt with gold-collar brass stepped out of the control room, the officers stood at attention. The captain proceeded to inspect the array of officers to make sure they were in proper uniform. He purposely brushed past Sierra, making her cringe with disgust. The captain briefed the small roll call and dismissed them shortly after so that they could report to their respective posts. As Sierra walked toward the small window to retrieve her equipment, the captain approached her. He leaned over her, blowing in her ear. Sierra, who was taken by surprise, was visibly annoyed.

"Yes, Captain Simmons, may I help you?" Sierra asked as she rolled her eyes at him. Her voice dripped with sarcasm and frustration. Captain Lamont Simmons was Sierra's former boyfriend. They had broken up almost a year before after an intense three-year relationship.

"I was just making sure you was all right," Lamont answered. He slowly undressed her with his eyes.

Sierra sighed with irritation. She tried to calm herself down, not wanting to embarrass herself in front of the other officers. When she told Lamont off, she wouldn't need an audience.

"Lamont, don't worry about me. I'm cool. Worry about ya damn self," Sierra callously commented. She hoped her attitude toward him would make him go away. She was wrong.

Lamont chuckled softly. He found her resistance irresistible. "What up, Sierra? I know you ain't feelin' me no more but can't we at least be friends? I mean, damn, you keep givin' me da cold shoulder and it's been almost a year now!"

Sierra sucked her teeth. She knew that once a man hurt you the way Lamont had hurt her, they could never be friends.

"Whateva, negro! And how old is ya son? Do you think I need ta be friends wit'a man dat cheated on me wit' another woman and ta add insult ta injury, you got her pregnant? Please, Lamont, kiss my ass!"

Sierra's mouth was ruthless. A no-nonsense type of sister, she was one to be reckoned with. Although she had the tough exterior, she had a heart of gold until you tried to break it. Unfortunately, Lamont had chosen to do the latter.

Lamont looked around and was embarrassed by the stares of the remaining officers. This made him angry. "You know what, Sierra?" Lamont paused. "I'm fuckin' tired of kissin' ya ass! You wanna act like you wasn't lovin' da shit outta me when we was together when we both know da truth!"

Sierra batted her thick eyelashes while she calmly put her long hair in a loose ponytail. She couldn't believe this motherfucker had the nerve to get upset with her for his infidelities. "Oh, I was lovin' you ah-ight. It was obvious you wasn't lovin' me enough, you got a bitch fuckin' pregnant, you bastard! Now get out my face before I write you up fuh harassment!"

After the outburst, Lamont reluctantly knocked on the thick glass to summon one of the control-room staff to buzz him back inside. Sierra knew that on any given day, Lamont would have slapped the hell out of her for trying to humiliate him. She wanted to let him know that she was serious about their breakup. He violated her trust, so with that he was immediately removed from her cipher.

Sierra held her head up and much to her dismay, she turned around to be face-to-face with her childhood buddy turned nemesis, Monique Phillips. Monique had seen the whole thing transpire between Sierra and Lamont. Sierra knew she was waiting to leap like a lioness attacking her prey, by sinking her acrylic claws into Lamont.

"Well, well, well, if it ain't Miss Sierra Howell and Mr. Lamont Simmons with their soap opera! A little trouble in paradise, huh?" Monique purred from behind the glass partition, inside the control room. Sierra knew that sinister smile. Monique was up to no good.

Sierra flipped Monique the middle finger. She wasn't even going to entertain her. It was hard to believe that as children they were inseparable, growing up in Tilden Projects together in the rough streets of Brownsville. As time went on, though, Monique chose to run the streets and act like a whore. Monique's mom, Miss Ann, accepted a lot of disrespect from her daughter. On the other hand, Sierra's mother, Marjorie Howell, was not tolerating that type of behavior from her only daughter. Even though Sierra and Monique's relationship took a turn for the worst, their mothers remained close.

"Monique, gimme the damn equipment so I can go to my post!" Sierra exclaimed through clenched teeth. "I don't have time to deal with your shenanigans this mornin'!"

"Looky here, lil' girl, you need to watch yo' mouth! Don't

get a 'tude with me cause yo' man, Lamont, dissed yo' ass! Seems like a chick like you would be able to hold her man down so he wouldn't have to cheat!" Monique paused. "Oh, but then again, you not me!" Monique cackled as she placed Sierra's departmental equipment into a metal sliding tray.

Sierra huffed. Lord knew, she wanted to put her hands on Monique but she knew that wasn't going to solve anything. She was not going to allow some weave-wearing hussy to irritate her.

Sierra retrieved her equipment and nodded her head at Monique. "All righty, Monique, since you such an expert on how to fuck and suck a man, you can have da triflin' bastard. Y'all was made for each other! I'm out!" Sierra walked through the large door toward her post. Even though her morning started out with a little chaos, she was able to shut both Monique and Lamont down in a New York minute.

When Sierra arrived at her post, she relieved the officer on duty. Her duties consisted of supervising the AM feeding in her housing area. She had to make sure there was always enough food to feed all of the inmates in the housing area. Most of the inmates refused to get up early, exhausted from staying up all night, doing God knows what, so there was always more than enough food to go around.

While Sierra sat at the round plastic desk, looking through her logbook entries, she thought about her relationship with Lamont. They were the envy of most couples. Sierra remembered being so enamored with him, especially after their first date. He was a complete gentleman; he wined and dined her, and of course made passionate love to her anytime she wanted. She was happy to have a different flavor in her life. Normally she was attracted to the same type of brothers she had to babysit at work. With Lamont, she felt she was on the right track after dealing with numerous gangsters and hustlers. It wasn't every day that she could meet a brother who was fine as hell, physically fit, had a good job with benefits, own car and crib—the list was endless. She was beside herself when she realized that he still had the bad-boy swagger she loved. Sierra knew then that Lamont Terrell Simmons was the ultimate package.

The beginning stages of their relationship were wonderful. They would spend so much time together and he gave her almost anything she wanted. Being with the hottest guy at work also had its benefits. She never imagined she would have a meaningful relationship with anyone on the job, let alone someone in the same facility. They made their coworkers wonder how they remained so happy with each other because marriages and relationships were destroyed on that job. What she didn't realize at the time is that it was the people who sabotaged the relationships, not the Department of Corrections.

Sierra remembered that fateful day like it just happened. She just happened to be out on sick leave and had to report to the health management division at LeFrak. Before officers were to report back to work, they had to be cleared by the departmental physician. Sierra saw the physician and waited for her "return to duty" papers. She struck up a conversation with an attractive young woman who was fashionably dressed, visibly pregnant, and just happened to be a corrections officer too. The young woman was transferred to HMD until she went on maternity leave. Sierra felt a twinge of jealousy because she couldn't wait until she and Lamont had a child of their own.

The woman looked at the signed paperwork. "Oh, wow, what a coincidence!" the woman stated to Sierra. "My boyfriend is a captain in your jail. Shoot, I know you know him," she said, subconsciously rubbing her swollen belly.

Sierra smiled at her. "I just might. What's his name?"

"His name is Captain Simmons—Lamont Simmons. You know him?" she asked, innocently enough. Sierra looked the woman in the face to see if there was any sign of vindictiveness, to see if the woman knew who she was talking to. The girl was clueless!

Sierra was mortified but she maintained her composure. "Lam—I mean, Captain Simmons, oh yes, I do! He's a really great guy. Do me a favor, when you talk to him, tell him that Sierra Howell said congratulations. So when are you due?"

"I have three more months to go, girl! I can't wait to drop this load, though. This bouncin' baby boy is bouncin' my big ass all over the place. It's our first and Lamont can't wait. He's so excited!"

"Umm," Sierra asked. "What's your name again?" She needed a little more information but didn't want to be too obvious.

"Oh," the woman chuckled. "Deja Sutton. And ya name is Sierra Howell, right?"

Sierra looked at Deja with a slight smirk. "Yeah, Sierra Howell, that's right."

Sierra wished Deja well, immediately snatched her paperwork, and ran out of there like a bat out of hell. When she reached her truck, she threw up all over the driver's-side door of her BMW truck. When she could finally gather enough strength to open her car door, she screamed at the top of her lungs until they burned. "*Why me, God, why?*" she yelled, as passersby looked at her like she had lost her mind. At that moment, she had. She never would have expected Lamont to do this to her. She had such high expectations of him and their future. She came to the realization that a man was still a man, regardless of race, color or creed, a "good" guy or "thug," that they were all the fucking same. Why would Lamont play himself and mess around behind her back and then get someone pregnant? She played everything over and over in her head, wondering where did she go wrong, what did she do or not do to make him fall into the arms of another woman? Sierra sighed and came to the conclusion that it didn't matter anymore. She would never be able to forgive him for his indiscretion.

The sounds of slamming cell doors brought Sierra back to

Chapter Two

LAMONT

Lamont watched Sierra as she walked down the corridor. *Damn, I still love dat bitch*, he thought. He knew that there could never be a relationship between them but he just wasn't ready to let go of her. Lamont knew Sierra would make someone a good woman; too bad he didn't deserve her.

As he leaned back in the raggedy recliner chair, he smiled as he thought about his sixteen years on the job. He was only thirty-seven years old with four more years until his retirement. He had accomplished everything he wanted to and more. Throughout the years as a corrections officer, he held up through riots, fights, rivalries, you name it. It was funny because Lamont never had any intentions of being a CO. He had aspired to become a professional basketball player in college. Lamont attended the University of North Carolina at Chapel Hill on a full athletic scholarship and was one of the best players in his division until a mind-blowing knee injury in his s‑ nior year. Lamont was so crushed that he dropped out school and looked for work, against his father's wishes. / he took a couple of civil service examinations, the D her dismal reality. She was lonely, single, and almost a virgin again because she hadn't been with a man in so long. But she was not about to become someone she didn't like. From that moment on, she was going to live her life to the fullest and do whatever the hell she wanted. What didn't kill her would only make her stronger.

ment of Corrections notified him and he jumped on it. It felt so good to make Pops proud of him once again.

Lamont was raised by his father. His mother, Linda, left when Lamont was six years old. He never understood the reason why. Lamont grew up thinking she left because being his mother was too much to handle, although Pops told him it had nothing to with him. Because of this, Lamont couldn't stand to be without a woman for too long. It was only a hurtful reminder of how he was never able to have the nurturing that a young boy needs from his mother, causing him to be insensitive and domineering. With Sierra, it was different. She was a beautiful woman who understood him and had compassion for him, regardless of his shortcomings. She loved him unconditionally, but unfortunately Lamont couldn't let go of the fact that one day she might leave him, causing him to sabotage their relationship. He couldn't have dealt with her leaving and him not have a backup plan.

Deja's pregnancy was untimely. He knew her for a while; they worked in another facility together a while back. Unbeknownst to Sierra, Lamont always kept an extra chick or two in his stash, with Deja being one of them. One night, he got weak and didn't use any protection, and Deja ended up pregnant. He could have kicked himself for it. Deja constantly talked about wanting children and with him wanting the pussy, he heard her but never listened. By the time she told him she was pregnant, it was too late to turn back. He crossed his fingers, hoping that he would be able to hide the child. He could have beat Deja's ass for running her mouth to Sierra.

"What da fuck is wrong wit' you, Deja?" he remembered asking her. "You dumb bitch! Why would you be runnin' ya mouth to her? I know you knew who she was!"

Deja smiled. "Okay, we even now. Now she knows who da fuck I am! Why you protectin' her, Lamont? You act like she a fuckin' princess or somebody!"

Lamont covered his face with his hands. He was so aggravated! Why did he even fuck this crazy broad?

"You know what, Deja? When you drop dat load, I'm gonna bust yo' ass. I swear I'm gonna show you dat I am not da one ta fuck wit'. When me and you started doin' our thing, I tol' yo' dumb ass, I had a girl, I'm not leavin' her. You said fine—it is what it is. Dat was da fuckin' deal. Now you pregnant, nigga, you . . ." Lamont couldn't even find the words to explain the way he felt. He realized he couldn't even be angry with Deja. It was all his fault. He knew Sierra was gone for good.

Deja stood in front of him with her arms folded. She had finally gotten what she wanted—Lamont—and now their love child was on the way. She tried several different methods to try to knock Sierra out of the box and she finally did it.

"Lamont, I'm sorry dat you upset, but I refuse to allow our child to be a secret. You wanted to fuck me wit' no protection, and you a grown-ass man; you knew da outcome so now go tell ya lil' girlfriend da truth. I did most of the dirty work for you so it shouldn't be dat hard." Deja gathered her things and walked out Lamont's front door. He just stood there in awe. His mind was going several different directions. He made up his mind to face Sierra and to be a father to his unborn child.

As he opened his eyes, he was surprised to see Monique Phillips standing over him and staring at him. She'd seen the earlier incident between him and Sierra take place so Lamont already knew what her agenda was. Monique always had a big crush on him but she just wasn't his speed. She was what he called your typical "hoodrat"chick, with the long weaves and fake nails, looking like she had just stepped out a rap video. Her enormous behind made the title *video ho* even more of a suitable description of her. Lamont was an attractive brother, with women waiting like vultures to swoop down on him after it was officially confirmed that he and Sierra were no longer together. His slanted eyes and Hershey's chocolate skin were the perfect combination, paired off with his full, kissable lips.

His perfect, white teeth were enough to have women, young and old, mesmerized. His crooked smile made him hard to resist and only added to his arrogance.

He ran his fingers through his curly hair as he contemplated what he was about to do. With Monique standing there, she seemed as if she was just asking for it. He'd had an erection ever since the argument with Sierra, swearing to himself if he could have gotten his hand on her, he would have ripped off her clothing, bent her over his desk, and screwed her right in front of everybody. That's just how horny he was right now.

"Phillips." Lamont beckoned her as she walked back to her corner of the control room. Monique sashayed toward her desk. He looked her up and down. *She don't look half bad for a slut*, Lamont thought. He stroked his goatee while Monique waited patiently for him to complete his inspection of her. She wasn't a raving beauty by Lamont's standards, but she had a lot of sex appeal.

Monique licked her glossy, M•A•C•-covered lips. "Yes, Captain Simmons, may I help you?" she asked, as she flirted shamelessly in front of her coworkers. They looked at her and cut their eyes.

"I'm gonna need you to go into da equipment room and count da radios. I think we got a few dat's missin'. Do you think you can handle dat?" Lamont grabbed his oversized penis under the desk. Monique glanced at the gesture and smiled.

"Oh, of course, Cap! I'll get on dat, right now!" Monique answered, making references to his private area.

Lamont smirked as he watched her eyes widen with pleasure. She couldn't contain her glee as she walked into the small equipment room, located in the back of the control room. Lamont got up from the desk and walked in behind her, not wanting to be too obvious. When they disappeared, the other staff members immediately began to whisper. Unfortunately, Monique's reputation at work was scarred because of the type of behavior she was about to exhibit.

"Oh, well," one of the senior officers stated. "They both hoes, so it's not like none of y'all should be surprised!" Everyone laughed in agreement and continued to work like everything was normal.

Inside the small room, Lamont and Monique were standing up, facing each other for a few moments.

"What do you want, Phillips? I know all about you and Sierra being old friends and I was just wonderin' is dis some type of setup?" Lamont laughed to himself as he used reverse psychology on Monique, just to see what her motive was.

"You know what I want, Lamont! I want you to put da dick in my mouth so I could suck da life outta you. I know you heard about my skills."

Lamont chuckled. "Yeah, I heard 'bout you. But what dat mean? Hearin' 'bout it and knowin' 'bout your skills is two different things."

"Well, let's find out." With that, Monique squatted in front of Lamont and released his dick from his pants.

Lamont loved a female who took what she wanted. He closed his eyes, envisioning Sierra wrapping her full lips around the head of his penis. He pushed Monique's head toward his groin area as she took him in her mouth. She deep-throated and massaged him like a professional, squeezing the base of his penis. Lamont felt himself grow and grow as Monique made soft humming noises while pleasuring him. Lamont moaned with pleasure as he watched his rod glisten with Monique's saliva and lip gloss, causing his knees to buckle slightly. Saliva dripped down Monique's chin as she played with the pre-cum and wrapped it around her tongue. She continued to create a suctioning effect on him and this went on for the next ten minutes. She gently tugged his balls and licked those too. Lamont went crazy, almost forgetting that he was at work. He couldn't be as loud as he wanted to be. Monique's skills were outstanding. Unable to withstand it anymore, Lamont released his babies in her throat and Monique gulped down the semen like a power shake. She took his penis out of her mouth and licked and sucked every drip drop of cum until his dick was completely dry. She licked her lips and removed any remnants of Lamont from the corners of her mouth. He watched in earnest while he wished that they were in a bedroom, or anywhere else except work. He would have fucked the hell out of her.

"Damn, you a good bitch!" Lamont said, after he got back enough energy to speak. "I see why you got these cats chasin' after ya ho ass."

Monique smiled. She knew that Lamont was disrespectful but she was about to make a mockery of him.

"Yep, call me what you want, nigga, but I'll bet before it's all over, you'll be chasin' too."

"Ha, ha, ha, you funny, shorty. Look at me. Do you think I have to chase?"

"No, do you think I have to chase? I got niggas lined up to get at me. Don't let 'em fool ya."

Not to make you wifey, Lamont thought. *Dat's for damn sure.*

"Phillips, who chasin' you? You loose as hell. Let's face it, you dun' got right wit' a couple of cats 'round here."

"Well, do you know who ya ex-chick, Sierra, got wit'? Don't let her corny ass fool you!"

Lamont grabbed Monique by her neck. "Watch ya mouth. I know you don't care for Sierra but don't be thinkin' you could be suckin' my joint to get back at Si. I ain't got shit ta do wit' you and her!" He let her go and Monique began coughing as she rubbed her throat.

Monique stared at Lamont. He didn't have any remorse at all. Even though he was no longer with Sierra, he wasn't going to allow this slut to disrespect her. Sierra told him a few stories about Monique and how conniving she was. Secretly, that made him even more curious to "test" her waters. He also had to make it clear that he was not the one to fuck with. He was always the user, not the "usee."

"What da fuck you tryin' ta do? Dis me over dat chick? She don't even want you no more!"

Lamont was pissed! He raised his hand like he wanted to slap Monique but decided against it. The more she popped her mess, the more he liked it.

"Phillips, you a whore! I mean, you just sucked me off in da equipment room. You act like we was togetha or somethin'. So don't worry about Sierra wantin' me or not, that shouldn't concern you. Just be concerned 'bout you getting dis dick again."

Monique walked up to Lamont as he fixed his clothing. She was so close to him, he could feel her breath on his face.

"Nigga, don't speak too soon 'cause I just might end up bein' da bitch you end up with!" After that, Monique excused herself and walked back to her post like nothing ever happened.

Lamont tried to fight it but for some reason was intrigued by Monique's nasty ass. He was thinking that he'd met his match. He'd never had a woman like her before—a woman who took what she wanted. He was always the one in control. Although he was still in love with Sierra, he figured that maybe Monique might be just what the doctor ordered.

Chapter Three

MONIQUE

Monique Phillips walked into the neat home in Jamaica, Queens that she shared with her younger brother, Timothy, her mother, and fourteen-year-old daughter, Destiny. Her mother's car was not in the driveway so she assumed that no one was home. As she climbed the stairs to her bedroom, she heaved a sigh of relief, knowing she would have the house all to herself.

She thought about the episode with Lamont and smiled. She felt like she had gotten revenge on Sierra for trying to embarrass her in front of their coworkers. "I'm gonna have dat bitch's man in a minute," she said aloud. Lamont had never paid her any attention, so she jumped at the opportunity to finally get her hands on him after the argument between him and Sierra. Sierra was a thorn in her side as they were growing up, with her mother, Ann, practically shoving the poor child down Monique's throat. Their mothers were good friends and they wanted their daughters to be just as close. Monique was always an envious child and secretly despised Sierra. She couldn't stand the fact that Sierra was the only child who got almost everything she wanted, especially before her father died. Monique was buddies with her until she got old enough to understand how she really felt about Sierra.

Monique was always at the center of controversy. For as long as she could remember, drama followed her for most of her life. She was not trustworthy enough to keep any female friends or even a man. She didn't see anything wrong with this because she never knew any better. Turmoil was a way of life for her.

She was a product of an affair that her mother had with a married man. Although Monique's biological father financially supported her throughout her young life, he never found the time to build a relationship with her. Monique thought about this from time to time and blamed her mother for her father's absence.

When her brother's father, Michael, entered their life, the jealousy that Monique felt consumed her. Ann seemed so happy and diverted all of her attention to her man. By the time Monique was nine, Ann gave birth to Timothy, who was the spitting image of Mike. He spent a lot of time with Timothy and tried everything in his power to develop a relationship with Monique, but to no avail. She wanted her own daddy. Wanting Michael out of the picture, at thirteen she concocted a story and told everyone who listened that Michael touched her on occasion. The truth was Monique had tried to seduce him several times but was unsuccessful. Michael eventually left but still continued to have a relationship with his son. He was so hurt from Monique's lies that he vowed never to lay eyes on her again for as long as he was alive and he stayed true to his word.

Monique spent those years as an unruly teen, trying to find father figures in men.

During this time, she met Destiny's father, Ali, who was an around-the-way guy, a neighborhood resident of Brownsville projects. Monique was fourteen years old at the time and even though she did not have any sexual partners under her belt at that tender age, she felt like she was a match for the young thug. She watched him constantly, waiting for that opportunity to spring into action. When Ali finally broke her virginity, he sexually manipulated her young, underdeveloped body to no end. He made her do things that no young girl should have been subjected to. Monique became sexually mature beyond her years and was no stranger to anal and oral sex. Ali was her only sex partner at the time and with his refusal to allow anyone else to get next to her, she became his personal project. Monique thought he loved her and she loved him until she found out that he was really a pimp and that she was another one on his plate after discovering at fifteen, she was pregnant. Ali denied the baby. Monique was devastated and hid her pregnancy until her last trimester. Luckily, Destiny was a healthy baby. Monique let the experience with Ali affect the relationship with her only child. She loved her daughter dearly but unfortunately was not able to provide the love and attention Destiny needed. She felt guilty sometimes but every time she felt Destiny getting close to her, she pushed the girl away.

Monique felt safer being a "friend" to her daughter. It just took away the harsh reality that Destiny was a product of something that was nasty and vile to Monique. With Destiny being a carbon copy of Ali, who ended up dying of AIDS five years before, it just made matters worse. Destiny, who was nine years old at the time, had never met her father, so his death was met with anger in the Phillips household.

Her thoughts were disrupted by her cell phone vibrating on the oak nightstand in her bedroom. She grabbed the phone and without looking at the caller ID, she answered.

"Yo, what up, ma?" the caller yelled into the phone.

Monique turned down the volume. "These niggas be actin' stupid in here, man. A nigga on da jack and they actin' like fools, yo!"

"What's up, sweetie?" she answered in her sexy voice. She

knew who it was instantly. She was expecting his phone call. "Ya miss me?"

"Hell, yeah. When you gon' see Daddy? You gonna gimme some da next time, right?"

"Why, of course! I know you need it, and shit, I need some o' ya chocolate too. But you gonna see me Monday."

The male on the other end of the phone began to smile. Monique wondered what was going through his head. She had been watching him for quite some time now and he was just what she liked—a cocoa-complexioned, bald, muscular brother whose voice could make a sister cream in her panties. They had had plenty of conversations before she could convince herself to finally give him the phone number. She was glad that she did.

"Good, ma. Dat's real good. Don't forget to bring dat stuff wit' you, ah-ight? I'm starving for it. You won't forget, will you, baby?"

"I got you, boo. 'Nuff said. Didn't I tell you that I was gonna take care of you?"

"No doubt." Scooter hurried the conversation. After everything was confirmed, there was nothing else left to say. "Look, ma, I gotta go hop in this shower but I see when I see you." He paused. "Gimme a kiss." Monique gave him a loud smooch through the receiver, they said their good-byes, and hung up.

Monique felt sexually charged while taking a shower, so she held her vagina open with her left hand while holding the showerhead with the right for the full effect. She let the powerful stream of warm water massage her protruding clitoris as she thought about Lamont's chocolate love muscle entering her. Monique was in another world as she felt waves of pleasure sweep across her body, almost reaching her climax. She held back, not wanting the feeling to end. "I need you, Lamont, I need you," she repeated to herself over and over again, as she envisioned him grabbing her juicy ass while pumping his large rod in and out her wet pussy. As Monique was about to reach her peak, she grabbed her titties and began to rub them, putting one into her mouth, sucking on her hard nipples. As the water pummeled her clit, her eyes rolled to the back of her head, and she fell against the wall, totally spent from an orgasm.

Chapter Four

RASHEED

Rasheed Gordon was awakened by the opening and closing of cell doors in the 5 North housing area. He was dreaming all night about his plans and couldn't get comfortable. He made a promise to himself that after this last "skid bid," he wasn't trying to come back to jail. He'd been in and out of jail since he was fifteen years old, and his "gangsta" days were now officially over. What he wanted and needed in his life was a strong sister to be by his side with morals. A woman who would be the mother of his children, someone he could treat like a queen. He glanced at the visit calendar on the small concrete slab that was supposed to be a desk and sat up when he realized that he had a visit today.

Born and raised in Bedford-Stuyvesant, Rasheed was definitely a product of his environment. He was the youngest member of the Gordon family and the second child of his mother, Lavon, and his father, Jihad Morton. Jihad was a self-proclaimed Muslim and extremely controlling and jealous of his wife. A young mother at sixteen, Lavon was devoted to her two young sons, Karim and Rasheed, who watched Jihad beat her mercilessly on occasion. Lavon was breathtakingly gorgeous, and men of all races admired her beauty. Although she was 100 percent faithful to her husband, Jihad believed that she was having an affair with another man.

One day, Lavon finally got the nerve to leave Jihad with some coaxing from her family. "Leave Jihad alone or else we gonna kill him," her brothers warned. They had whipped his ass a couple of times already, but Lavon continued to go back to him. Lavon had four brothers, Peppy, Nayshawn, Shaka, along with Kemp, who was only a couple of years older than her own sons. The last time she went back to Jihad, he shot her to death then took his own life as well. With no questions asked, Rasheed and Karim, who were five and seven years old at the time, came to live with their grandmother, Miss Carrie Gordon. Rasheed and Karim always said they owed their lives to their beloved Nana, in return for everything she did for them.

Rasheed was more than happy to be with his extended family. There, he learned how to be a man at an early age. Being raised in a household with uncles who were big-time hustlers, money or his career choices were never an issue. He was a hustler by nature, a trait passed down from his uncles. As much as Miss Carrie chided her wayward sons about their antics, they brushed her off and proceeded to fall victim to the fast life. The Gordon boys were notorious for raising hell in their hood and citywide. They eventually purchased two brownstones that were next door to each other and located on Halsey Street. With their money, they transformed the two brownstones into a massive one-family, providing a comfortable home for the brothers, Miss Carrie, the one of the two remaining sisters, Carrie and Sharee, and of course Karim and Rasheed. Then, unfortunately, Peppy—the eldest of the Gordon siblings—was murdered in East New York, coming from his son's mother's house. Things weren't the same but everyone had to move on with their lives. Carrie, Sharee, Shaka, and Nayshawn eventually moved out on their own and Karim moved to Atlanta.

Rasheed and Kemp opted to stay in the family home, which had more than enough room for the three people who lived there.

Rasheed stood up from the concrete slab with a mattress that the Department of Corrections called a bed. He stretched his six feet four frame and proceeded to stand over the small sink to brush his teeth and wash his face. He looked in the so-called mirror, which was nothing but a piece of metal nailed to the wall, and brushed his full beard. Rasheed put his lengthy locks into a ponytail and retrieved his toiletries from the desk so that he could take them with him to the shower. While waiting for the duty officer to open cells, he dropped to the floor of the concrete box and began his daily regimen of crunches, push-ups, and sit-ups. He had to maintain his physique of 220 pounds of muscle. With his chiseled features, long eyelashes, and reddish-brown complexion—compliments of his Sioux Indian ancestry—Rasheed looked more like a runway model than an inmate on Rikers Island. Surprisingly, he was very modest about his looks. He just took great pride in being healthy and exercising, which was good for his mind, body, and soul.

Rasheed cut his workout short and rushed to his cell window when he heard the sounds of keys. He knew that this day he would tell the CO on duty, Miss Sierra Howell, how he really felt about her. He had been studying her since he'd been in 5 North, and he was infatuated with her. He was feeling the sassy, hood-chick persona she gave off. Sierra was a pro at handling guys like Rasheed and he liked that. Suddenly, the sounds of keys were getting closer and closer to his cell.

When she got to his cell, she jumped when she realized Rasheed was standing in the window.

Rasheed laughed. "I'm sorry, Miss H," he apologized. "I didn't mean to scare you. I heard your keys and I ran to the window to see who it was."

She held her chest. "It's ah-ight, Gordon." Rasheed watched as she scoped his muscular chest through the small window and he repositioned himself so that she could see his well-toned arms too. He felt an erection coming on.

He noticed her fidgeting. There was an unequivocal attraction between the two. There was also a line that couldn't be crossed and they both knew it.

"I apologize, ma-ma. I didn't mean to make you uncomfortable. It's just dat . . . forget it. Um, could you tell 'em to open my cell so I could take a shower?"

Sierra smiled.

Damn, Rasheed thought. *She is so fuckin' gorgeous*.

"Yeah, Gordon, I got you, man. As soon as I get my shower list finished, I'll open your cell first. You know cats be hatin' when I don't take down their cells for da list."

"Oh, yeah, I know about these hatin'-ass dudes. I'm in here wit' 'em twenty-four hours a damn day! But anyway, sweetheart, I would appreciate if you can get me outta dis cell so I could take care o' my business."

As Sierra walked away, Rasheed was mesmerized as her round butt moved up and down in her uniform pants. They fit her just right, not like so many other CO women whose pants were way too tight. While she was talking to another inmate in a cell directly across from Rasheed's, he watched her closely. Every inmate in the housing area was on their cell door, glaring at Miss Howell. Rasheed fell back as he felt the green-eyed monster rearing its ugly head. He wanted her all to himself.

Rasheed gathered his shower supplies and neatly placed them in the jail-issued mesh bag. He then proceeded to go back to his exercise regimen and do his fifty crunches to keep his six-pack tight. When his cell finally opened, he walked out and glanced at Sierra, who was sitting at the desk, writing in her logbook. He wondered if she had any idea how he felt about her. He walked around the tier to where the showers were located and much to his dismay, someone was already in the only shower he liked to use. Rasheed liked to take a shower before everybody else did. He wanted to be in and out without all the conversation. He mumbled under his breath when he realized it was Scooter. Scooter, whose real name was Shamel Abrams, was a typical Harlem cat to Rasheed. He was a flashy, loud-mouthed braggart who took great pride in having the tightest game when it came to the ladies. Scooter was very good-looking and oddly enough, very cultured, having been raised by Senegalese parents. From what Rasheed knew about Scooter, the man didn't have to work or hustle because his family was well-off. His mother owned hair-braiding shops all over Manhattan and his father was a big-shot diplomat. He figured that they pretty much had given up on their son, who was American-born and who obviously got caught up in the street life. Rasheed shook his head every time he thought about how good some people had it, but they chose this jail shit.

Rasheed sighed as he entered the shower and let the lukewarm water hit his bare chest. He stood in the shower with his boxer underwear on, usually scrubbing them by hand after he washed his body. He noticed Scooter, who was in the next shower, standing there butt-naked and masturbating.

"Nigga, what da fuck are you doin'?" Rasheed exclaimed. He heard rumors about Scooter being on the "downlow" and he didn't want to take any chances. "Why you can't wait 'til I'm outta here to do dat shit?!"

Scooter laughed. "Nigga, I ain't thinkin' 'bout ya ass. I'm checkin' out Miss H, ya know, usin' my imagination. Picturin' puttin' my joint in her mouth!"

Suddenly, Rasheed felt hot. "Muthafucka, don't play wit' me! It ain't no need for you to dis shorty, man. Dat could be somebody doin' dat to ya motha or sista, man!"

Scooter, who apparently had finished his dirty deed, immediately began washing his hands. "Yo, Rah, you feelin' dat bitch or somethin'? You takin' it real personal, bruh, like you diggin' her out. She promised you some pussy or somethin', nigga?"

Rasheed cringed. This was the reason he disliked coming in

the shower when other dudes were in. "No, mu'fucka, I just got respect for women, man. What da fuck, is you gay, nigga? What is it, you don't like women?" Rasheed waited for the answer.

Scooter paused. He wondered if he was on to him. "Yeah, of course, I like chicks, paw, don't try me like dat!"

"Well, don't let me hear 'bout you disrespectin' no other female up in here, 'specially Miss H. She's my peoples!"

Scooter sucked his teeth. *Did this nigga just threaten me?* Scooter thought. He wasn't going to ask. Rasheed was a dude that nobody messed with, behind the walls or in the streets. His reputation preceded him.

Rasheed waited for Scooter to say something slick. He promised himself that if Scooter did say something, he was going to knock his block off. He didn't want anyone being disrespectful to his future woman. Nobody.

Chapter Five

TAMIR

Tamir opened up her overstuffed closet and carefully chose an outfit from her enormous selection of clothing. She and the twins, Asia and India, who were her best friends, went shopping the day before. Their "shopping" consisted of numerous items that were purchased with some stolen credit cards they received from a connect they had. They would buy the items, sell most of the goods, and keep a couple of items for themselves. They would split money and items with the connect so they could keep the cards coming. Tamir was so good at what she did that it became her second nature. Her man, Rasheed, wanted her to stop but she couldn't help herself. She had to have it all.

Tamir Armstrong, who was twenty-four years old, came from a financially comfortable background. Unlike her friends, she did not have one single reason to commit fraud or any other type of crime, for that matter. Her parents always provided Tamir with the best that they could, but unfortunately she didn't feel that way. She wanted more and her excessive greed led her into criminal activities.

Tamir wanted desperately to fit in with the "hood rich" and

live her life like the videos she continuously watched on BET. She was fascinated with the flashy clothes and fly cars. Most of all, she was completely in love with Rasheed. In her eyes, Rasheed could do no wrong. He represented everything Tamir wanted in a man. He was an intelligent thug, a hustler who had the cars, money, and reputation. People respected him but feared him. Belonging to one of the most thorough families in Bed-Stuy, Rasheed was well-known for his gunplay, only using it when it was really necessary.

One of the problems in their relationship was the fact that Rasheed was continuously locked up. He did a few stretches in prison before and during their union, but Tamir held it down. She was willing to ride with her man, even if she wasn't happy with his jail stints. She felt that was one of the requirements of a "thug wifey."

Rasheed was her first love. Having been a couple for five years, they had their ups and downs. Tamir thought about the day she had actually met him, even though she already knew of him from the neighborhood. She used to see him riding around in a black Mercedes CLK and knew then that she had to have him. Unfortunately, he never paid her any attention; that is, until he happened to spot her walking from the A train with a girlfriend one day.

"Hey, shorty," she recalled Rasheed calling out to her. She looked around and pointed at herself.

"Who, me?" Tamir replied, with a surprised look on her face. She hoped he wasn't talking to her homegirl.

Rasheed pointed at Tamir and laughed. "Yeah, you. Come here." Rasheed gestured for Tamir to walk over to his car, which was parked on the corner of Hancock and Stuyvesant.

Tamir walked toward the shiny black car, motioning to her friend to wait for her. She did everything in her power to keep from running toward him. Rasheed was her star and she was his biggest fan!

"What up, sweetheart? I'm Rasheed but you can call me Big

Rah. How you doin', baby?" His question was accompanied by the prettiest smile Tamir had ever seen on a man.

"Hello," Tamir replied with a hint of nervousness in her voice. Rasheed was a few years older than she was, but she had the biggest crush on him. Tamir wasn't used to dealing with a man of his caliber.

Rasheed laughed. "What's ya name, shorty?" Tamir didn't know until later that Rasheed already knew about her from his aunts. Tamir was a steady customer in his aunt's beauty salon. She had to expressed to them that she had a thing for Rasheed.

Tamir." She paused. "Your aunt does my hair." Rasheed looked at Tamir up and down. He liked her style and she had a very pretty face. Her hair was a deep red, which was cut short and stylishly, compliments of his Aunt Carrie. Her clothing was couture and fashionable. They complemented her shapely, petite frame.

Rasheed examined her thoroughly and rubbed his chin. "Looks good, looks good. You wearin' the hell outta dat hairdo, shorty. You ain't lettin' it wear you." He leaned to the side to get a glimpse of Tamir's perky butt. "Dat's wassup!" He stared into her green eyes. "Yo, how ol' are you anyway?"

Tamir swallowed real hard because she usually lied about her age. "I'm nineteen, going on twenty. Is dat too young for you?"

Rasheed smiled again. "Damn, how ol' do you think I am? Shit, I'm only twenty-six! Is dat too ol' fa you?"

Hell no, Tamir thought. "Nah, dat's good." Rasheed touched her arm and she thought she was going to faint!

"Shorty, I be seein' you aroun' da way. You a lil' cutie-pie. My aunts tol' me dat you was feelin' me, but they was sayin' you was too young fuh me. But listen, I'm my own man. You think you can handle me?" Rasheed smirked, causing Tamir to almost have an orgasm right there on the spot.

"Yeah, Rah, no doubt. I can handle you, anytime." She was starting to feel a little sexy. She was glad he acknowledged her after all this time. They exchanged phone numbers and he drove off. When he called Tamir that evening, she knew that he was going to be hers and that she would do whatever it took to keep him.

Tamir finally chose a bebe T-shirt with studs and a matching denim skirt. She was also going to surprise Rasheed with a ballon of weed that she had stored in her "chocha" so she decided to wear the skirt for easy access. She knew that he had female mules coming to Rikers to bring him drugs that he would sell to the other inmates. She wanted to put a stop to the mules. It didn't matter that Rasheed had told her not to do it, but she was going to ride with him to no end. This would prove her loyalty and devotion to him.

After she put on her Louis Vuitton sneakers, she ran downstairs to check herself out in the large mirror located in the foyer by the front door. Just as she picked her Louis bag and was about to walk out the door, her brother, Tajir, walked downstairs. Tajir, who was older than his sister, was graduating with a master's degree in engineering. Tamir couldn't stand Taj and rolled her eyes at him. Her parents always threw his achievements in her face. She knew that he was going to have something to say to her.

"Where you goin'?" Taj asked as he inspected her outfit. He knew that it was probably one of her "booster specials" because she didn't have a job.

"To see Rah," she answered with a defensive tone. "Why?"

Taj ripped into her almost immediately. "Dat's why homie can't stay da fuck outta jail 'cause you always runnin' up there to see him! Why don't you fall back and try to get ya own shit together?"

Tamir sucked her teeth. "Listen, nigga! Mind ya fuckin' business, ah-ight! Rah is my man and I do what da fuck I want to do fuh him and wit' him!"

Taj shook his head. "You know, you are stupid. Dat dude is gonna drop ya ass one day for a female dat got some common sense 'cause you ain't about shit. All you do is lay up, steal, and chase after him all da time."

Tamir brushed past Taj, walked outside, and beeped the alarm on her Honda Accord coupe. She knew what Taj was saying was true, but she didn't care. She was going to do exactly what she wanted to do. As she put on her Christian Dior shades and looked in the rearview mirror at herself, she knew that she was ghetto fabulous and that was what she was going to be until she felt like being something different.

Chapter Six

TYKE

Tyke exited the home he shared with his wife and two children. He briskly walked to his car, a cream-colored Chrysler 300. He entered the vehicle and immediately began rapping along with Jay-Z's *Black Album* as he drove down Gates Avenue. He had just been released from prison last week and had business to attend.

As he cruised down the streets, Tyke laughed to himself as he sucked in all the attention from the ladies and watched as dealers ran for cover. The young up-and-coming hustlers knew to steer clear of Tyke, in order to protect their street turf, where their money was being made. Soldiers, as they were referred to, were supplied with ammunition and were instructed to shoot first and ask questions later. Tyke was notorious for having low-level dealers robbed of their product, and of course, forcing them to lead him to their suppliers, which he would eventually rob too. This is why he earned the nickname "Robin Hood." Tyke was no longer interested in taking drug money. He was into bigger things like promoting. That's where the money was.

Tyquan Williams was stickup kid most of his life. His

mother and father had died when he was very young and he was raised by various family members, so he never had any real stability in his life. At thirty-four years old, the streets were all he knew. He learned a couple of trades while serving time in jail, but never put any of those skills to use.

While waiting at a stoplight, he observed the Benzes and the Beemers around the neighborhood. Tyke liked being flashy and was working on those vehicles being the next on his list. He pulled out his new Nextel BlackBerry and began scanning through his contacts old and new. One phone number caught his eye. Sierra. He dreamed about having her again and now he would finally have the opportunity. As he dialed her number, her voice mail came on instantly, giving him the indication that she might be at work. He left a message with his new phone number, knowing that she would call him back with no hesitation.

Suddenly, the light changed and Tyke turned the corner of the block. He noticed a black Yukon Denali parked on the corner and two men talking to each other. One of the men looked familiar. Tyke looked closer and realized that the taller of the two was his longtime cohort, Kemper Gordon. Kemp and Tyke were friends since they were young boys and started committing crimes at the tender ages of twelve years old. They had been through the ringer and back, making them loyal cronies for what seemed like a lifetime. Tyke parked his car and walked over to Kemp, who gave him a bear hug.

"Yo," Kemp yelled. "Whaddup, son, when you came home?"

Tyke laughed. "Yo, I jus' got home last week, son. I was layin' low. You know I had ta get my shit right before I came outside. Especially wit' wifey and da kids." Tyke looked inside Kemp's truck. It was hooked up. "Son, dis shit is nice. I see you got ya shit on twenty-fours!"

Kemp glanced at his truck. It was nothing for him to have a nice ride. "Yeah, I jus' got dis cause all dat fancy fly shit be gettin' too much attention in da hood. Where you headed?"

"I'm headed uptown ta meet up wit' these Harlem dudes I know. We about ta promote dis party fah some rapper nigga—I'm about ta get dis money. You know how I gets my money!" Tyke slapped Kemp on the back.

Kemp smiled. "Same ol' Tyke. Shit, youse a money-getting' mufucka, I know dat much about you."

"How ya family doin? Miss Carrie and all of 'em?"

"They good. Oh, Rah locked up on da Island on a parole violation and um, I found out who killed my brother, Peppy. Some Dominican cats from East New York."

"Word? Did y'all get at dem dudes yet?" Tyke wanted to know.

Suddenly, Kemp had a solemn look on his face. He missed his oldest brother but he had left that life alone and really didn't want to think about it too much. He had grieved enough already.

"Son, it ain't even worth it. My brother is dead and da shit nearly killed my moms, yo. I jus' moved his baby moms and his son closer ta us and left da shit alone."

Tyke was impressed. Kemp had always been a better man than he was because he would have killed those motherfuckers. He was curious to hear more about Rasheed. He never liked Rasheed, and Rasheed felt the same about him. Tyke always felt that Rasheed was jealous of the relationship that he had with Kemp. Some of the things that Rasheed had said to him and about him behind his back would get a man murdered in these streets, but with the loyalty that Tyke had to Kemp, Rasheed's life was spared. Just barely.

"So, Rah locked up again, huh?" Tyke asked, with a hint of sarcasm.

"Yeah, he'll be home in a couple of weeks, parole-free. I know he happy as hell cause you know he like ta be out and about," Kemp answered, oblivious to the snide remark Tyke made about his nephew.

"Yo, maybe I could get my shorty, Sierra Howell, ta look out for 'em, you know, while he in there."

"Sierra? Oh yeah, shorty you was messin' with. Your ex. Oooh, she official, son. You still rockin' wit' her?"

"I'm about to see dat ass tonight. You know, dat's my baby girl! She'll look out fuh Rah, if I ask her to."

Kemp shook his head. He knew that Rasheed was no fan of Tyke's and would never except anything from him. "He good, Tyke. Good lookin' out, man."

Tyke looked at his watch. "Yo, take my math and hit me up later. I gotta shoot uptown real quick." They exchanged numbers and hugs, pulling off in their vehicles at the same time. Tyke continued to play his music and thought about Sierra. He got an instant erection as he thought about their sexual escapades. He still loved Sierra and he was pretty sure she felt the same way about him. Now that he was home, he would make it his business to lay her down real good. He wanted to make sure that he had her all to himself because this time he wasn't going to let her slip through his hands like he had so many other times.

As he headed to his meeting, Tyke smiled as he rubbed his bald head while looking in the rearview mirror at his handsome face. He beeped his horn at two young ladies in a car, idling at the light. After a brief conversation, Tyke had the young ladies following him to Manhattan for a night on the town.

Chapter Seven

SIERRA

Sierra sat at the desk and proceeded to write in the logbook. She made sure that every inmate in her housing area was accounted for and was where they were supposed to be at all times. Inmates had an uncanny way of trying to "play" COs, and Sierra refused to be one of them. She let them know that she was from the streets just like them.

One inmate was the exception. That was Rasheed Gordon. She thought he was fine and made her damn knees buckle every time she saw him. She could never share her feelings with anyone because they would never understand. He was an inmate and feeling or even being remotely attracted to one was the ultimate violation if you were an officer. Sierra was considered a great employee, and showing any interest in Inmate Gordon would be going against the oath she took when she first got the job.

Sierra held her breath as Rasheed walked toward the desk, which was tucked in the corner by the phones. She hoped that he was going to use one so that he could avoid having him talk to her for too long. She didn't want to run the risk of saying something wrong or being too forward with him. Sierra had a weak spot for fine brothers, especially tall, handsome men with a whole lot of swagger and big dicks. Little did Rasheed know, Sierra had viewed him a couple of times, pleasuring himself in his cell while he thought no one was looking.

Sierra looked up and before she knew it, Rasheed was standing over her. They were silent for a brief moment. She was at a loss for words, as he thought of something to say to her. Sierra began shifting in the plastic chair.

"Miss H, did I get called for a visit yet?" Rasheed asked, as Sierra wiped the small beads of sweat from her forehead.

"Huh? Uh, not yet." She paused for a moment. She didn't want to keep stumbling over her words. "Ya girl comin' to see you today?" She couldn't think of anything else to say.

Rasheed frowned and took a deep breath. He seemed as if he didn't want to be reminded. "Yeah, she comin' up here. How you know my girl comin' up here? It could be somebody else." He winked at her.

Sierra blushed. "It could be. I just figured it would be ya girl cause she always comes up on da visits." *Damn, why I say dat?* Sierra thought.

"Lemme find out you been watchin' me." Rasheed casually flirted. He changed the subject. He needed to throw out his résumé while he had the chance. "You know, Miss H, I made a promise to myself, dat I ain't comin' back here. I been doin' dis for a minute and after this parole violation, I decided to hang it up."

Sierra wasn't impressed. She heard this just about every day from different inmates and she always ended up seeing them locked up again.

"Word. What plans do you have out there?"

"Well, my older brother, Karim, got a couple of business ventures in Atlanta. We got a couple of things we about to get poppin' in NY and I'm gonna help him out. He does a lot of promotin' down there in ATL too."

Sierra was impressed. "Oh, okay, dats good, Gordon. I wish

you da best. I know ya girl would be happy about you gettin' this new lease on life."

"Man, I wasn't really tryin' to include her in my new lifestyle. She's more in love wit' da old Rah. She's in love wit' da hype."

"How would you know dat, Gordon? Give her a chance. Just talk to her dis visit and see where her head at."

"Yeah, ah-ight. I'm tellin' you, she not gonna be feelin' it. But anyway, it ain't about her. It's about changin' me and what's best for Rah."

Sierra smiled. "You right, Gordon. It is about you. You sound like you got a good head on ya shoulders."

Rasheed looked at Sierra with a seductive glare. She could tell that he was doing everything he could to compose himself in front of her. She stared off into space when she noticed the huge bulge in his Rocawear sweatpants.

The phone rang. It was the visit officer calling for Rasheed Gordon and some other inmates in 5 North for visits.

"I know dat dis is kinda personal but do you have a man, Miss H?" Sierra frowned. *Dat is personal*, she thought. She didn't know what to say.

"Not exactly. Why do you ask?" She knew why he asked but she just wanted to hear him say it.

" 'Cause I want you," Rasheed replied and walked out the door.

Sierra picked up the phone on her desk to check her voice mails. As she scanned through a few messages, she replayed one over and over again in order to retrieve the phone number. The message was from her ex, Tyquan.

She was surprised that Tyke was home and calling her from the streets of Brooklyn, no less. They had a long-running relationship with each other, probably more emotional than physical. He was the one man that she knew had unconditional love for her. They were only together exclusively for two years but were still involved with each other way after they separated. Sierra broke it off with Tyke after she saw that his profession was going to be going back and forth to prison. Love still prevailed, and with a simple phone call, Tyke would probably end up in her bed.

She put aside her duties for a moment and made the phone call. Her heart began to beat real fast as the phone rang over and over.

"Hullo?" Tyke screamed into the phone. The number Sierra had called him from came up unknown on his caller ID.

"It's Si Si, Tyke. What up, baby?" she said. "You in da town? You couldn't tell me dat you was comin' home?"

"Hey, baaaaaaby! I miss you! You home?"

"Hell no, Tyke. I'm at work. When did you touch down?"

"Last week, baby. You know I had to do da family thing fuh a minute. But I'm good right now. I'm about to go meet these promoters in da city. I got a party to do in two weeks."

"Damn, what's up wit' da promotin'? I need to be down. Dat's good money. How ya kids doin'?" Sierra always asked about Tyke's children. She knew he loved children with a passion, even though she had to get an abortion. Sierra and his wife were once pregnant at the same time.

"Oh, they good, baby. Got big. Yo, could I see ya pretty ass tonight or what?"

Sierra felt tingly all over. Tyke did it for her. She knew that a good session was guaranteed with him and maybe a good nut was what she needed for the stress.

"Why, of course, Tyke. Call me later, we'll hook up."

"Oh, just one thing," Tyke added, "Mel gonna be hangin' wit' me, so bring ya girl."

Sierra knew who he was talking about. She did not want to bring her friend, Red, with her anywhere that Melvin was. They all grew up together in Brownsville, and Melvin was the person who introduced Sierra to Tyquan. Red and Melvin had a long-term relationship when they were much younger, with

Red ending up pregnant at sixteen. Her mother took her to get an abortion and Red blamed her misfortune on Mel, even though she was just as guilty as he was. Sierra guessed that Red's disdain for Mel was a defense mechanism because she was no longer allowed to see him after that.

"Oh, shit, Tyke," Sierra exclaimed. "Why you gotta bring Melvin? You know how Red is about him."

Tyke chuckled. He knew that Mel was feeling Red and this was his opportunity to reconnect with her.

"Man, tell Red to get out da house. All she do is work. She need ta have a good time. Shit, she need some dick and my man is tryin' ta give her some!"

Sierra laughed because she knew that he was telling the truth. Over the years, her friend Red had become real uptight. Sierra guessed it was because she was a registered nurse and she had to be that way working in that type of environment. Maybe she did need some loving!

"You a grimy muthafucka, Tyke, I swear. You leave me ta do da dirty work. I might be able ta get her out but dat's my girl so I gotta tell her about Mel."

"You want some of this grimy muthafucka in you, right? You miss me?" he asked.

"Hell yeah," Sierra replied. "Look, I can't talk right now, but I'll get her to come out. Red is ah-ight."

"Okay, meet us at PK's. Around nine o'clock. Okay, baby girl?"

Sierra agreed. "All right, baby. Nine o'clock it is. Later." Sierra hung up. Tyke was something else. She had already caught on that Tyke had to bring Mel as a decoy so that he could hang out with Sierra in public, just in case any of his wife's friends spotted them. Tyke would just blame it all on Mel, the single friend. Game recognized game.

Her mind drifted back to Lamont. He had taught her a lot about game. He had hidden his affairs well, making sure Sierra didn't know a thing about his indiscretions until Deja. She recalled their meeting after she found out about the pregnancy. She had agreed to meet him by the Verrazano Bridge off of the Belt Parkway. They needed a place to air out their gripes.

"Lamont, you played me. You been playin' my ass all along. I won't ever forgive ya ass for dis shit!" she shouted.

"Si, you don't understand, I never meant for her ta get pregnant," Lamont replied. He couldn't think of anything else to say.

Sierra's eyes widened with amazement. "Are you fuckin' serious? You mean, you neva meant fuh da bitch to keep it. You know if you screw without protection, it's a possibility da bitch could get pregnant."

"Sierra, da fuckin' condom broke, ah-ight? I didn't know it broke—I, I woulda stopped, I woul—"

Sierra put her hand up for him to stop. "Lamont, you are a liar. I gave you da benefit of da doubt. I trusted you and look what you did ta me, to us! You ain't give a fuck about nobody but yo damn self! It's ah-ight 'cause I'm finished wit' you!" Sierra screamed with a tear-streaked face. "Go on wit' ya baby mama!"

Sierra turned around to walk away from Lamont. He grabbed her arm and pulled her to him.

"Don't leave me, Sierra! I'm so sorry!" He attempted to kiss her but she resisted.

"Get da hell off of me, you piece o'shit! You don't deserve dis pussy anymore! I'll give it to da next man before I give it to you again!"

Suddenly, Lamont slapped her. Sierra fell to the ground, holding her face. She looked at him and all she saw was rage.

"Dat is my pussy! Yeah, I fucked up but don't you sit here in my got-damn face and tell me you givin' away ya ass to nobody! You think I'm a fuckin' sucka or somethin'?"

Sierra was afraid and as much as she hated to admit it, was turned on at the same time. She got up from the ground and brushed herself off. She stared at him with contempt in her eyes, while contemplating on going to her truck to retrieve her personal firearm from her Gucci handbag. She was going to shoot Lamont dead in his ass!

She ran toward her truck with Lamont on her heels. Before she could grab the gun, they tussled for a few moments, with Sierra digging her nails into Lamont's face. He instantly wrapped his large hands around her neck, causing her to gag for air. With the other free hand, he managed to unbuckle her tight jeans, yanking them down to her ankles. Sierra was no match for the six feet three, 210-pound Lamont. He threw her across the front passenger seat of her truck and held her down as he pushed his dick inside her smoldering pussy. At first, Sierra attempted to resist, but as the loving strokes continued, she succumbed to passion, prompting her to kick one leg out of her jeans and wrap it around Lamont's chiseled back. He grinded deep in her walls, as she screamed and yelled his name over and over. They kissed, not caring that their faces were drenched in each other's saliva. Lamont grabbed Sierra's ass, causing her to scream in ecstasy. She allowed him to immerse himself in her love with reckless abandon. They carried on for what seemed like eternity but apparently not long enough for the both of them. They had orgasms simultaneously, with no inhibitions, not caring who saw or heard them.

As Lamont fixed his clothes, Sierra continued to lie on her back. She was embarrassed and heartbroken. She had allowed Lamont to once again make a fool of her. That wasn't her intention. She needed him to feel her pain, but unfortunately Sierra was in love with the gorgeous man standing before her. At one time, he was everything she could have possibly wanted.

Sierra covered her face and began crying again. Lamont kissed her softly and helped her from the seat. He slowly redressed her, feeling like shit for the way he treated her. They both stood under the iridescent lights of the Verrazano Bridge and held each other. At that moment, they both knew that it was over.

Sierra wiped a small teardrop from her eye. She was not about to lose her composure over Lamont for what seemed like the millionth time. The pain was still fresh and left Sierra to deal with trust issues and insecurities. She could never subject herself to that pain again.

If Daddy was here, he would know what ta do, Sierra thought. Her father had died in a car accident when she was nine years old. He was the best father a girl could have, giving her everything that a man could possibly give his child. He loved her to death, leaving Sierra to expect that from any man she dealt with on a serious level. Unfortunately, there weren't many "serious" relationships. Her family and friends said that she was too picky. It wasn't that; it was just that she was cautious with her heart. She knew the caliber of men that she dealt with. She felt that she could protect herself sexually, but it was harder to protect her heart. Resorting to using the men in her life for her physical needs, Sierra never pretended she was an angel.

Chapter Eight

RASHEED

Rasheed looked at the small calendar he had taped to his wall. He only had a week before he went home. He continuously made a vow to never come back behind the walls again. He was going to give himself a couple of months before he left to go to Atlanta. He needed to take care of a couple of things first. One of the things on his to-do list was Sierra Howell. He would love for her to leave the job and come with him. He knew that was wishful thinking when she hadn't even really given him the time of day. He didn't want to leave New York until he knew where he stood with her. He was persistent.

As Rasheed commenced to straightening out his living quarters, Scooter appeared in his doorway. Rasheed never liked Scooter, and since he'd been in 5 North, the man made it his business to talk to Rasheed every chance he got.

"What's good, Rah?" Scooter said.

Rasheed didn't bother to look up at Scooter. "Yeah, what up?" Rasheed answered.

"What's been up wit' you, nigga? You ain't talkin' ta a nigga, no more?"

Rasheed stood up. He towered over Scooter's five feet ten frame. "What are you talkin' about?"

"You just been actin' kinda distant lately. I'm figurin' since you been tryin' ta holla at Miss H, you ain't got time fuh da peoples."

This gay muthafucka, Rasheed thought to himself. "Nigga, you ain't my bitch. I ain't gotta talk ta you every day!"

Scooter laughed. Secretly, he wished he was Rasheed's "bitch." "I was just wonderin'. So how Miss H doin' anyway?"

Rasheed frowned. He knew that Scooter was testing him, so he could not lose his cool. He turned around quickly so that Scooter wouldn't see him grimace. He was the last person Rasheed needed to pick up on any sign of him feeling Sierra.

"She cool, I guess. I ain't her keeper." Rasheed was too close to getting out of jail to whip Scooter's ass. He would have to speak to a couple of his comrades about Scooter. He didn't trust him.

"I just asked 'cause you seem to spendin' a lot of time talkin' ta her. Her fine ass. I know I'll fuck her."

Rasheed felt his blood boil. He knew that if Scooter stood in that doorway any longer, he was going to get a beatdown. Rasheed took a quick look at the calendar again for inspiration and decided to dismiss Scooter. He knew that Scooter was trying to gather information on anyone he could to try to get out of jail.

"Yo, son, back out my doorway. You askin' me too many questions."

Scooter smirked. "Excuuse me, nigga. I'll leave you alone, gettin' all sensitive over me askin' 'bout some CO bitch!" Scooter quickly disappeared.

Rasheed wiped the sweat from his forehead. He was on fire. He wanted to pop Scooter real bad but he had too much to lose. That was the problem with jail—someone was always gonna try you, especially if they knew you was about to go home. His thoughts were interrupted when Miss H called his name for a visit.

The facility visiting room was bustling with people. Inmates, dressed in DOC-issued jumpsuits, stood in the visit holding pen, waiting as patiently as they could to see their families and friends. It was Saturday, one of the busiest days for visits, and the noise level was astounding. The radio was blasting the hottest hip-hop and R&B as the COs kept tabs of visitor registration cards at the tattered desk that was strategically placed on the visit floor. Couples argued, babies cried, and children played, while others tried to steal a kiss or a feel in the midst of all the commotion. This type of distraction was the perfect situation for smuggled goods to be passed back and forth between visitors and inmates. COs attempted to keep a watchful eye on some, but there was always one or two that managed to get over. Visitors would smuggle drugs, razors, or cash anywhere they could—small pockets, their hair, baby's diapers, etc., even the most undesirable places like their rectums and for women, their vaginas. The inmate would then retrieve the impermissibles and attempt to swallow it, only to retrieve it from their feces later on.

Tamir entered the room and gave the registration paperwork to the female CO sitting at the desk. Tamir cut her eyes as the officer gave her the table number. The table was located within eyeshot of the CO's desk. *Bitch probably did dat on purpose*, Tamir thought. She had gotten through the search with the balloon of weed, and now she sat in the seat and adjusted her short skirt. The other female visitors scolded their boyfriends for staring at the pretty Tamir.

As the large metal door slid open, her eyes lit up when Rasheed stepped out. She watched as he quickly scanned the room for his girl. He smiled when he saw Tamir, waving to him from the left side of the room. He made his way over to her and greeted her with a big hug and passionate kiss. Once they were seated, he observed her attire.

"Why you wearin' dat short-ass skirt?" he asked. He looked around, daring to catch somebody looking at her. He knew that the male COs were notorious for flirting with inmates' girlfriends.

Tamir smiled. She loved to make Rasheed jealous. "I wanted to wear it. Besides, I got somethin' fuh you in da kitty kat."

Rasheed frowned. "What?" He paused. "I know you ain't talkin' about what I think you talkin' about?"

Tamir grinned from ear to ear. "Yeah, I got a balloon." She pointed to her private area.

Rasheed leaned back in the plastic chair. He was pissed! He was not happy with the fact Tamir would risk her freedom to bring him drugs. He had other people to do the dirty work for him.

"Why would you do dat, 'Mir? Did I fuckin' ask you to do dat? I got muthafuckas dat bring me shit all da time!" Rasheed whispered.

Tamir was disappointed. She hated to disappoint her man. She just knew that he would be happy about it, about the fact that she was down for him.

"Rasheed, I—I . . . I figured you would be happy. Dat way you don't have to depend on none of dem Sumner Project chicks you fuck wit' to be comin' up here. I didn't like dem no way!"

Rasheed was irritated and did everything to try to keep his composure. He was starting to see Tamir for what she really was.

"Man, Tonya and dem ain't nuthin' to me but my home-girls! Dat's what dey get paid to do is bring me some product. I ain't da only nigga they do dat for! I tol' you before when you asked to do it dat I ain't gonna have my girl do dat! Why you so hardheaded?" Tamir's face flushed with embarrassment. "Rasheed, why is you mad at me, now? I got it, so go get it!" She pointed to her area, hoping he would go for it and possibly give her a little pleasure too.

Rasheed sucked his teeth and ignored Tamir. He decided that he was going to give her the ultimatum today. It was now or never.

"Look, 'Mir, I decided to stop dis bullshit! No more biddin', no more hustlin'. I'm tryin' ta get up outta here and shoot to ATL with Karim. I wanted to know if you was wit' it—if you was wit' comin' wit' me ta begin dis new life?"

Tamir stared at Rasheed. She hoped she didn't hear what she thought she heard. She was not ready to give up her life in New York. She loved the fast life; it gave her a rush. Rasheed was her life. He was the epitome of everything she glorified. Now he was talking about leaving it all behind.

"Rasheed, what is you talkin' about? You a gangsta! You hangin' it up now at da peak of ya career?!"

"My fuckin' career? What? Dis ain't no career, man! Frankly, I'm tired o' shit, these dirty-ass dudes! Shit, I could be makin' somethin' happen in them streets, good shit, but I chose ta be up in here! My uncles done hung up their street cards and I'm da only fool in da family dat ain't got it together, ain't doin' nuthin' but endin up in the slamma! I'm not tryin' to end up like Uncle Peppy, so it's a wrap! Now I'm gonna ask you one mo' time, you rollin' with me or what?"

Tamir was livid. She wasn't ready to make a life-changing decision yet. "Why you gotta do dis now? I mean, I'm gettin' money too. I just can't pick up and move down somebody's south and I ain't got no hustle. What da hell am I supposed ta do while I'm down there? Huh, Rasheed? Shit, ya fuckin' brotha don't even like me!"

"Man, my brotha ain't even thinking 'bout yo ass. He wants what's best fuh me. Now if you gonna get wit' me and change ya ways, like put dat credit-card bullshit to a rest, then it's all good. I tol' you ta stop wit' dat credit-card shit anyway so don't expect me ta come see yo ass if you get locked up!"

Tamir froze in her seat. She didn't comprehend anything else he'd said except that he wouldn't visit her in jail.

"You mean ta tell me if I get locked up, you ain't comin' ta see me? After I done trucked my behind up here ta see you every time you looked around?" Rasheed stared at Tamir with no emotion. "You know what, fuck you, Rah! I'm outta here. You don't really wanna be wit' me. You probably fuckin' one of these CO bitches in here!" Tamir was raising her voice and drawing attention to herself. Rasheed didn't like that, especially since Tamir had drugs on her. COs began walking toward their table. He had to hurry and get her out of there before she really caused a scene and got the both of them into hot water.

"Yo, Tamir, shut the fuck up, man! You causin' a scene! Jus' leave now and I'll call you later, ah-ight?"

Tamir stood up. "No, you shut da fuck up, Rasheed Hakim Gordon! Don't call me no more, you lame muthafucka! Talkin' 'bout you won't come see me! After all da shit I did fuh you, nigga, I don't need yo ass!" Two female COs came and gently escorted Tamir from the visit floor. She realized she still had the drugs on her, causing her to calm down as she was walking out. "Go to Atlanta by yo' self, you bastard!" Tamir screamed out as the metal doors closed behind her.

Rasheed covered his face in frustration as three male COs prodded him to leave the area. They knew he was upset so they were real patient with him, not wanting him to cause a melee, with a possibility of other inmates and visitors getting hurt. He got up and walked toward the holding area to change out of the dingy gray jumpsuit. He knew that Tamir wasn't going to be easy to convince of his plans, but he never expected for it to go the way that it did. The one good thing that did come out of the incident was that he could finally get at Miss Howell with no guilty feelings.

As he knocked on the glass for the officer to let him in 5 North, he prayed that Miss Howell would still be on post. To his surprise, she was. He wanted to talk to her before she was relieved of her duties. He glanced at his unauthorized leather-strapped Rolex and saw that he had fifteen minutes before she left.

As the large gate opened, Sierra turned around and was surprised to see Rasheed come back from his visit early.

"Gordon, don't tell me you got in trouble."

Rasheed sighed. "Nah, Miss H," he answered. "My visit was terminated. Dis girl was wildin'out. It was da worst."

Sierra raised her eyebrows, curious to know what was going on with Rasheed and his girlfriend, although she couldn't figure out why she cared. "What happened, if you don't mind me askin'?"

"Well, I told her about my plans, about ATL, about givin' dis jail shit up and she was givin' me da runaround. Ya see, Tamir is into da credit cards heavy and I been tryin' ta get her ta stop. She don't wanna listen. Her main concern is she not gonna be able ta do her own thing in Atlanta and of course, me just givin' up on dis street shit, period. I tol' her if she get locked up doin' dat credit-card bullshit, I ain't comin' ta see her. Do you know she cussed me out? We supposed ta be talkin' about me and once again, she was da topic of da conversation. She flipped it on me!"

Sierra frowned. "Gordon, I'm sorry ta hear dat. Sounds like you really love dat girl."

"I did, Miss H. I really *did* love Tamir. She was jus' a pretty, lil' round-da-way girl who had a big crush on me for a minute so I decided ta holla at her, see what she was about. She was cool, dat is, 'till she started getting involved wit' these twins dat she be runnin' around callin' her best friends. They got her involved wit' dat credit-card stuff. Our relationship was doomed after dat. She started gettin'caught up in da hype, you know, wit' my reputation and all, she just got da big head from all dat."

"Well, Gordon, what you gonna do? Are you cuttin' her off fuh good?"

"Oh, yeah, it's ova! I can't be with her no more, Miss H! I

got big plans fuh myself and she ain't gonna be a part of the equation. I'm ready fuh somebody dat's gon' build wit' me. A woman I could be wit' and start a family wit'. A woman wit' a good head on her shoulders."

Rasheed stared at Sierra. She shifted in her seat. "Do ya feel me, Miss H?" He wanted her to catch on to what he was saying and he stood there wondering if she did. He was about to really get at her when her relief walked through the door. He was pissed but he knew tomorrow would just be another day for him to say something. He would break her down real slow. She was what he wanted in a woman; she was assertive, hardworking and of course, sexy as hell. But she was a CO.

Tamir

As Tamir boarded the Q-101 bus to take her off of the Island to the visitor's parking lot, she thought about how she may have overreacted. She knew that Rasheed did not take embarrassment lightly, so she figured that she would avoid his phone calls for a couple of days. She hoped that with them not speaking to each other, it would make him come to his senses. *Rasheed is a thug and will always be a thug*, Tamir thought. She couldn't understand why he wanted to give up his life, his reputation, to live in Atlanta with that square-ass brother of his. Tamir exited the bus and got in her car, peeling off as the thoughts of being without Rasheed saturated her heart with self-pity. What she didn't realize was that she had done Rasheed a favor.

Chapter Nine

LAMONT

Lamont entered Deja's apartment. She had asked him to come over to watch their son while she went out. As he walked in, he smiled as his son, Lamont Terrell Simmons II, scooted toward him.

"Hey, man," Lamont said, as he scooped Trey up into his big arms. Lamont kissed his adorable son. Trey was his heart. Even though he and Deja didn't see eye to eye on things, they did agree on one thing, and that was his son. He sat on the couch in the living room and watched Trey play with his toys as his mother ran around getting prepared for her night on the town. Lamont didn't really care where Deja went, as long his son was okay. He was pretty sure Deja was doing her thing. He thought about how he reacted when he found out that Deja was pregnant.

"You what?" Lamont yelled. "How you pregnant?"

Deja looked at Lamont in amazement. "What da hell do you mean? How did I get pregnant? I'm not goin' ta answer dat question. You a grown-ass man, I'll let you figure da shit out!" she screamed. "Here's da damn test from my personal physician. I'm eight weeks' pregnant so man up, okay?"

Lamont was pissed. He knew that having unprotected sex was a no-no. He did it anyway. He had fucked up big-time.

"Man, you keepin' it? I got a girl—what da fuck am I gonna tell her? You gotta get rid of it, Deja."

Deja smiled. "Lamont, I'm keepin' my baby! How dare you tell me what ta do wit' my baby!"

Lamont ran his hand through his hair. He was so frustrated. Even though he had never been in an official relationship with Deja, they continued to have sex with each other even after he was with Sierra. Deja never let on that his situation with Sierra was a problem. That is, until now.

"Fuck ya lil' girlfriend, fuck you. I'm havin' my damn baby, with or without ya help! So I don't give a fuck what you tell her. Do you want me ta tell da bitch?"

Lamont stared at Deja with a blank look on his face. He neglected to tell Sierra about Deja but after the chance meeting between the two women, it was over for him and the woman he was in love with. The only woman that he ever was in love with.

He picked up Trey so that he could give him a bath. He didn't understand how someone that was so special to him could come from a woman that he couldn't stand. He admitted to himself that he wasn't ready for a child but because his mother had left him as a child, he promised that he would be there for his every step of the way.

Deja exited the bedroom, fully dressed. She was a very attractive woman, with high cheekbones and bronze skin. She fell back from Lamont after the baby and kept him on a string. She had everything she wanted: her baby, her space; and of course, Lamont Simmons, by the balls.

"I'm outta here, Lamont" she announced. "Thanks for comin' over here."

Lamont's jaw tightened. He figured that Deja had already lined up another "victim" to trap off with a baby.

"Where you goin', anyway? You goin' ta meet up wit' ya boyfriend?" he asked, while inspecting her sexy outfit.

Deja smirked. "I will see you in a couple of hours, Lamont, and don't worry about where I'm goin'. Now dat you don't have ya lil' girlfriend, you seem to be real curious 'bout what I do wit' my time."

Lamont clenched his teeth. He looked at his son, who was in his arms and put him down on the floor. He approached Deja.

"I'm real tired of you throwin' dat shit in my face! When you gonna realize dat you neva was my woman? You was my side bitch, and you always gon' be a side bitch!"

Deja was emotionless. "Yep, I was ya side bitch, but you was fuckin' me probably as much as you was screwin' your lil' girlfriend! But get over it 'cause I have ya son now. Not bad work fuh a side bitch, huh?"

Before he knew it, Lamont grabbed Deja by her neck and pushed her up against the wall in the hallway of her apartment. Trey looked up at his parents and smiled, not knowing what was going on.

"Look, girl," Lamont began. "I'm real sick of ya fuckin' mouth. I'm real tired of you bringin' up Sierra. Keep it up and I'm gon' whip yo' ass. Do you understand me?"

Deja was struggling to remove Lamont's large hand from her throat. She couldn't breathe. He finally released the hold and she fell back, gasping for air. She was unusually calm while rubbing her throat.

"Put ya paws on me again and dat's ya job! I'm tired of you tryin' ta put ya hands on me, Lamont!"

"What you gon' do, call da police? Fuck wit' my job, bitch, and I'll kill you!" Deja looked at the crazed look on Lamont's face and quickly exited the apartment. He watched as the door slammed and proceeded to give his son a bath and a warm bottle. Trey eventually fell asleep in his father's arms.

After Lamont put Trey in his bedroom, he decided to call

someone. He was bored with watching sports on the Madison Square Garden cable channel on Deja's big-screen TV; he needed some company. He felt his doggish ways coming on and couldn't resist the sexual urges he felt. He picked up the phone and dialed Monique Phillips's phone number. After three rings, she finally picked up.

"Hello," Monique answered, as she turned down the music in the background.

"Hey, Phillips, what up, girl?" Lamont shouted.

"Who is dis?"

"Girl, it's me, Lamont. You don't recognize my voice now?"

"Heyyyy, Lamont! What do I owe dis phone call?"

"I need you to do me a fava. Come bring dat pussy ta me, right now."

"Mmm, no doubt, Mr. Simmons, I was about ta go ta a party but I can definitely come see you first. Where you at?"

Lamont gave her the address. Monique must have been in the neighborhood because it took her ten minutes to get over there. When she walked in, Lamont was impressed with her. She was dressed in a pair of Apple Bottoms jeans that fit her to a T, with a sequined gold shirt, which slightly hung off of her left shoulder, revealing a sexy tattoo. Her long weave was tied into a neat bun on the side of her head, and her large hoop earrings added to her stylish appearance. Lamont stared at Monique as she walked toward the living room and plopped down in front of the television. Lamont joined her.

"So, is dis ya apartment, Lamont? It's really nice."

"Somethin' like dat. Okay, let's get to it." He began kissing all over Monique. She pushed him away.

"Wait, boy! Damn, could I at least get a conversation before we get busy? I jus' walked through da door!"

Lamont didn't have time for Monique's antics. She came over, she wanted to have sex. That's all he wanted anyway.

Lamont stood up. Monique was resisting his advances, and

he was getting impatient. "What is ya problem, Monique? What you came ova here ta do? Talk or screw?"

Her feelings seemed hurt. "I came to have sex wit' you, Lamont, but you ain't even give me a chance to get warmed up. I mean, I really like you and I thought you really wanted me ta come over 'cause you wanted ta see me other than ta get a quick nut."

He laughed. Was she serious? This was a woman, in Lamont's mind, who would fuck whatever man the wind blew in, as long as he was suitable to her taste. He didn't want to tell her that she was about to get sexed in his son's mother's house, so he had to take care of business and get her out of there.

"Take ya clothes off, Phillips."

Monique got up to leave. Lamont pushed her back down on the couch. He was horny as hell and he couldn't let Monique leave without him having his way with her. Monique followed his request and undressed. She stood in the middle of the living room floor, with nothing on but her Victoria Secret's underwear. Lamont's penis rose instantly. He immediately put on a condom and opened her legs.

"What's wrong, girl? Don't you want me?" Lamont whispered, as he entered Monique and began having sex with her on Deja's couch. Monique closed her eyes and began to get into it after a couple of strokes. Lamont was able to get his rocks off, not caring if Monique enjoyed herself or not.

After they were cleaned up, Monique stood by the door. She had a somber look on her face, like she was expecting a kiss from him. Lamont ignored her attitude.

"Ah-ight, Phillips, good lookin' out," he said, as he held out his hand for a pound. Monique just stared at it and gave him a quick hug.

"I guess dat's it, huh, Lamont?" she asked.

"What are you talkin' about, Monique? I mean, we just had a good time. Why spoil da mood?"

She shook her head. She opened the door to walk down the hallway toward the stairs. "I'll see you at work, Captain."

Monique did not look up when she walked out the door.

"Yeah, fine." Lamont watched Monique disappear in the stairwell before he shut the door. He ran to the window and saw her pull off in her Mercedes, causing the tires to screech a little. He knew he was inconsiderate from time to time but he really felt sorry for Monique. He knew that she was looking for love and the only way she felt that she could find it was with sex. Who was he to tell her any different when their lives mirrored each other?

Just then, he heard Trey crying in his bedroom. Lamont grabbed a bottle from the kitchen counter and went to comfort his son.

Chapter Ten

MONIQUE

It was going into Monday morning and Monique walked to her post after roll call was dismissed. She was pissed off because she had to stare at Lamont, who for some reason would not give her the time of day after they had sex the night before. She had other plans tonight. She took a deep breath as she prepared to relieve the 3:00 to 11:00 PM officer. As she walked inside 5 North to do a count, she was happy it was quiet, meaning most of the inmates were settled in for the night. Tomorrow was court for most of them and that meant an early night.

Monique walked up to one cell door and tapped lightly. The inmate inside the cell was lying down, reading a book with his back turned to the door. He smiled as he turned around and saw Monique standing there. He immediately ran to the door.

"Hey, Miss P," he said. "What's up for tonight?"

"I'm ready. I got da things you asked for," she replied. He smiled, showing his pretty white teeth. "Good, good. Just holla at me when you finish takin' care of ya business."

Monique played her position until the housing-area captain

made his rounds and signed the large logbook. On the midnight shift, the captains usually shuffled into their offices, disappearing for most of the shift, until the court inmates were about to move. Monique knew that the captain would not be visible for another couple of hours so she would have to move quickly.

She tiptoed inside the small control room that separated the two large housing areas. She was bombarded by loud snores coming from the officers, who were laid back in worn recliner chairs and with rolls of toilet paper under their necks for pillows. Monique made a quick observation of the control panel. She noticed that all the cells had green lights next to the control button, meaning that they were closed. There were two or three cells that had red lights, which meant they could be opened by just jerking the handle. Monique was relieved because she could open her guy's cell without it being so obvious.

As she reentered the dark 5 North, there were a few cell lights on. Inmates that wanted extra privacy had their cell windows covered. Monique put her keys in her pocket as she crept up the stairs. She had some food and other items in her hands, also some Magnum condoms in her pocket. She was slightly nervous because she was about to do what so many female officers had done and were fired for. It felt good to be genuinely desired or so she thought by a man, without any agenda or financial gain on her part. Her heart skipped a beat as she realized that she was about to do the unthinkable: have sex with an inmate inside his cell. When she arrived at the cell door, she was startled when she saw him standing there, obviously waiting for her.

Monique held her chest. "Oh, damn!" she whispered. "You scared the hell outta me!"

Scooter pulled her inside the cell, quickly removing the articles from her hands. "I'm sorry, baby . . . let's go. You know we don't have much time," he whispered back.

Monique instantly dropped her uniform pants to reveal a red lace thong. He instantly pulled her to him by grabbing her round butt. She pulled his wife beater over his head and squatted in front of him, pulling his boxers down to his ankles. She opened her uniform shirt to reveal a red lacy bra so while she gave him the blow job of his life, he could have a slight visual of her perky breasts. She licked and sucked him, forcing him to pull back, with him not wanting to have an orgasm too quickly. Scooter laid Monique on the thin mattress. He put on a Magnum and he slid inside of her. Their bodies moved rhythmically as the moon glared through the cell window. He took long, deep strokes, making sure he touched every crevice of her insides. Monique did everything to keep from screaming because she was feeling so good. Her body tingled as he grabbed her ass and pulled himself deeper inside her, touching her G-spot. "Oooh, right there, baby!" she whispered softly, as she wrapped her long legs around his butt and he pumped harder and harder, almost forgetting where he was. They both climaxed together, not even remembering if they had screamed out loud in their fits of ecstasy. Monique rapidly dressed as she watched him eat the seafood dinner she brought him.

Suddenly, a wave of shame, guilt, and fear swept through her body. She hoped she hadn't made a big mistake. Monique had just played out an illicit fantasy of hers that could possibly cost her the job. The strangest thing was that she still felt unfulfilled. To make matters worse, she was number thirteen on the promotional list to become a captain. What was she thinking?

Scooter passed her the tray with small remnants of food on it so that she could dispose of the evidence. He had already made himself comfortable and was about to fall asleep. Monique gathered the used condom and her belongings as she left the cell, making sure that it was locked when she walked out.

Just as she walked back to her desk, the assistant deputy warden walked in. Luckily, she had discarded everything just in time. She never saw Rasheed, who had been at his cell door the entire time. As he watched her enter and exit Scooter's cell, he shook his head in disgust.

Chapter Eleven

SIERRA

Sierra and Red exited the parked vehicle and immediately began walking down the long block to PK's. Sierra was more than exited to see her longtime lover and friend. Red, who was just basically along for the night, was none too anxious to see her childhood flame, Melvin. She was pissed that Sierra waited until the last minute to tell her that he would be there tonight. She felt that Sierra was just thinking about herself.

"Si, I know dat you brought me along for da third wheel but it's ah-ight. You lucky I got love fuh yo ass."

Sierra rolled her eyes in her head. "Red, please!" she screamed. "You know Tyke is married and yeah, maybe you are my fall guy tonight but at least you got company. Mel is gonna be there. Just try ta have fun!"

Red huffed and brushed her naturally red-colored hair out her face. "I don't give a fuck if I'm gettin' on ya nerves, Miss Thang, but you know dat chapter of my life has been closed fuh some years now. I don't deal wit' da thugs anymore. I gotta new life and new career and unlike you, I ain't tryin' to ruin my life by dealin' wit' certain people!"

Sierra stopped dead in her tracks. Why was Red taking potshots at her? She just wanted everyone to enjoy themselves. Tyke was hanging out with his best friend and she thought she was hanging out with hers.

"Hey! We are goin' in here ta have a good time wit' two ol' friends of ours. Okay, some of da shit they done in their lives might not have been socially acceptable but I ain't gon' forget about where da fuck I came from, whether I'm a CO or not! Remember, you from da fuckin' projects just like me! Don't go get brand-new on me!"

Red smirked. She was glad that she had gotten Sierra just as annoyed as she was right now. She remembered ending up pregnant by Melvin when she was sixteen years old and she couldn't stand him for it. Sierra felt that Red's pregnancy was just as much as her fault as it was Mel's. Red refused to take responsibility for her part and continually blamed Melvin all of these years.

Sierra walked in silence. Red had pissed her off as usual even though deep down in her heart she knew that the things her friend were saying were true. If she felt like that about Tyke and Melvin, imagine what she would say if Sierra told her about her attraction to Rasheed? She knew at that point that her little secret was going to remain a secret.

Red grabbed Sierra's arm. She wanted to clear the air before they stepped inside. "Si, I'm sorry. I know I been gettin' on ya nerves and I give you a hard time. It's just dat I go to work and come home—I don't have a life anymore and I'm miserable. Yeah, I admitted it. I'm tired of bein' by myself. But you got ya peeps, Tyke, in there waitin' and he always loved you. I ain't gonna ruin the night wit' my stank-ass attitude. I just want you to have a good time, okay?"

Sierra smiled as she gave Red a quick hug. "Thanks, Red. Shiiit, as horny as I am, I can't wait ta get me some of dat fine-ass man up in there! And you need ta be hollerin' at Melvin too!"

Red turned her lip up. "I don't think so. Melvin probably look old and funky now. I ain't seen him in years!"

The ladies entered the lounge and walked to the back where everybody was jamming to the music. Sierra spotted Tyke, who was by the bar and signaling for them to join him. She walked in his direction and gave him the tightest hug that she could. Tyke had gained weight while he was locked up, which looked good on him. He looked clean-cut and muscular with the form-fitting T and jeans he was wearing. Sierra stole a brief glance at the Raymond Weil watch he had on his wrist and his pinky ring, which was flooded with diamonds. She frowned as she tried to figure out where Tyke had gotten the money to afford the expensive items but pushed any negative thoughts of out her mind.

"Heyyy, Tyke!" Sierra yelled over the loud music. "I see dat you gettin' ya grown man on. You look good!"

Tyke flashed a smile. "Yeah, baby girl!" he replied. "I can't come home and not be able ta fuck wit' these young niggas! I had ta step my game up!" He looked at Red and pulled her to him for a hug. Red was only five feet tall and looked like a midget in comparison to Tyke. "What up, Red? Ya ready fuh my man, Mel?"

Red rolled her eyes. She remembered Melvin being a scrawny teenager. She hadn't seen him in years and she assumed he was probably no bigger that what he was as an adolescent.

Just then, Melvin appeared out of the crowd of people on the dance floor. Red was pleasantly surprised as the six feet one Melvin engaged in conversation with Sierra and Tyke, purposely ignoring Red. His wavy hair and full beard were shaped up perfectly. His Cartier glasses completed his chiseled looks. His body was toned and he exuded the scent of Armani Code cologne. Sierra looked at Red's stunned expression. She knew that Red expected him to be broke down. Little did she know that the same Melvin who used to terrorize Brownsville as a young man was now an entrepreneur, flipping his money into lucrative businesses and investments. Sierra withheld the information from Red because she wanted her to find out for herself.

Melvin finally walked over and hugged Red. Red hugged him tightly for what seemed like a long time and they casually walked away from Tyke and Sierra to talk outside on the veranda, located at the back of PK's. Sierra focused her attention on her old lover. He looked so handsome tonight that she wanted to eat him alive.

"So," Sierra began. "What you been gettin' into, Mr. Williams?"

Tyke rubbed Sierra's mocha-colored cheek. "Hopefully, I'm gettin' into you, baby," he replied softly in her ear. He made her skin quiver as his lips brushed up against her ear.

"You look real good, Tyke. I hate ta say it, but dat bid did you some good. I mean, it saved ya life and it seem like it changed ya attitude too."

"Yeah, man, it did. I'm hookin' up wit' Mel and I got a lot of ideas I wanna put together ta get dis money, Si."

She was impressed. "I hope it's all legal money, Tyke. You know how you do. You be doin' mad good fuh a hot minute then you right back on dem streets!"

He shook his head in agreement. "You right, you right. But dis time I'm on some otha shit. Whut you been up to? How dat job treatin' my baby?"

"It's good, Tyke. Same shit, different day. Jail is jail."

"I be knowin'." Tyke looked on the dance floor. "C'mon, boo, let's dance."

Sierra turned over as she thought about her night with Tyke. They had ended up in her bed together and she was exhausted from a night of passionate lovemaking. He hadn't left until 7:00 that morning. Before he left, he asked her if they could start a relationship with each other again. She couldn't accept. She had made a promise to herself that she wasn't going to settle for less and although Tyke was a good man to her, he wasn't the man for her. He was married with kids, she was single with no kids; it wouldn't work out.

Lately, Rasheed Gordon had been on her mind. His sex appeal was overpowering but she didn't think it was just about lust with him. He seemed so endearing and she was captivated by him. If only she could find out more about him, she probably would give him a chance. She never considered having any type of dealings with an inmate, but she had to wonder what was it about Rasheed that made her want to get to know him.

Chapter Twelve

RASHEED

Rasheed packed his belongings as he prepared to go home. He was happy because his family had prepared a coming-home party just for him. He not only was coming home but he was finally off of parole. He served his time and that was it. No more bids, no more bullshit, no more Tamir.

Rasheed had not tried to contact Tamir since she came to visit him. He heard about her still being up to her same old tricks and hanging around his aunt's shop, leaving messages with them for him to call her. That chapter was closed. He felt like a free man now that he didn't have to carry Tamir's dead-weight around. He hated that she was so dependent on him. He wanted a woman like Sierra—no, he wanted Sierra. She had been off for a couple of days and he was happy when he looked up and saw her in 5 North. She instantly walked to his cell after the count.

"Hey, Gordon." She greeted him with a warm smile. "I hear you goin' home. I know you glad."

Rasheed stared at her. Was this the time to tell her how he felt? "Yeah, I'm glad." He paused. "Yo, listen, Miss H. I'm feelin' you, hard. What's up, can I talk to you when I get out?"

Sierra seemed taken aback by the question. "Gordon, I don't think dat would be a good idea."

"Why not? I'll be home, nobody don't have to know."

Sierra laughed. He could tell she wanted to take him up on his offer so bad but she couldn't. She told him many other females went down the same way and she didn't feel bad for them—until now. She thought that they were gullible and careless but what would she be if she was to actually act on her feelings?

Sierra took a deep breath. "Gordon, that's why I really can't. It's not right. I mean, don't get me wrong, you are fine as hell and you seem mad cool, but I can't take a chance like dat. It could cost me my job and then what?"

Rasheed was disappointed but he was determined. "It's cool, Miss H. I'm gonna see you out in da streets." He looked at his cell. "Yo, ma, let me get back to getting myself together. Could you give a call ta da general office and see when they comin' ta get me? I'm ready to get outta here!"

Sierra watched Rasheed for a minute more and walked away from his cell. When she got back to her desk, the phone began ringing. They were on their way to get Rasheed Gordon. He was going home. Sierra happily walked back to his cell.

"Gordon, they comin' ta get you. You ready?" she asked. Rasheed nodded his head and she motioned for the control-room officer to open his cell door. She stepped into his cell, grabbed his face, and gave him the most passionate kiss he had probably ever had in his life. He was shocked as he watched her back out of his cell.

Rasheed walked down the stairs with a small bag of personal belongings. Sierra wondered what he did with the rest of the items.

"Gordon, where is ya stuff? You ain't takin' it wit' you?" Rasheed shook his head.

"I ain't takin' none of dat shit home. I got a couple o' personal papers in dis bag right here and some other things but da clothes you can give it to my young boys, Pretty and Valentine. They can have dat shit." Rasheed looked at Sierra and touched his lips. "What was dat for?"

"It was somethin' I wanted ta do fuh a while now. A farewell kiss. Hoping I see you one day, dat's all."

"Damn, I can only imagine what comes wit' dat. Too bad, I may neva find out."

"You neva can say, Gordon. You neva know how things will turn out."

Rasheed had one more thing he had to do before he left. Scooter was running his mouth and he heard that he called the inspector general's office on Miss Phillips. He didn't want to put Miss Phillips's business out there but he had to speak with Pretty and Valentine, who were young five-star generals of the sex, money, murder bloods set. Scooter would have to be taken care of and now that Rasheed was going home, he wouldn't have to be involved. In jail, snitching is a no-no and Scooter had violated that rule in so many ways by talking too much. Rasheed walked to Pretty and Valentine's cell door and tapped lightly. They both emerged from their sleep and came to the cell window.

"What up, Pretty? What's poppin', Val? I hate ta wake y'all, man, but listen, remember dat shit I told you and Val ta do fuh me. Y'all blow dat nigga face off. Dat frontin'-ass nigga is runnin' round tryin' ta be somethin' he not and he a rat."

"Yeah, son, good lookin'. We got him. Today when Daniels come in on da three-to-eleven, we gon' make dat move," whispered Pretty Blood, a tall, good-looking young man, with a small scar above his right eye.

"Good, son. I ain't gonna say no names but somebody was lookin' out for him in here and he done called IG on they ass. Fuck dat dude!"

"Nah, we don't tolerate dat!" replied Valentine, a short square-faced man with a muscular build. "If he could rat on somebody dat's lookin' out for his lame ass, he won't have no problem snitchin' on one of us! Shiiit, he makin' it hard fuh da other niggas in here dat wanna eat! COs ain't gonna do shit fuh niggas up in here after awhile!"

Rasheed laughed. He knew that Valentine was telling the truth. There were inmates who respected COs that looked out for them while they were locked up. Then there were the ungrateful scavengers, like Scooter, who were always looking to get over on staff.

"Anotha thing," Rasheed added. "Dat nigga is a Crip. A reliable Crip source confirmed da shit."

"Wooord, Rah?" announced a surprised Pretty, causing Valentine to have a stunned look on his face. "Dat muthafucka be frontin' then. He stay comin' at me and Val talkin' in codes and tryin' ta participate in our roll call and all dat. I ain't never heard otherwise 'bout dis lame-o, so more or less, I thought he was a homie."

"Fuck dat bird-ass nigga!" Val exclaimed, who was quite upset and couldn't wait to get at Scooter. "We gonna make a movie in here, son. Put dat crab on da menu. Put in dat work!"

Pretty finally gathered his senses and realized Rasheed was out of his cell early in the morning. "Oh shit, Rah, you outta here?"

"Yeah, man, I'm out. Yo, do me anotha favor. Look out for dat young lady. She real special."

Pretty had an idea Rasheed and Sierra were feeling each other. Rasheed was his people and he had no problem granting his requests.

"Miss H? Don't worry, kid, she good wit' us. Dat's a good officer right there and a good person too."

"I had my people put some money in y'all commissary, so take care of dat nigga. Oh, and I tol' Miss H ta let you and Val go get all those clothes and stuff outta my ol' cell—y'all can have whateva you want. Whateva you do, wait 'till Miss H leave ta get at dat nigga, son. We don't need her gettin' in no trouble. Daniels is my man and I done already put him on ta da shit so he gon' leave post fuh a lil' while so y'all can handle ya business. He got family ties so he'll be able ta get outta dis shit." Rasheed heard his name being called in the front. "Y'all lil' niggas, take care, and hold ya heads. You got my home number, Pretty, so call me if you need anything, ah-ight?"

Pretty was a little teary-eyed. Rasheed had been like a big brother to him for years and they had even been upstate together before. Pretty had no family and Rasheed had treated him like a brother, which was all he needed. "No doubt, son. Love is love. I'ma holla, Rah, be easy!" He watched as Rasheed disappeared to the front of the housing area.

The intake officer was there to pick Rasheed up but he was waiting outside the housing-area door. Rasheed winked at Sierra and placed a piece of paper with his information on her desk. As he walked out, he inconspicuously blew a kiss at her. Sierra sat in her seat and stared at the crinkled piece of paper. It had Rasheed's address and phone numbers on it. Also, it had information about a party for him. He wanted her to come.

At approximately 6:00 PM, 5 North was buzzing with activity. It was the 3:00 to 11:00 PM shift and if anything was going to happen in jail, it would usually occur at this time of the day. Some inmates were watching TV in the dayroom, some were playing cards, taking showers, etc. CO Daniels was on post, making sure everything was going smoothly. He found out that his old neighborhood running buddy, Rasheed Gordon, had gone home. CO Daniels could have easily been in the cell next to Rasheed's at the rate he was going in his younger years. Thanks to his mother and his uncles, who were also on the job, they kept him in line. He knew what was about to go down but had to look as ordinary as possible. Daniels walked around and talked smack with the inmates, giving Valentine and Pretty the sign to take care of their business. It was perfect because he really wanted to be inside the control station with a new female officer, who was cute as hell and had a nice, firm ass. He loved new meat and like so many other male correction officers, was trying to hit that before anyone else got to her. He did one more visual of 5 North and walked out of the housing area to talk to the rookie officer, who looked like she needed a little help with the count slips.

Pretty and Valentine watched as Daniels left the post. They knew that they would have to get on the ball. They watched Scooter walk around bragging about how they didn't take a lot of his impermissible items during the routine search. Scooter went to his cell, unaware that Pretty and Valentine were lagging behind him. As he was about to walk back out of his cell after using the toilet, he was shocked to see that Valentine and Pretty had blocked him in. Scooter backed up, looking like he knew what was about to happen to him. The housing area was quiet, like everyone was waiting for something to pop off. Pretty spoke first. "What up, Scooter? We been hearin'a lot of shit about you dat we not feelin'!"

Scooter squinted. "Yo, Pretty, man, why is you even entertainin' dat bullshit? These niggas don't be talkin' about nuthin' in here!"

Valentine spoke next. "Nigga, I'm hearin' you a crab, a fuckin' Crip. You been frontin' like you Damu. Tellin' niggas, zero-three-one and shit! You know dat's a direct violation!"

"Oh, yeah," Pretty Blood blurted out, almost forgetting some other disturbing news he heard about Scooter. "Heard dis nigga is a faggot too, Val! He got a lil' boyfriend in da town. Da nigga Sandman from four Main sent me a kite about dis dude. You know him, Scoot. Y'all both from Grant Projects. Sandman said Scoot like a lil' shit on his dick."

Valentine was shocked and disgusted. "What?! Aww, man, come on! You a fuckin' snitch and you like dudes? Damn, I woulda never thought you get down like dat!"

"Sandman don't know me from a muthafucka!" Scooter

lied. Sandman was his lover's first cousin so he knew everything. "Man, these cats be hatin' on me! Y'all lil' niggas don't know what da fuck y'all talkin' about!"

Pretty looked around Scooter's cell. He noticed all kind of unauthorized items that Scooter obviously was allowed to keep.

"Dis muthafucka got all kinds o' shit in his cell. Damn, Timberland boots, Nikes, damn, they took my shit and put it in property. How you get ta keep dis stuff, crab?" Pretty asked.

At that moment, Scooter attempted to push past the two young men, who overpowered him and knocked him to the floor. Pretty and Valentine were only twenty-two years old, but they had a lot of anger and hostility, not to mention lengthy criminal histories and jail infractions. They could care less about beating someone senseless and were paid very well by other inmates, who recruited the young thugs to do their dirty work. They beat Scooter mercilessly and cut him from his left temple to his jawbone. Before they walked out of the cell, they flushed the evidence down the toilet, while Scooter was laid out bleeding on the cold, cement floor. They stepped over his limp body as they walked out of the cell. Their mission was accomplished.

Chapter Thirteen

LAMONT

Captain Simmons responded to 5 North, just as the response team was called down. Lamont found out that Daniels was off of his post at the time of the slashing and wasn't doing his thirty-minute tours like he was supposed to. Lamont knew the warden was going to be asking him a shitload of questions that he refused to take the fall for.

Lamont was not pleased as the gate opened to the housing area. He spoke to Daniels, who told him that he discovered Inmate Shamel Abrams on the floor of his cell, covered with blood. Daniels was not sure if he had been cut by someone else or if he had cut himself. Surrounded by a sea of white shirts, as the COs called supervisory staff members, Lamont felt nervous and anxious. He also thought about his promotion. Daniels was on the bottom of the totem pole. He could afford a couple of days on suspension. He had no dreams or aspiration to ever be promoted like Lamont wanted to be.

Lamont walked to directly to cell 45, which housed Scooter, where medical and uniformed staff placed him on the gurney to take him to the clinic. EMTs were waiting in the jail clinic to rush Scooter to Elmhurst Hospital.

"Mr. Abrams, I'm Captain Simmons," Lamont introduced himself to a barely conscious Scooter. "I'm goin' ta da clinic with you to speak about the incident. I need you to tell me if CO Daniels was on post when this happened. That's very important!" The other officers that were within earshot of Lamont's comments shook their heads in earnest. They wouldn't want to be in Daniels's shoes right now.

"But, Cap, this inmate has to go to the hospital!" the medical escort stated. Lamont looked at him like he had grown two heads.

"Wait until I get there to question him! After I question him, he could go to West Hell for all I care! That is a direct order!" Lamont demanded.

After the injured Scooter was removed from the housing area, CO Daniels and the new officer in the control station were ordered to write incident reports about what happened. As the new officer cried her eyes out, tenured COs assisted her in writing a report. Lamont ran around 5 North, asking inmates to write statements about what they saw. He was aggravated as inmates either ignored him or cussed him out. They weren't telling on nobody! Daniels had a smirk on his face as Lamont approached him and the tour commander, Assistant Deputy Warden Miller, who was already discussing the incident. Daniels had a personal vendetta against Lamont, especially after the way he treated Sierra, who happened to be a very good friend of his.

"Mr. Daniels," Lamont announced, "I'm hearin' you left this post! Do you know that this crook could sue the department because of your negligence?"

"Look, Cap," Daniels replied, trying to remain calm. "I had ta take a personal and I left my post for a few minutes. When I came back, all dis bullshit had went down! Plus, I apologized ta Dep. Miller already. I ain't even gotta talk ta you."

At this moment, inmates began yelling at Lamont to leave their steady officer, Daniels, alone. The inmates had a lot of respect for Daniels and didn't like Lamont reprimanding him in front of everybody. This made Lamont even more upset.

"Daniels, I'm writin' you up! You fucked up big-time and now it's gonna be a lot of repercussions behind dis incident. I mean, a search team just left this housin' area at four PM and now all of a sudden, a weapon appears and an inmate is cut. How do you think dat looks?"

Daniels frowned. Captain Simmons was pushing his buttons. "What da hell you tryin' ta say, Cap? You tryin' ta say I had somethin' ta do wit' dis shit?"

"I just find it funny—"

Daniels cut Lamont off. "Yo, man, I don't have no fuckin' time ta bring in a damn thing fuh one o' these mufuckas in here. No razors, no cigarettes, no food. Personally, I don't give a fuck if they fuckin' kill each other! Besides, nigga, dis is jail! Y'all mufuckas act like shit don't happen in jail!"

Lamont counterattacked. He couldn't allow Daniels to disrespect him in front of Dep. Miller, who was unusually quiet as they exchanged angry diatribes.

"You know what, Daniels? I'm writin' yo ass up fuh insurbordination, abandonment of post, and conduct unbecoming an officer! Now I'm gonna give you a direct order to relinquish your equipment. I want you off dis fuckin' post!"

At that point, Dep. Miller ordered the two men outside of the housing area into the small corridor by the stairway. He had a feeling it was going to get uglier and the inmates had already seen too much of a show as it is.

Daniels cleared his throat to get Lamont's attention again. "Why you writin' me up, Cap?"

Lamont, clearly agitated by Daniels and the slashing, instantly lashed out. "Because you a fuckin' assho—"

With that being said, Daniels drew back his right fist and laid Lamont out with a hook to the jaw. Daniels dropped the equipment on the floor alongside Lamont's semiconscious body, watching the picture slide out his hands.

"There's ya fuckin' equipment, sir!" Daniels said, with disgust. He gestured for Dep. Miller, who had a grin on his face. "C'mon, Uncle Tony, let's get outta here!" Dep. Miller and CO Sean Daniels, his sister's son, stepped over Lamont and walked the corridor toward the front of the building.

During the course of the day, the inspector general's office and the gang intelligence officers, were walking around questioning inmates, to no avail. Some inmates were moved from the housing area, including Pretty and Valentine, whose commissary accounts had $500 apiece for their effort, thanks to Rasheed.

The housing area was turned upside down. Mattresses were searched and inmates were taken to the B.O.S.S. chair, which could detect if they had any metal objects on their body by them just sitting upright. The jail was on lockdown and a T.S.O (Tactical Search Operation) was in full swing. COs from jails all over the city were there searching everything from the ceiling to the floor. Weapons and other contraband were found in the strangest places and officers were writing reports like crazy. The warden was furious because it made him look bad. If he looked bad, somebody was going to have to pay.

An officer walked from cell 45, Scooter's old cell, with a disturbing picture. He handed the flick to a captain. It was a picture of a woman with a CO uniform shirt on.

The shirt was open to reveal the woman's bare chest and she had on panties. The face was cut off but she had a small tattoo on her groin area. The captain just shook his head and sadly passed it on to an IG officer.

Chapter Fourteen

SIERRA

Sierra walked into 5 North, which was unusually quiet. She had gotten wind of what happened that day from Daniels, who called her at home. She laughed when he told her he had to knock Lamont out. She felt the punch was long overdue.

The housing area wasn't the same now that Rasheed was gone. On one note, she was relieved he wasn't there. She wouldn't have to fight off her attraction to him. But for some strange reason, she missed him. He had been in 5 North for at least six months and she became accustomed to seeing him every day. She thought about the information Rasheed had given her that she had neatly tucked in her underwear drawer at home. She looked at the number one time too much that night before contemplating calling him. Sierra knew that if she did, she would be violated the rules and regulations of the department. Officers were not allowed to fraternize with present or former inmates. It was called "undue familiarity" and Sierra wanted no part of it. There was a rumor swirling around the jail that a female officer's seminude picture was found near an inmate's cell. She didn't ever want to be in that position.

What was that officer thinking? She probably could figure out how she felt. The taboo of an officer and inmate being together made it even more exciting to some. They didn't realize that there were limits to that kind of behavior.

As she sat on the post throughout the day, she was blessed with the unfortunate presence of Monique Phillips. Monique was on overtime that day and just happened to relieve Sierra for lunch. Sierra noticed Monique wasn't her usual self, which she found odd. Monique strolled into the housing area, accepted the radio, keys, and personal body alarm, and proceeded to make her logbook entries, all in silence. Sierra felt compelled to ask Monique if she felt okay, unsure of what the response would be. She decided she would take a chance anyway.

"Umm, Monique," Sierra began cautiously. "I'm not tryin' ta be in ya business but are you okay? I mean, you ain't cussin' me out like you usually do."

Monique gave Sierra a faint smile. "I'm okay. I'm just goin' through a lot, I guess."

Sierra sighed. She was really reaching, but someone had to be the mature one. Their feud had been going on for too long and although they probably would not ever be the best of friends, they could at least respect each other.

"Oh, okay. Whateva it is, I hope you feel better."

Monique didn't look up as she continued to write. "Thank you. Take ya time comin' back from meal. I ain't got nuthin' else ta do."

Sierra banged on the glass for the control-station officer to open the gate. She had to get out of there before Monique changed her mind. She wondered what was going on with her. She walked in 5 North like it was the end of the world; like she had lost her best friend, if she had any friends at all. The job was stressful and Monique had a teenaged daughter, so she probably had it coming from both ends.

While out on meal, Sierra slid into the K.K. The K.K., or keepers' kitchen, was similar to a small cafeteria where food was served by the inmates to officers. She sat at a table by herself as other officers conversed at the tables all around her. She didn't feel like participating in the rumor mill and just settled on watching the large-screen floor television for the latest news. Nothing was wrong with eavesdropping, though. No one could ever say that she said anything if she just listened.

"Dat bitch was fuckin' wit' Abrams," claimed a buxom officer with bad skin. "Dat was the only muthafucka in here who would be stupid enough to give a inmate a flick of her in her damn uniform shirt!"

"Girl, please!" a petite senior officer exclaimed. "It could be any fuckin' body. I know it definitely ain't you wit' ya fat ass!" They both laughed.

"Shit, I'm glad it ain't me wit' my fat ass! I wouldn't want nobody ta catch a picture of me or my body, fat or otherwise, in a crook's cell!"

Miss Petite laughed. "I hope it ain't her. I mean, she a ho, but dat shit would be embarassin'. Oh yeah, ain't she fuckin' wit' Captain Simmons now?"

"Whaaaat? She ain't even his type! He look like he into those cutesy females! She sure ain't no cutesy!" said Big Breasts.

"Well, anyway, Miss Phillips betta get right wit' God 'cause if dat is her in dem pictures, it's a wrap for her dumb behind!"

Sierra sat very still. *Dat's why she look so depressed,* Sierra thought to herself. She figured that Lamont probably put the mack down on her; that was nothing new. The part she heard about Abrams was a little disturbing. If Monique was messing with him, how did he end up cut up? Was she the woman in the picture? Sierra didn't want to speculate, and after her forty minutes were up, she returned to her post.

Monique was on the phone when she arrived. Sierra gestured for her to finish her conversation and that she would be inside the control station until she was ready. After ten minutes had passed, Monique exited the housing area and Sierra met her in the small corridor to retrieve the equipment.

"Sierra, I need to talk ta you." Monique looked worried. Sierra sighed, hoping that it was no drama. She was not in the mood and promised that this time, sad or not, Monique was going to get her ass whipped.

"About what, Monique? I'm not up fuh da drama. And if it's about Lamont, I don't—"

Monique sucked her teeth. "Girl, it ain't about Lamont. It's about me. Can I have ya number?"

Sierra looked at her. Was this a setup? "Fuh what?"

Monique looked desperate. "Si, I'm serious. I need ta speak ta somebody. I feel like—I feel like . . . killin' myself."

Sierra stopped breathing for a moment and stared at Monique, who seemed unusually calm. There were no tears, no expression. It looked like her mind was made up. Sierra didn't know what to do, but knew that she didn't want to be responsible for Monique taking her life when she probably could have stopped her.

"Hey, Monique, do you want me ta call somebody? A captain or somethin'—"

"Look at dis." Monique handed Sierra the paper she had balled up in her hand. It was letter to appear to 60 Hudson Street, the inspector general's office, for a hearing. It was an allegation made against her.

"I—I don't know where it's comin' from" she said. "It's so many peop . . . if I lose dis job, Si . . . dis job is my life. I don't have anything else."

Sierra looked around the corridor to see if anyone was around. The coast was clear.

"Monique, you have a life. You have ya health, ya family, ya daughter. I mean, you have a lot to live for. Dis job is not da end of da world!"

Monique shook her head. Sierra held her breath and gave

Monique her phone number. Monique crumpled the paper in her hand and held it up to her chest. Sierra ran to the phone and called the captain in the main control room about Monique's mental condition. She was taken by ambulance to Bellevue Hospital that night.

Sierra looked in her full-length mirror in her bedroom at her outfit. She had on a pair of 7 For All Mankind jeans, which fit her nicely. Her form fitting-blouse allowed a little cleavage to show. Her hair dropped down her back in a cascade of loose curls. She had look of satisfaction as she realized this day would change everything she stood for, professionally, if not morally. Tonight, she was going to Rasheed's coming-home party. Daniels had called her to tell her he had a message from someone. That someone was Rasheed. She had just found out that Rasheed and Daniels had grew up together and their families were very close with each other. Daniels insisted that Sierra come to the party, jokingly stating that Rasheed was going to "kick his ass" if Daniels didn't walk in the party with her.

"Sean, I can't go ta dat fuckin' party! Dat's goin' against da grain, man!"

Sean Daniels huffed. "Man, Si, who do you really fuck wit' on dat job? Nobody! Nobody but me! And I ain't telling ya business!"

"I know, Sean, but I'm nervous. I like Gordon, I mean, Rasheed, but what if I see somebody there and—"

"Nigga, you take dat job too damn serious! You know how many mufuckas on dat job dat's doin' grimy shit? Look at ya girl, Phillips. She in Bellevue right now probably bein' sedated cause dat nigga, Scooter, done tol'on her ass."

Sierra stopped in her tracks. "Ohh, dat's why she was so fucked-up today. She was my meal relief." Sierra continued to get ready. "See, Sean, I don't wanna be like Monique. I don't want nobody ta blow me up to IG and I'll be outta my job cause o' my own stupidity."

Sean laughed. "Sierra, dat nigga is home now. You ain't goin' round fuckin' dudes in da jail like Phillips. She was fuckin' Abrams right in his cell!"

"Oooh, Sean, say dat's ya word? Oh, my gosh, she played herself!"

"Look, you got me on bitch mode right now, gossipin' and shit, like I'm a broad. Get ready and meet me at my house. You can park ya truck over here and we could ride in mine. Ya know I gotta ride up in style, in my Escalade!"

Sierra laughed. "You so crazy!" She hung up, grabbed her purse and keys, and flew out the door. She was happy to have a good male friend like Sean. Even better, it felt good to have him as a cosigner. Ever since Rasheed had obviously talked to Sean about how he felt about Sierra, it would make it easier for her to come forward with her feelings.

As she was driving to Sean's house, her cell phone rang. It was Tyke, who she had not heard from since they hung out two weeks before. She smiled as she answered the phone.

"Hey, Tyke." There was a brief silence. "Helloo?"

"Hello, my ass!" a female voice came through loud and clear on Sierra's Sprint phone. "So you still fuckin' my husband, huh?"

Sierra's heart dropped. It was Tyke's wife, NeeNee. She was not up for her bullshit. "What da fuck you doin' callin' my damn phone, NeeNee? I'm not thinkin' about ya fuckin' husband, okay? I got my own man ta fuck wit'!"

"Bitch, you ain't got no man, don't lie ta me! You too busy screwin' everybody else's man ta go get ya own!" NeeNee screamed.

"Sweetie, did you forget dat Tyquan was my man first and you start screwin' him behind my fuckin' back?! What a tangled web we weave, you fuckin' slut! Anyhoo, you had better go take care of ya muthafuckin' kids and stop worryin' bout me—I ain't got no fuckin' kids fuh Tyke—I done swallowed dem all!"

"You lil' bit—"

Sierra hung up on the screaming woman. She was tight from the unexpected phone call and she made a promise that Tyke would not have to worry about her picking up her phone to call him for a while. She was too old to be going through it with his crazy-ass wife.

Chapter Fifteen

RASHEED

The music was blaring from the speakers as people milled inside the club. The place that Rasheed's party was being held was a neighborhood social club that was a fixture in Bedford-Stuyvesant. All of the Gordon family was there, dressed to the nines, as they greeted well-wishers and old friends who came to congratulate Rasheed on his new beginnings. His older brother, Karim, couldn't be there but had surprised him with a late-model Range Rover as a coming-home gift. Rasheed stood at the door, looking handsome as ever, with a crisp button-down with French cuffs, expensive designer jeans, and Gucci loafers. His three-karat diamond earring twinkled as he pulled his long locks into a ponytail. It was still early and people were just coming in, getting a plate of catered soul food, and sitting at the various tables that were lined up around the huge dance floor. The DJ was busy blending and mixing assorted R&B, not wanting to get too hype until the right amount of people was ready to get on the dance floor.

As Rasheed was smiling at and hugging his guests, Sean Daniels and Sierra walked in. Rasheed hadn't seen them yet because his back was turned. Sean waited patiently to be acknowledged, while Sierra looked like she was about to faint. When Rasheed turned around and saw Sierra standing there, he looked like he was about to faint too.

"What up, Rah?" Sean greeted Rasheed with his hand extended. He laughed as Rasheed casually ignored his hand and walked toward Sierra.

"Hey, ma!" Rasheed exclaimed, with a warm smile on his face. "I'm so glad you came."

Sierra blushed. "Yeah, Sean convinced me ta come. You look real handsome!"

"Thank you, thank you, sweetie." He inspected Sierra from head to toe. She was fly as hell, just like he expected her to be. "You lookin' real good too. Damn!"

"What up, Rah?" Sean said again.

Rasheed laughed loudly. "Oh, shit, Sean, I ain't even notice you!"

Sean looked at Sierra. "Damn. See? You got dis mufucka open like a twenty-four-hour store! And you worried 'bout him? Girl, go 'head!" Sean suggested, then quickly drifted off into the crowd and instantly began chatting with old friends. Sierra and Rasheed stood there alone and feeling awkward.

Sierra smiled. Rasheed wanted to melt from just looking at her. He did everything to try to contain himself from kissing her right there in the middle of the party.

"So, what you been up to, Miss Howell?"

"You can call me Sierra, Rasheed. It's okay, we not on da Island no more!"

"Yeah, I know. I'm so happy ta be home, man! I'll never take my freedom fuh granted no more."

"Good. You look too good to be behin' dem bars. Umm, I'm gonna mingle wit' Sean so when you get settled, save me a dance, please."

Rasheed watched as Sierra walked away, looking extra sexy. He was so happy he could have told everybody to go home and leave him and her there by themselves to dance to some slow jams. He was going to get her information tonight because he wanted her. He wanted her that bad.

Rasheed's aunt, Sharee, walked up to him, whispering in his ear that Tamir was outside and wanted to talk to him. He had not seen her since he'd come home and didn't want to see her now. He reluctantly went outside to talk with the love-struck woman, not wanting her to ruin his chances of getting with Sierra Howell.

Tamir was dressed up like she was invited to Rasheed's party. She was adamant as Rasheed told her that she would not be allowed inside. He grabbed her arm and guided her to the corner, where it was dark.

"You ain't comin' in my fuckin' party! I'm not gonna raise my voice and I'm not gonna whip yo ass out here 'cause I'm tryin' ta have a good time. Leave now and don't come back!"

Tamir was persistent. "Why won't you talk ta me, Rah? I'm sorry. I tried ta tell you I was sorry before. Why you not listenin' ta me?"

"Tamir, it's ova, man. I don't want you. You don't want da new me. So go and find you da next gangsta nigga and ride his nuts! We don't have da same dreams, baby, so I can't do it wit' you!"

Tamir began to cry. She buried her face in her hands. "I love you, Rah. I'm nuthin' wit'out you. Nuthin'. I need you, Rah!"

Rasheed turned up his face like he smelled something foul. Tamir looked pathetic as she stood in front of him and begged for his forgiveness.

"Tamir, I forgive you, but it's over. Good-bye and don't think about ruinin' my party. Sharee and her dyke friends is just waitin' ta whip ya ass! I already warned you!"

Rasheed turned around and walked away. He looked at Tamir drive away and went back into the party to search for Sierra. One of the male guests at the party had her posted up, trying to talk to her. Rasheed rudely interrupted.

"Hey, dis is my girl, man!"

The guy politely backed off and Sierra laughed.

"You are so rude, Rasheed. Why you do dat ta dat poor guy?" she asked.

"Fuck him. He ain't nobody; you my guest tonight, not his."

"I didn't know you was funny too. I like you, Gordon. You cool."

"If you like me so much," he said, as he pulled out his phone, "put ya number in dis phone right now before we get too drunk tonight and forget." She gave him the number. "Now I'm gonna really get my party on. I got da best coming-home gift I could get tonight."

Sierra giggled. They partied hard and had a great time together. Even though Sierra went home alone that night, Rasheed told himself that she wouldn't have to worry about going home too many nights alone if he had anything to do with it.

The next day, Rasheed sat on the stoop of his house with his uncle, Kemp. They were having a man-to-man conversation about his plans for the future when Kemp asked him about the female he was with at his party.

"Yo, Unc, I'm tellin' you, dis female is proper! She had da smooth brown complexion, da beautiful eyes, dimples, and nice lil' ass! She's what I want in a girl."

Kemp laughed. "Son, sound like you really diggin' her *personality*!" he sarcastically replied. "Did you get da panties, 'cause it sound like you got da panties."

"Nah, I ain't got da panties. Damn, I ain't even thought about da panties! I been feelin' her ass so hard, I ain't even been thinkin' about gettin' pussy since I been home!"

Kemp looked at Rasheed like he lost his mind. "You, ain't been thinkin' about no punanny? I can't believe it! You must really love dis chick. I gotta meet her."

"I can't put it out there and have her meetin' da fam' yet. I might scare her off. We ain't even sure if we bumpin' like dat yet."

"Let's get dis shit straight. You feelin' shorty, you think she beautiful, blah, blah, blah, she came ta da party last night, and you still ain't sure if y'all rockin' wit' each other yet? Rah, you about to be swaggerless! I'm revokin' ya swag, son. You supposed ta be havin' her eatin' out da palm of ya hands! Damn, Big Rah, you a Gordon, nigga!"

Rasheed knew that his uncle was talking junk, but on the other hand, he was right. He didn't want to keep putting himself out there to Sierra and she ending up hurting his feelings. She still seemed kind of hesitant, even at the party last night. Kemp was going to be on his back about it because he knew that his nephew had always been a womanizer and was always under control. This time, Rasheed didn't feel like he was in control. He was accustomed to having whatever he wanted, whenever he wanted. Sierra was no different but she was giving him a challenge and strangely enough, that made him want her even more.

Kemp rubbed his goatee as he looked at Rasheed, who seemed as if he was in a dreamworld. Kemp was a player indeed and hoped his nephew wasn't hanging his player card up for no woman. It didn't matter how good she looked. Kemp was very macho and he felt men who got soft all over a woman were suckers, which was the reason why he was still single. Now that Rasheed was home, Kemp felt it was his duty to get him hooked up with some good ass and quick.

"Man, I know I'm a Gordon! Dat's da fuckin' problem with the Gordons. We ain't neva been married ta nobody, we ain't neva in no stable relationships. Don't you feel like you just wastin' a good nigga on some o' these triflin'-ass women out here?" Rasheed asked Kemp.

Kemp paused. "What da hell are you talkin' about? I ain't tryin' ta wife a damn body. If I ain't wife my son's mama, why da hell would I put a ring on any bitch's finger except hers and she sure as hell ain't gettin' a ring from me!"

Rasheed was getting annoyed with Kemp's attitude toward women. Clearly, he didn't have much respect for them. "Man, I wanna get married one day and have kids! I ain't got time to be dealin' with these crazy-ass broads out here. Look at Tamir's stupid ass. Dat chick done made me want ta put my hands on her a couple o' times and I don't like to even think about hittin' a woman."

"Fuck Tamir. She da exception. Somebody need ta whip her ass—man or woman. She musta called dis house like a hundred times dat week tryin' ta find out if you came home yet. You know, Ma don't like her. Always thought she was real simple-minded."

"Well, I shoulda listened to Nana when she tol' me about Tamir. She be tryin' ta tell me a lot of shit and I don't listen. I'm listenin' now."

"So, when am I gonna meet dis female? You gon' let ol' Unc meet her?"

"I dunno about you, nigga. You get a lil' disrespectful sometimes. . . ."

Kemp spread his arms out. "C'mon, youngin," he exclaimed, hitting his broad chest in the process. "You know, she gotta get my stamp o' approval. Fuh all I know she could be a dog. Where you meet her, anyway?"

Rasheed hesitated. He really didn't want to tell Kemp that Sierra was a correction officer. "Umm, five North."

"Five North? She a CO, son?" Kemp looked amazed. "Wow. How you bag dat, youngblood? I guess you get ya swagger pass back fuh dat catch! What's her name?"

"Oh, yeah, Si . . . Sierra Howell. Yeah, Sierra. Miss Howell."

The expression on Kemp's face suddenly turned very serious. "Sierra Howell?" Rasheed stared at Kemp.

"Yeah, Sierra Howell. What's da matter?" Rasheed inquired.

"Yo, you need ta leave her alone." Rasheed waited for his uncle to tell him why, but the answer didn't come right away.

"Why? Don't tell me you used ta fuck wit' her!"

"I didn't but my peoples did," Kemp answered.

"So what? Fuck ya peoples! They ain't my friends! I ain't got no loyalty ta those cats like dat—"

"Tyquan, Rasheed. Tyke is her ex-man, nigga!"

Rasheed's face felt hot. He was not a fan of Tyke's and he knew that Tyke surely wasn't a big fan of his. The only thing that saved both of them from trying to kill each other was their love for Kemp, who was caught in the middle. Instead of choosing blood over water, Kemp just made sure that everything was peaceful between the two hotheads instead of an all-out brawl.

Rasheed stood up and walked to the bottom of the steps. He was clearly aggravated with the news. "Damn, Unc, damn! Why her? I want dis fuckin' girl, yo! You know what, fuck Tyke! I don't like dat nigga any fuckin' way!"

"Look, Rah, you just came home, son. I mean, shorty might be a nice young lady but she ain't da one. Ain't no chick worth da bullshit dat Tyke gonna try ta bring over here. Dat's my man but if he fucks wit' you, Rah, I'm gonna have ta kill dat muthafucka! Remember, we tryin' ta get our lives on track after Peppy's murder!"

Rasheed paced up and down. He didn't give a fuck about Tyke and he sure didn't care about Sierra being his old girlfriend. She was about to be Rasheed's new girlfriend.

"Well, you know what, Unc? I ain't tellin' her shit. I'm gonna act like I don't even know dat lame-ass nigga. He don't have ta know nuthin'! And if he find out, let him find out on his own."

"Well, if ya think I'm tellin' him, I ain't. I'm just gonna let da chips fall where they may. Now, what if shorty is still fuckin' wit' him, then what you gonna do, Rah?"

Rasheed laughed. "I hope she is still fuckin' wit' 'im. Dat would give me a even better excuse ta do what I wanted ta do fuh so long and dat's blow his head off!"

"Rah, why you hate dat nigga so much?" Kemp asked. He couldn't understand why they couldn't stand each other.

"Nigga, I got my reasons fuh not likin' dat dude. It's a lot o' shit wit' Tyke, I'll let you know one day. I like ta have da facts before I put a bullet in a nigga ass!"

Kemp sighed. Suddenly, Rasheed's cell phone began to ring. He smiled as he picked up the phone. "Hey, sweetheart, I been waitin' fuh ya call. . . ." It was Sierra. Rasheed frowned as he watched Kemp cover his face with his hands. It was then he knew that he better pull out the guns because it was about to be nothing but drama.

Chapter Sixteen

TYKE

Tyke attempted to call Sierra's phone over and over. He even called her home phone and the voice mail came on. He needed to talk to her after his wife, NeeNee, managed to get a hold of his phone and started calling every female's number that was stored in his phone. She had even called his business associates. Tyke felt that he had no other choice but to whip her behind, and she got the message after a few bumps and bruises.

The last time Tyke called Sierra, she finally picked up the phone. He instantly began yelling at her.

"What da fuck, you ain't pickin' up ya damn phone now?" he shouted.

"Who you talkin' to, Tyke?! Let's not even start dis shit, I don't need it!" she replied.

Tyke got his senses together. He wanted to see her so he knew that he would have to do a little sucking up.

"My bad, baby girl. I know you mad at me 'cause NeeNee called you da other day. I'm gonna apologize for dat."

Sierra was unmoved. "Keep ya fuckin' wife from callin' my

phone, Tyke! You know how I do and she lucky I ain't tryin' ta get arrested or else I would kick her ass—again!"

Tyke laughed. He remembered the day Sierra tore a chunk of hair out of his wife's head. It wasn't funny then but he found humor in it now that so many years went by.

"Ah-ight, ah-ight, there will be no fightin', Laila Ali! You beat her before so we gonna leave it alone!"

"Thank you. Anyway, I'm still mad at you. But fuck dat, when you comin' over here?" Sierra whined.

"Wow, I like your mad! What about later on tonight? You wanna go out?"

"Nah," she said. "I gotta go ta work tomorrow so it gotta be an early night. Dat five in the mornin' is no joke."

"Okay, ma-ma. Look, let me handle my biz and I'm gonna call you later before I come. Tell dat nigga ta stay his ass home tonight. You'll see him later on in da week when dat cat is all nice and healed up after dis beating I'm about ta put on it!"

Sierra gushed. He loved to talk junk to her. "Okay, big daddy. I'll tell 'im. I'll see you later."

Tyke smiled to himself as he did a recap of their conversation. He knew that Sierra could only be mad at him for so long. Secretly, he didn't want her to be with anyone else but him. With his situation, his wife and kids, it would be difficult to try to lock down an independent woman like Sierra. He would just have to take what he could get from her, which would hopefully be a whole lot.

Tyke had heard through the grapevine that Rasheed had came home and threw a little coming-home party for himself. *How sweet*, Tyke thought. He had also happened to pass through the block and caught a glimpse of Rasheed's new Range Rover. *Impressive*, Tyke thought. Rasheed had always been competition for Tyke and he still was. They were both in the same type of hustle at one time or another, with Rasheed sometimes robbing the drug supplier before he did. Tyke didn't know how

Rasheed found out about his plans to this day, because it definitely wasn't from Kemp because he wasn't involved with Tyke on that level anymore. He didn't want to have to smoke his man's nephew if any problems were to arise.

Tyke pulled over on a dark block to check out a run-down house that he had been watching for some time now. He knew that it was a stash house. It was surrounded by empty lots and abandoned warehouses, which was perfect for a hit. He felt the adrenaline rush through his veins, as he contemplated how much money and drugs were inside of the dilapidated two-story. He would have to set up shop before he could attempt to come near it because it was guarded like a fortress, making it almost impossible for anyone to make in or out alive. He had run the plan by Melvin, who refused to participate. When he drove off, he knew he would have to recruit but it would have to be someone who was capable and, of course, trustworthy. He would give it a while, though. He wanted it to be his last robbery before he retired his 9 mm.

Chapter Seventeen

TAMIR

Tamir exited the restaurant with her food in tow. She had the twins, India and Asia, waiting for her in her car. They had just returned from their weekly crime spree and had came off with a variety of different items that they were going to sell in the hood. She was still pissed at Rasheed for not allowing her to come his party but she was not going to let herself get caught up. She had chased Rasheed for years and now it was time for him to chase her.

The twins were inside of Tamir's Honda Accord, blasting Mary J. Blige's CD and singing along to all the songs. Tamir laughed.

"Hey, y'all, please stop singin'! Damn, y'all sound like some sick hyenas!" she teased.

"Oh, chile, don't hate! We about to get up on the Apollo and do our thang. When we get dis record deal, don't hate now!" Asia shot back.

Tamir giggled. "Ookay, I won't hate, trust me!"

"Tee, what was da deal wit' Rah not lettin' you in his party, girl? You don't wanna talk about it?" India asked.

Tamir shot her a look. "Who tol' you dat?"

"Man, you know Missy and them was in there. They get their hair done at Cuttaz, right? Okay, you know Carrie and Sharee invited they ass ta da party! They cool wit' them," India replied.

Tamir was anxious to hear what was going on at the party. She already knew that she came up there and made a fool out of herself for Rasheed.

"What was goin' on? Y'all heard anything?"

"Dag, homegirl, you beastin' a lil' too much for info. Rasheed was just chillin'. Even though it was some chick there he was type sweatin' a lil' somethin' somethin'!" India said.

Tamir squinted her face into a slight frown. "What da fuck you mean, sweatin' some chick? My Rasheed don't sweat no females."

"Your Rasheed?? Ha! He was 'your' Rasheed at one time but he ain't 'your' Rasheed no more. He's sweatin' da next chick," said the envious Asia. Asia always had a crush on Rasheed and was secretly happy that they had finally broken up.

Tamir rolled her eyes at Asia. She would have to get to the bottom of this mystery. Whoever this female was, she probably was the woman that Rasheed had got all soft on her for. This unidentified woman was probably the one filling his head with all the "time to change your life" bullshit.

"I don't wanna hear y'all say nothin' else about dis chick and Rasheed 'till y'all come back wit' some facts. The female coulda been anybody from aroun' da way," Tamir stated.

India cut her off. "No, girlfriend. Nobody never seen dis one before. She ain't from aroun' here. She's fresh meat."

Tamir sulked in silence as she drove through the neighborhood. The twins were running their mouths as usual, while she felt completely miserable. She didn't know whether to be angry or sad. Rasheed had moved on from her and for the first time, she felt that their relationship had finally come to an end.

The twins suddenly began yelling like they just saw a superstar. It was a dark-skinned man with a bald head and goatee in a cream Chrysler 300.

"Mmm," Asia began. "Look at dat nigga, looking luscious in dat pretty car. Ooh, he look good!"

India agreed. "Yes, ma'am. I would love ta taste his chocolate!"

Tamir was clueless. "Who da fuck is dat? Y'all actin' he Puff Daddy or somebody!"

Asia sucked her teeth. She was getting tired of Tamir's miserable attitude. "Girl, dat's Tyquan! Everybody call him Tyke. He about one of da most thoroughest niggas in the Stuy right now!"

"Please, Rah is—"

India shut Tamir down immediately. "Tamir, Rah is an official dude, there is no denyin' dat. But Tyke set it off fuh these lil' niggas in the hood. He had everything aroun' here in a smash. He got locked up, came home, and still got muthafuckas on lock!"

Tamir sighed. As Tyke rolled by, he honked the horn at Tamir and the twins. Tamir got a good look at Tyke. *Damn, he is fine*, she thought to herself as she caught him blowing a kiss at her.

Chapter Eighteen

MONIQUE

Monique exited Bellevue Hospital in Manhattan with her brother, Timothy. Timothy had stayed with her overnight at the hospital while she was evaluated. After Monique was cleared by the doctors, she was told that she was just stressed-out and that she would need some time off from work. Two captains from CARE (Corrections Assistance Response for Employees) came to make a routine visit to Monique during her stay. They were notified that Monique stated she wanted to kill herself and wanted to make sure she was all right. The captains were genuinely concerned for her because they knew that so many officers had taken their own lives behind constant worry. Monique was appreciative but she was skeptical about telling them the real reason she was stressed.

As Timothy drove toward the FDR Drive, Monique began to cry. Timothy looked at her.

"What's up, Mo? The doctors already told you dat you wasn't crazy, why are you cryin'?"

Monique wiped her eyes and continued to look out the window. "Tim, I fucked up. My life is one big fuckup. I did some things dat made me realize I hit an all-time low."

Timothy shrugged his shoulders. "Like what? I mean, you do ya thing but for da most part, you ain't half as bad as so many other triflin'-ass bitches I know!"

Monique looked at her brother and gave him a faint smile. If only he knew the other side to his sister. He surely didn't know about her accusing his father, Mike, of molestation. He didn't know that Monique had a problem with screwing her friends' boyfriends, which is why she didn't have many. He didn't realize that she was mess and everywhere she went, she started mess. If he didn't know those things about her, she sure as hell wasn't going to tell him!

Monique was silent for the rest of the ride home. When she walked inside the house, her mother and daughter burst into tears of joy, happy that she was alive and well. She was more than surprised that Destiny, who usually went toe for toe with Monique, was so relieved to see her mother that she didn't want to leave her side. The family was also able to sit down for dinner that night and have a conversation without arguing.

After retiring to her bedroom, Monique could not help thinking about what she going to say when she was questioned at the inspector general's office. She already knew that the union lawyers weren't worth shit and that she would basically be thrown to the wolves, if they had a case against her. The sad part was that she had crossed so many people until she had no idea where the allegation came from. So far, everything pointed to Scooter. After she found out that he had gotten cut, she knew that Scooter probably had run his mouth about her. In jail, the term *snitches get stitches* was true. Monique was so accustomed to seeing inmates walking around with cuts on their faces that had bubbled up from keloid skin. Upon seeing this, she always wondered in the back of her mind that they may have made the fateful decision to sing like a bird.

Monique sat upright in her bed. She grabbed a piece of wrinkled paper from her nightstand and stared at Sierra's phone number. She wanted to thank Sierra for helping her that day but she had no idea how. Suddenly, her cell phone began to ring. She was in no mood for talking but she went ahead and picked up her phone anyway.

"Hello?" Monique answered with a hint of annoyance in her voice.

"Hey, girl, what up?" boomed the baritone voice through her phone. She immediately held the phone away from her ear. She had no interest in trying to recognize the voice.

"Hey, who is this?" she asked.

The male voice chuckled slightly. "Wow, I was just tryin' ta see if you was ah-ight. Damn, are you ah-ight?" he asked in return.

Monique became agitated. "Who is this?"

"It's Lamont, girl! You okay?" She was able to let out a meek "yes."

"I heard about you leavin' out da jail in a ambulance. I was worried 'bout you."

A week earlier, Monique would have been excited. In the past two days, she had become quite cynical and she was questioning the motives of Lamont's concerns.

"Well, thank you, Cap. It's good ta know you was worried about me." She paused. "Now thanks for callin', I gotta go—"

Lamont cut her off. "Phillips, don't hang up. I was callin' because I need ta help you."

Monique was confused. "What you mean—help me? Help me wit' what?"

"I heard about ya situation, you know, havin' ta report to IG and all. I wasn't tryin' ta get into ya business but I have a couple of peeps dat work at headquarters. I inquired about you and they tol' me about da allegations somebody had made against you. Come ta find out, it was a female dat made da phone call."

"Is anything sacred? How do you know if I wanted you in my business like dat?"

"Don't be upset wit' me, Phillips. I wanted to help you get ta da bottom of this."

"Look, I don't know what female it is. I always had problems with females, dat's why I don't have any friends now! Sierra coulda made dat phone call for all I know!"

"Nah, you wrong on dat one. I don't care how much Sierra dislikes a person, she would never try to get them twisted up in some bullshit. She just not dat type of person and you should know dat. You know her better than I do."

"Well, I know dat she doesn't care fuh me."

"Man, Si don't hate you. She just never understood why you stop talkin' ta her. Do you even remember why you not feelin' her?"

Monique remembered why. She was jealous of Sierra, it was that simple. She was the only child with loving parents, that is, until one day her father got into a car accident. Sierra was always prettier, smarter, and more popular than Monique was. With all those positive attributes and with Sierra being the tough cookie that she was, Monique wanted to be Sierra Howell. Single, sexy, childless Sierra. She was not about to tell Lamont the real reason she stopped speaking to her childhood friend.

"It wasn't really dat serious. Childhood issues, I guess," she replied. "You really think that she wasn't da one that made a phone call on me, huh? I was real fucked-up toward Si Si all these years."

"Look, we don't know who did da shit and I'm gonna help you find out. Do you want my help?"

She hesitated. "Um, okay, Lamont, you can help me." She was relieved it wasn't a male caller, even though it didn't really mean a thing. "Could you tell me what da allegation was about?"

"Dat you was fuckin' wit' da female caller's baby daddy, and how it's a known fact you fuck wit' inmates. Ta be honest wit' you, I heard dat same thing about ya ass."

"Oh, please! They are haters. They wish I was fuckin' with a inmate just to give 'em somethin' ta talk about!"

"I hope it's not true. I heard Shamel Abrams was the dude you was fuckin' wit'. I really hope it's not true."

Monique was shocked that Lamont even asked her that. "Heeelll no! I ain't got time ta mess with—"

"Ah-ight, ma. It's not important. Let's just find out what's goin' on, okay?" he stated.

"Lemme ask you a question. Why are you tryin' ta help me? You treated me like shit da last couple o' times I seen you and now you wanna be my knight in shinin' armor?"

Lamont chuckled. "I know it sounds suspect but I was checkin' out da captains list and I see dat you are number thirteen on there. Okay, so you a lil' hot in ya ass but you got potential if you made thirteen on a promotions list of four hundred people. You a good officer, Phillips. You know da job and ya do it well. But you need ta do your eight hours and go home. Stop mixin' ya business wit' pleasure. Shit, I need ta take my own advice. Ya see what happened wit' me and Sierra. I was fuckin' around wit' my baby mama on da side and she got pregnant. Do you understand what I mean?"

"Yeah, I get it. You right. Oh, and I appreciate this talk, Lamont, I do. I don't have too many people dat would keep it real wit' me."

"I know, I know and it's not a problem. I mean, I felt bad dat night when you left my son's mother's crib—I treated you like a trick. I apologize."

Suddenly, Monique heard a crash on Lamont's end of the phone. She listened closely as he dropped the phone and she figured that he wanted to investigate. She held on until Lamont came back to the phone. When he came back on the line, he was huffing and puffing. "Phillips, let me call you back." The phone went dead.

Chapter Nineteen

LAMONT

Lamont ran outside his house to the driveway. He looked at the damage to his windshield and began to cuss loudly. He went to the end of the driveway and looked in both directions. There was no one in sight. He scratched his head. "Who in the fuck did this shit?" he said aloud. He couldn't understand why he was going through so much in a matter of days. First, he got knocked out at work and now some unknown person threw a brick through his windshield. Lamont looked on the front seat, removing a brick with a note tied to it. He observed the note carefully.

Dear Asshole,

You fucked me over too many times and you gonna pay for it. This right here is a warning, so take heed. I could have killed your ass if I really wanted to but that would be too good for a bastard like you!

Sincerely, Yours Truly

Lamont looked at the note over and over again, trying to figure out who it was. The handwriting was unfamiliar and even worse, like Monique, he couldn't weed out the suspect because he had made so many enemies. He grabbed the brick and the note, walking back in his house. Lamont made sure he double-bolted the front door. He had seen enough scary movies. He didn't want to be like so many black actors who had starred in those movies—a dead nigga!

Any noise that Lamont heard for the rest of the night, he jumped up. He was unable to have a restful sleep that night. The people that ran though his mind were key suspects—Sierra, who probably had better things to do with her time. Daniels, who just didn't give a fuck about him and he knew it wasn't Monique because he was on the phone with her, and last but not least, Deja. He was not about to put anything past her. She had been acting real strange lately by not really letting him see Trey and certainly not leaving the baby with him while she went out. She would rather take the baby to her mother's house before asking him.

"Why da fuck are you takin' Trey over his grandmother house and I'm right here? He could stay wit' me!" Lamont recalled asking her a couple of days ago.

"I don't need yo ass ta do nuthin'. He got other family dat he could stay wit'!"

Lamont tried to remain calm. He loved his son to death and he didn't want to ruin his opportunity to see him. "Deja, what's goin' on? Why you don't want me ta see my baby?"

Deja sighed. "We don't need you, Lamont, and dat's it. You wasn't very happy wit' him when I was pregnant so why act like ya give a fuck now? You don't care, Lamont. All ya think about is ya self."

"Why are we still havin' this same conversation? I love my son, he's da best thing dat ever happened to me—"

"But dat's da damn problem right there, Lamont. You love ya son, dat's fine, but you don't respect me. So how can you say you love someone dat came from me when you don't show me love. You don't have ta be in love wit' me, but have love fuh da woman dat gave you this beautiful lil' boy, your firstborn!"

Lamont snapped out of his daydream and rolled over in his bed. He knew what Deja said was true but it was hard for him to have respect for a woman who underhandedly manipulated him with an untimely pregnancy. He was not ready for fatherhood, although he neglected to protect himself. He wanted to kick himself every day for not using a condom but his son was one of the few things in his life that he had done right. He was proud of that. Deja wanted a relationship with him and thought that having Trey would seal the deal. Unfortunately, things didn't quite go her way.

The next morning, Lamont took his Expedition to the glass shop to get his windshield fixed. When he came home, he parked it in his garage. He still was reeling from the mysterious note but he wasn't going to let fear get the best of him. As he picked up the study guide for a promotional test for the assistant deputy warden test that he was taking, his doorbell rang. Lamont grabbed his personal firearm and looked out the window. He was surprised to see Monique standing on his front doorstep. He opened the door and quickly let her inside.

"How did you get my address?" he asked.

"I got it from ya personal file at work. I jacked it when I was workin' in administration," she responded.

Lamont looked at Monique like she was crazy. "Girl, you a nutcase! Comin' ta people house without callin'!"

Monique shrugged her shoulders. "You could think I'm crazy but last night when you didn't call me back after dat commotion in da background, I got kinda nervous. I was worried about you."

Lamont smiled. "Okay, Phil—I mean, Monique. Thanks. Thanks a lot. I'm glad dat I got somebody dat care about me!"

"I'm sorry fuh da stalker move. I don't normally do this, but

I really was worried. Now dat I know you okay, I can go back home and relax. Oh yeah, thanks once again fuh da talk, I needed dat."

"You welcome." Lamont paused. "Well, you don't have ta leave. Stay and have lunch wit' me."

Monique seemed skeptical. "Oh, it's okay, I don't wanna trouble you—"

Lamont grabbed her hand. "Nah, Monique. It's okay. Trust me. It's fine."

As Lamont prepared some salad and grilled chicken for their lunch, they talked nonstop. Lamont found out a lot about Monique and was amazed by all the things she had been through. He even shared some things about himself. They ate lunch together, laughing and having a good time without any sexual comments toward each other. They didn't realize that they had so many similarities, like Monique missing out on a father-daughter relationship and Lamont's estranged relationship with his mother. They also spoke about the incident that occurred the night before.

"So you don't know who did it? You can't think of anybody dat might just hate you dat much?" Monique asked between bites of her lunch.

"Nah, man. I got a few enemies. It could be anybody," he answered.

"Except Sierra! You tol' me dat, remember?"

"I know, I know, even though, I ain't gonna lie, she was da first person to pop up in my head. But then I realized dat girl is not thinkin' about me!"

"You really loved Sierra, didn't you?" she asked.

Lamont sighed. "Yeah, I did. I shitted on dat girl, I really did. She was mad cool, had flava and just a good woman. I don't even think about it anymore."

"Yeah, I know what ya mean. I ain't no better. I couldn't stand da sight of Sierra! She's pretty, she just almost damn perfect ta me. I think da talk we had last night made me understand dat she got feelings too. She a human bein' just like me and all da smart-ass comments I used ta have fuh her, actin' like a asshole toward her, wasn't cool. Actually, it was confirmed when after all dat I did ta her, she helped me at work dat day. It's no tellin' what I would have done."

Lamont seemed pleased with Monique's new attitude. He felt his blood warm up as he really got a good look at Monique, who actually was very pretty without all the makeup and fake stuff on. Her hair, which was a medium length, was cut into a bob and her outfit consisted of a fitted T-shirt and jeans. Lamont licked his lips. As he collected their dishes from the kitchen table and put them in the dishwasher, he leaned over Monique and slowly started to kiss her. Monique responded by returning the kiss, which was what she needed at the time. He guided her to the living room couch, where they continued to exchange saliva, suck each other's tongues, and bite each other's lips. Lamont massaged Monique's ample buttocks with his large palms, causing her to throw her leg around him. They stayed in the position for a long time, with Monique finally coming up for air. Lamont looked at her, wondering why she had stopped their make-out session.

"Lamont, I really like you but I can't do this. We went there already and I can't get played like I did da last time," Monique blurted out.

"No, it won't happen again, Monique. I just got caught up in da moment da last time. I want ta make love ta you this time around!" he replied.

Monique gathered her purse and walked toward the door. " I like us bein' cool wit' each other. I need ya talks, ya friendship. I can't do da sex thing right now."

Lamont was disappointed but he couldn't let her know it. "Okay, baby, dat's fine. I don't blame you." He opened the door. His dick was protruding from his G-Unit sweats. "Call me, okay?"

Monique waved at him as she walked to her car. Lamont

closed the door and slid down to the floor. He didn't want to admit it, but he was started to have feelings for Monique. He kept reminding himself of her past but after today, after seeing the "real" Monique, he actually liked her. She was funny and best of all, they were two of a kind. But there was one problem. Sierra would have a fit.

Chapter Twenty

SIERRA

Two days after the party and Tyke, Sierra rolled up on Halsey Street. She was trying to catch a glimpse of Rasheed, thinking he would just be around the way. She looked at the address and smiled as she approached the house. She double-parked and was amazed at how massive the house was. It took her a minute to realize that the Gordon home was two brownstones put together, which she thought was a superb idea for such a large family. Being the only child, Sierra always wanted a large family. They just seemed like they had so much fun together.

She pulled up a little when she saw someone exiting Rasheed's front door. It wasn't Rasheed but they favored each other. She figured it was one of his uncles. Immediately after the man exited the door, Rasheed came running out behind him. She almost jumped out of the truck, trying to get to him before they got into the black Range Rover and pull off. Rasheed was surprised to see her.

"Oh shit! What's up, Mommy?" Rasheed asked as he gave her a tight hug. "What you doin' over here? I thought you was busy!"

Sierra laughed. "Busy, drivin' ta see you. Where you goin'?" she inquired.

"Oh, me and my Uncle Kemp was goin' ta get somethin' ta eat. Ya wanna come?"

Sierra hesitated. She hadn't anticipated on being seen in public with Rasheed so soon, but she couldn't resist him and his charm so she ended up parking her truck and riding with him. Sierra sat in the backseat.

"Why you back there, ma? Sit up here wit' Rah. I ain't gonna bite—yet!" Rasheed stated with a laugh.

"Nah, I'm okay, Rah. Right here in da back," she responded. Kemp turned around and introduced himself.

"Hello, beautiful. I'm Rasheed's uncle, Kemp. How ya feelin'?" he asked.

"Good, Kemp, good." Sierra frowned a little. "I hope you don't mind me sayin' so, but you look mad familiar. I swear, I met you before!"

Rasheed looked at Kemp on the sly. He knew that Kemp would never expose the truth about knowing Sierra.

"Well, ya know what they say about us black folks, shorty. We all look alike!" Kemp said.

Sierra leaned back in the leather seat, clicking her seat belt and preparing for the ride. She was not concerned about Tyke because she was exactly where she wanted to be and that was with Rasheed. She had been thinking about him all night, causing her to start touching herself. She must have had three orgasms back-to-back as she imagined Rasheed running his manly hands all over her body. She fanned herself thinking about their future lovemaking.

"So," Rasheed began, breaking Sierra's concentration. "What's on ya mind, sweetheart?"

"I'm just kinda buggin' right now, dat's all."

"I know why you buggin'. You woulda neva thought dat you be sittin' in da backseat of a Range Rover dat's owned by a former inmate. Is dat it?"

Sierra giggled. "Yeah, dat's a good point! But nah, I'm buggin' cause I'm in ya area, period. I ain't supposed ta be nowhere near you. You was in my jail, dammit!"

Kemp and Rasheed laughed. "I tol' you, Unc. She so cute, ain't she?" They seemed to get a kick out of Sierra's inhibitions. She could tell her resistance turned Rasheed on even more. "Ma, you are so straight right now and you don't even know it. I would treat you so good, I'll make yo ass forget you ever took dat muthafuckin' test, you hear me?"

Damn, Sierra thought. *This nigga gon' make me give him some pussy tonight!* "Okay!" was all she could say as the two men laughed hysterically at Rasheed's comment. She laughed too.

They traveled to downtown Brooklyn, where Rasheed pulled up in front of a Thai restaurant. Sierra loved Thai food and was amazed that Rasheed even knew about it. She didn't give him enough credit. As Rasheed helped her out of the backseat of the truck, he brushed his lips against her ear. "Didn't think I knew 'bout this shit right here, huh?" he whispered.

Sierra smiled. He stuck his tongue in her dimpled cheek. She felt her knees weaken.

They sat at the table, with Rasheed being the perfect gentleman. He opened doors for her and pulled out the chair for her to sit down. Kemp looked at Rasheed like the proud uncle and was genuinely impressed with the notion that Sierra was feeling Rasheed.

"Sierra, you seem like a nice young lady. I'm glad dat you decided ta hang out wit' us today cause this dude ain't stop talkin' 'bout you since he been home!" Kemp said.

"I ain't gonna lie, I was talkin' 'bout you. I want you; why wouldn't I talk about someone as lovely as you are?" Rasheed added.

"Well, thank you, Kemp and you too, Rah. Y'all are makin' me feel real good, even though I'm nervous as hell. . . ."

Rasheed continued. "Sierra, do you know how long I been

wantin' ta get at you? I couldn't wait ta get from behind them walls ta show you how official I am. Fuck dat job. I could take care of yo ass if you was to fuckin' quit tomorrow. My paper is long, baby, so don't ever feel like you losin' anything if you was to lose dat job. Shit, you know how many fucked-up dudes done tol' on female correction officers. A hell of a lot! But I'm different. I'm tryin' ta make you my fuckin' girl. Dem niggas was playin'!"

Sierra stopped eating. "You right, Rah. I just don't wanna be a victim. I'm not sayin' you would tell on me. It could be anybody, another inmate, another officer, a bitch in da street, whoever. I seen too many of my peeps go down 'cause some jail nigga is feelin' them, they get caught up with da dude and he end up tellin' cause da reality is homegirl can't fuck wit' him da way he want her to because she's a correction officer!"

Rasheed shook his head. "You right. But fuck dem niggas. I think they some snitch-ass, bitch-ass niggas dat can't stand ta know dat it's a possibility dat their chick might be hollerin' at da next dude like she hollered at him. It's a hate thing. It don't be 'cause they want a time cut!" Kemp nodded in agreement. "Dem niggas know they ain't gettin' out no fuckin' time cut if you got two life sentences for a double homicide! If you think dat, then youse a scary-ass dude dat don't wanna do ya bid!"

"Well, you won't have ta worry about me doin' this wit' nobody else. I'm feelin' you and only you!"

Kemp and Rasheed looked at each other. Rasheed's chest puffed out a little bit. "Aww, you feelin' me, baby?" He reached over and gave Sierra a quick kiss. She blushed.

"Yeah, I'm feelin' you, Mr. Gordon."

They continued to eat their dinner and enjoy each other's company. Upon returning to Rasheed's block, Kemp got out of the truck and walked in the house. Sierra hopped in the front seat of the parked truck and took in the summer breeze while she and Rasheed talked.

"I wanna thank you, Rah. I really enjoyed myself. I haven't had this much fun in a long time," Sierra said.

He rested his hand on her thigh. "Good, I'm glad. It's more where dat came from."

Sierra turned Rasheed's face to hers and she kissed him. She placed his hand on her breasts and he massaged them gently. Rasheed was excited but he chose to take it slow with Sierra. She stopped kissing him after she realized he had stopped fondling her breasts.

"Why you stop?" Sierra asked. "I wanted you ta do it."

Rasheed leaned back in the driver's seat. "Nah, I'ma chill, ma. You special like dat and I don't wanna ruin this with some quick nut. I really like you, Sierra."

Sierra looked away. "I understand. Let's take it slow." She kissed Rasheed and proceeded to get out of his truck. "I think I better go home now. I appreciated da dinner and I'm gonna call you tomorrow."

Rasheed got out of the truck and held Sierra close to him. "I hope you not mad at me. Just gimme a chance. I wanna do it da right way. I want you to believe in me."

Sierra smiled as she kissed Rasheed one more time. "Okay, Rah. I'll do dat." He walked to her truck and she pulled off. Sierra looked in her rearview mirror and saw him still standing in the spot she had just left him. Her heart fluttered as she thought about all the sweet things he said to her during their time together.

As Sierra turned the corner at Fulton Street, she saw Tyke in his car. She swerved a little bit and breathed a sigh of relief after she discovered he hadn't seen her. She knew that he would have had all kinds of questions as to what was she doing in that neighborhood, with Tyke knowing that she wasn't usually in Bed-Stuy like that. Her phone rang.

"Si, I'm on my way ta ya house, you home?" Tyke asked, with some loud music in the background.

"Yeah, okay. I'm home," Sierra lied. "Come through."

"Okay, sweetie. I'll be there in like fifteen minutes," he replied.

Sierra looked at her watch and pressed on the gas. It would take about ten minutes to get home but she needed to be showered and shaved before Tyke got there. She was angry with herself for giving him that power over her but she couldn't deny that she loved Tyke and he was her comfort zone.

Out of the blue, Sierra thought about Monique and how she used to judge her. She wondered how she was doing and why hadn't she called her yet. She knew that Monique felt awkward, considering Sierra did help her after all they had been through. With all the situations going on in Sierra's life, it was easy for her to let go of the bad blood between them and put herself in Monique's shoes. She hoped that Monique was willing to do the same.

Sierra entered her apartment and quickly undressed so that she could take a shower and prepare for Tyke's visit. The doorbell rang. Sierra checked in the mirror to make sure everything was in place. She opened the door and Tyke came through, sweeping her off her feet. They were loving kisses as Tyke took off her robe. Sierra unbuckled his jeans, which instantly fell to his feet. Tyke stepped out of the pants and kicked them to the side. He pulled off his boxers and shirt as he watched Sierra play with her pussy while waiting for him to get naked. He pushed her back on the sofa and spread her legs, submerging his face into her hot box. His face was saturated with her juices as he sucked Sierra's twat like it was dinner. He nibbled on her clit and stuck his tongue in and out of her, driving her crazy. Sierra grabbed Tyke's bald head as he made slurping noises while licking her, causing her to have an orgasm in a matter of minutes.

"Dat's right, baby, cum in Daddy's mouth!" Tyke whispered between licks. Satisfied with his work, Sierra licked the remainder of her juices off of his face and then put his raw dick into her dripping vagina. He stroked and stroked her pussy, going fast, then slow. Tyke whispered things in Sierra's ear like "This is my pussy" and "This shit is so good."

Sierra screamed Tyke's name over and over as he grabbed her ass, spreading her love box wide open. Sierra pulled him closer and screamed, "Harder, muthafucka, fuck me harder!" Her walls tightened around his dick every time he stroked. They both came and spread out on her couch, huffing and puffing from exhaustion and pleasure.

Tyke looked up at Sierra while laying his head on her stomach. Her eyes were still closed, looking like she was in la-la land.

"What up, baby? You ah-ight?" he asked. Sierra wiped her hair from her sweaty forehead. "Yeah, I'm so good right now. You don't know!" she exclaimed.

Tyke laughed. He got up from the awkward position they ended up in and sat upright on the couch. He put his arm around Sierra. "Our sex be crazy, don't it?"

"Hell yeah! Why you think you back over here after ya wife called me? Ya shit is da bomb! Ya know I can't resist," Sierra responded. "But I can't keep fuckin' you, Tyke, and not deal wit' nobody else. We ain't in no relationship with each other."

"I already tol' you dat I want you to be my girl. What's da problem?"

"I ain't tryin' ta be nobody side bitch! We cool like we are. We see each other when we see each other. Plus, I ain't gonna be the only female ya fuck wit' on da side. You love women, Tyke. Lots of 'em. I shoulda used a condom fuckin' wit you!"

Tyke waved his hand at Sierra. "Ah, whatever, man. You full o' shit. You wanna lead me on, callin' me over here ta fuck and now you wanna talk like we ain't feelin' each other. Do what da fuck you wanna do!"

Sierra was surprised by Tyke's response. She thought that it was going to be different but she must have guessed wrong. He was being selfish and she was not feeling him right now.

Sierra stood up and put her robe back on. "Ah-ight. Ya gotta go. Get da fuck out!"

Tyke looked at Sierra like she had lost her mind. "What da—for what, man?"

"I am fuckin' you 'cause I thought we had an understandin'. You married wit' a fuckin' family and here I am tryin' ta have a damn decent relationship and you mad 'cause I wanna have one? You ain't my friend, you just tryin' ta get over on me. Selfish bastard!"

Tyke got dressed. "Sierra, you buggin' out. I can't wanna be wit' you?"

"Be wit' me? Nigga, you had me. You wanted ta do jail bids and rob people. Then you went and married da same bitch you was fuckin' behind my back 'cause she was the only stupid broad dat would do dat damn time wit' ya dumb ass! I ain't havin' it, ya gotta go!"

Tyke stood fully dressed in Sierra's living room. He looked like he wanted to apologize, but he headed for the door. He turned around to look at Sierra with a gloomy look on his face. She had made up her mind. Tyke was the past and it was time for her to let him go ahead. As soon as he stepped into her hallway, she slammed the door in his face.

Sierra went into her bedroom, fell across her bed, and cried.

Chapter Twenty-one

RASHEED

Rasheed looked at the phone and was tempted to call Sierra. It was 4:00 in the morning and he couldn't sleep for the life of him. He was trying to get her off his mind but it was hard when he had finally gotten close to the woman that he admired for so long. He picked up his phone and put it down several times, hoping that she would call him, at least.

Rasheed got up from his queen-size bed and walked to his bedroom window. He took in the night air and watched as the various stragglers walked through his block. He was so happy to be home that he was going to make sure he took advantage of all the positives, by staying clear of drama. The only thing he was concerned about was Tyquan, who was starting to become a thorn in his side. He knew that Sierra probably rocked with Tyke since he'd been out of jail, considering they were old lovers. From what his uncle told him, Tyke really loved Sierra but she wasn't about to bid with him. He really couldn't say he blamed Sierra, with so many sisters throwing their lives away, waiting for their man to come home from jail. So many times he told Tamir and the other women he dealt with to move on with their lives. They insisted on coming to see him, sending him things and of course, accepting his collect phone calls. He thought about all the women he used and misused to do favors for him, even going as far as them breaking the law or having sex with him on a visit upstate. He never wanted to experience none of it again. Freedom had so much to offer, like money, family, and friends, and in this case, Sierra Howell. He was open!

Rasheed retrieved his phone from underneath his pillow and saw that he missed Sierra's call. *She must be on her way to work*, Rasheed thought and immediately picked up the phone to return her call.

"Hello, Miss, how you doin'?" he asked.

"Hey, Mr. Gordon. How you doin' cause I'm ah-ight," she responded.

"I'm so glad ta hear from you, ma. I miss you."

"Aww, you miss me? Dat's sweet. Why you bein' so sweet ta me?"

"Because I am feelin' da shit outta you. Because you are da woman fuh me. Because I just fuckin' want you so bad!"

Sierra was silent for a moment. "Wooww! I'm feelin you too, Rah. I ain't gonna lie."

"Sierra, can I ask you a question?"

"Sure you can. What up?"

"Do you trust me? Be honest."

"Umm, yeah, I mean, you got my number, we on da phone talkin' on da way ta my job as a correction officer, so yeah, I must trust you cause I ain't crazy . . . yet!"

"So let me love you."

Sierra began singing "Let Me Love You" by Mario. "Dat's da song—"

Rasheed cut her off. "No, I'm serious. I wanna love you. I want you ta be my fuckin' girl, yo. I am feelin' you so hard and no, I ain't no weirdo stalker nigga who is obsessed wit' ya pretty ass, neither!"

Sierra laughed. "Rasheed, I'm feelin' you too, but am I desperate or what? I feel like I'll be riskin' a lot ta be wit' you."

Rasheed sighed. He didn't want them to have this conversation over and over. He knew that he would never try to hurt her or put their relationship out there for the world to see.

"Sierra, I know you ain't met no man in a while dat is ready ta give you da world. I am. I know about ya relationship wit' dat captain and how he fucked you over. C'mon, do you think dat I would do dat to you?"

"Rah, I don't know what you'll do. When you start talkin' about my relationships wit' men in general, dat's a whole different topic."

Rasheed fell back onto his bed. "You know what, Sierra? Let's do it like this. Da ball is in ya court. When you ready ta fuck wit' me, holla at me." Rasheed hung up the phone. He looked at the phone over and over again, hoping she would call back but the call didn't come that night or even that day. He was about to get worried for a minute until his phone rang that next evening. Rasheed grinned ear to ear as he picked up the phone.

"Hey, Rasheed, have we met? You act like you don't know me no more!" she said.

"I ain't tryin' to be a pain in da ass, dat's why I tol' you da ball was in ya court. You musta thought I was playin'."

"Well, I thought about what you said. I wanna give us a chance, I just don't want no unnecessary drama wit' nobody."

Rasheed reflected on Tyke for a moment. He wanted to tell Sierra but he didn't want to spoil his chances of getting close to her. He felt like he was being dishonest but he would have to think about that later. He gave less than a fuck about Tyke. After they had a pleasant conversation, Rasheed jumped in his truck and decide to take a drive through his neighborhood. He rode up and down Stuyvesant Avenue and creeped through Malcom X Boulevard, where he waved at the old-timers sitting in front of the pool hall. As he turned down Gates Avenue, heading toward Ralph Avenue, he decided to go inside of the bodega on the corner. Rasheed just happened to walk in the store when he saw Tyke standing at the cash register. They looked at each other and nodded their heads. Rasheed kept his eye on Tyke, who didn't seem like he was ready to leave the store anytime soon. Tyke suddenly engaged in bullshit conversation with Pedro, the owner of the store. When Rasheed walked to the counter with his bottled water, Tyke was the first one to speak.

"What's poppin', youngin'?" Tyke exclaimed. He held out his hand to give Rasheed a pound. Rasheed relented.

"Yeah, what up, Tyke? What's good, my man? What up, Pedro?" Rasheed stated.

Tyke looked at Rasheed up and down, which was one of the reasons why Rasheed wasn't too fond of the man. "I see you doin' real good fuh ya'self. New truck, new clothes, looks like y'all lil' family businesses be doin' real good out here, huh?"

Rasheed gave the cashier his money. He had to get out of there before he punched Tyke in his face. He knew that Tyke was trying to antagonize him.

"Yeah, you could say dat," Rasheed responded. He grabbed his water and walked toward the door. "Ah-ight, son, I'm out."

Rasheed walked out the door, knowing that Tyke was burning a hole in his back. He was tired of trying to be cool whenever he saw Tyke. Any self-control was purely out of love for Kemp. He always told Kemp that he felt that Tyke was jealous of their family. He also knew that if Tyke would have run into the old Rasheed, with the slightest provocation, he would have put a few bullets in his ass with no problem. Rasheed smiled because he just couldn't wait to fuck Tyke's ex-girl and teach the self-proclaimed gangster a serious lesson. This made Rasheed want Sierra even more.

Chapter Twenty-two

TYKE

Tyke watched Rasheed pull off in the Range. It was confirmed—he couldn't stand Rasheed! He looked at his Chrysler 300. He was getting real tired of the rivalry. If it wasn't for his boy, Kemp, his nephew would be a dead man.

Tyke tried to call Sierra, who had not picked up the phone since he left her apartment the night before. After the time passed, Tyke just decided to leave her alone for a little while and she would eventually call him when she needed some loving.

As Tyke drove down Gates Avenue, he was surprised to see the female he blew a kiss at the other day. She was parked on the block and standing outside her car, talking to a few of her friends. He thought she looked real cute with her short haircut and expensive clothes. Looking at her made him forget about Sierra for a moment. He decided to pull over.

"Hey, ladies," Tyke shouted to the small crew of women. "What up?"

They all giggled. They knew Tyke as one of the "original gangstas" of the neighborhood. It was every hood girl's dream to have a piece of Tyke, but the female Tyke was interested in had her back turned. Tyke called out to her.

"Hey, shorty, with the cut, how you doin'?" Her friends poked at her.

She turned around. "Hey, boo." Tyke was pleased with her response. He smiled.

"Come here, sweetheart. I wanna talk ta you." She was hesitant. Tyke insisted. "Come over here, I ain't gonna kidnap you, baby." She walked to his car. "What's ya name?"

"Tamir, and I already know ya name, Tyke," she said. Tyke was even more impressed with Tamir. He figured if she knew his name, she had probably done a background check on his ass too. He wouldn't be surprised.

"Look, I'm in a rush right now, sweetness, so hit me wit' ya math and I'll call you later." Tamir put her number in his BlackBerry. He rubbed her chin. "You are so pretty, you know dat?"

Tamir blushed. "Thank you. When you callin' me?" Tyke laughed. From that statement alone, he knew that she was young, hot, and ready. That was perfect for him. The younger they are, the more he could have a bitch in check.

"I'll call you later, boo. Run along wit' ya lil' friends and I'll holla at you later, okay?" he replied, with a sneaky look on his face.

Tamir nodded her head at him and returned to the crew of females. Tyke watched them hover around Tamir like she had just won the lottery. She figured that he was just what she needed to get over Rasheed. Rasheed was a thorough dude and definitely had the wild reputation that Tamir was accustomed to having around her. What she didn't realize was that Tyke was cut from a different cloth. He was by no means like Rasheed at all, who was respectful to most. Tyke, on the other hand, was a whole different ballgame. A game that Tamir was not ready for.

Tyke made his stops and was able to collect some money from his clients. The party-promoting hustle was good, allowing Tyke to rub shoulders with a few rappers here and there. He was about to keep the extortion game going so that would surely bring him even more flow. The only problem was that it wasn't consistent cash and Tyke only thought for the present.

After he took care of his business, he decided to call Tamir. He hoped that she would answer the phone because she could be his new conquest. Since Sierra had opted to fall back from him, it would definitely have to be her loss. Tamir's voice got his attention.

"Hey, Tyke," she answered very quickly, like she was anticipating his phone call.

"What up, pretty girl? You wanna hang out tonight?" he asked.

Tamir paused. "Yeah, I would but . . ."

"But what, shorty? I know you ain't doin' shit but talkin' mess wit' ya girlfriends. Hang out wit' me."

"Nah, but fuh real, I'm doin' somethin' fuh my mother."

Tyke looked at the phone. He wondered what was going on. *Is this the same broad that was willing to give him the phone number a couple of hours ago?* They would have to have a nice talk because at the end of the day, he was going to hit it.

"What's da problem, shorty? You scared o' me? You musta heard about my rep."

"I did hear about you and yeah, you a lil' wild, even fuh me. I thought my ex-man was wild."

Tyke was curious. "Who ya ex-man, ma? I probably know homie."

"I think you know him. Rah. Rasheed from Halsey."

Tyke was quiet. He was tired of hearing Rasheed's fucking name! Now the attractive female on the other end of the phone was Rasheed ex-girl. He was kind of annoyed but he didn't want to let on that it was a problem.

"I heard of him. I don't really know him like dat." Tyke quickly changed the subject. "Look, maybe we could set somethin' up fuh anotha time then. Dat's cool?"

Tamir was thrown off guard. She didn't want him to lose interest in her. She had to think of something and quick.

"Hey, look Tyke, how 'bout me and you hang out tomorrow? My hair ain't done and I just don't feel right. So can I call you tomorrow?"

Tyke reluctantly agreed. She had tried to blow him off at first and he knew now that it was probably because of Rasheed.

"Yeah, ah-ight," Tyke mumbled. "See ya later."

Tyke was amped up, thinking that he could get into something tonight. Tamir had turned him off so he just decided to call it a night and go home.

Chapter Twenty-three

MONIQUE

Monique parked her car near 60 Hudson Street. The building housed the inspector general for the NYC Department of Corrections. She got out of her car and sighed as she walked into the building to find out what the allegations were about. She hoped that the day would just end on a happy note, not with her job hanging on a string.

As Monique walked out of the elevator toward the office, she was nervous as hell. Her palms started to sweat and her knees felt wobbly. She was greeted by an IG officer, who was gracious and led her into an office with a small desk loaded with paperwork. The officer walked out and left Monique in the room to practically hyperventilate.

"Oh, God," Monique prayed to herself. "Please, if you get me outta this jam, I'll promise ta stay outta trouble. I'll be a better mother, a better daughter, sister, a better woman. Please, Lord, please!"

Monique sat up as a stocky, white man with a comb-over walked in the office and sat at the desk in front of her. He held his hand out for a handshake.

"Hello, Miss Phillips, how are you doing today?" he asked with a smile.

"I'm fine, sir. And you?" Monique asked nervously. She realized that the man before her was Thomas Holden, the chief investigator for the inspector general's office.

"Miss Phillips, I know you are wondering why you're here today. Sorry for the scare but that was the only way we could get you down here without drawing any attention from your coworkers. We need you to be on our team."

Monique was stunned. She didn't know whether to feel honored or terrified. What the hell was she going to do for these people when she was just as corrupt as some of the most crooked officers in the department?

"Um, um, I don't know what to say, sir. I—"

"Just say yes. We did an extensive background check on you, Miss Phillips, and you got great recommendations from previous supervisors that worked with you. I see that you worked with wardens and chiefs who praised your overall performance and commitment to the Department of Corrections. We need a team player like you to stand up and protect the integrity of NYC's boldest." He continued after a slight pause. "Do you understand that you may have to report your colleagues and that you may have to cut several ties to different people in your life? We need your know-how to bring down some of the dirtiest employees in this department, and given your history, you are one of our better candidates for the job." Monique was at a loss for words. "Umm, Mr. Holden, may I ask what you're talking about?"

The man stood up. "Miss Phillips, you are in a position where you don't have any choice but to work with us. You have to provide us with any information about corruption that you could get your hands on. You have to save your job, Miss Phillips."

Monique was mortified. Her worst nightmare didn't come

true but she would be practically selling her soul to the devil if she agreed to his offer. She put her head in her hands.

Mr. Holden spoke sternly. "I understand that you are confused, Miss Phillips, but when you choose to violate the rules and regulations of this department, you have to take what is given to you. I see that you are about to be promoted and unless you do a lot of ass-kissing, your whole career and everything you worked for will be down the drain. You make the decision and I'll be expecting a phone call tomorrow morning at ten AM."

Monique was amazed. She was relieved that her job was going to be saved but at what cost? Was it worth it?

She finally had the energy to speak up. "Mr. Holden, sir, there's no need for me to wait until tomorrow. I accept the offer."

As Monique drove toward the Queensboro Bridge, she was a complete wreck. All this time, she thought she had gotten over with everything she done but obviously not. A couple of weeks ago, she would have been offered that position and she would have jumped at the opportunity to bring down some officers with no problem. Was she becoming soft?

Her cell phone rang and she saw that it was Lamont. She didn't want to answer the phone but she took the call anyway.

"Hey, Lamont," she answered, trying to sound as cheerful as possible. "I was just gonna call you."

"What's up, girl, did you go? What happened?" he asked. Monique's eyes filled up with tears. She didn't have anyone that she could trust with her secret, not even Lamont Simmons.

"Everything was ah-ight. It was some bullshit allegation dat couldn't be proven."

Lamont breathed a sigh of relief. "Good, good. Are you okay? You don't sound too good."

Monique held her composure. "Oh, no, I'm good. As a matter of fact, I'm great. I'm still standin' and ain't no bullshit involved."

"Yo, Monique, ya need me ta come over? I will, ya know."

She shook her head, not realizing that he couldn't see her through the phone.

"Thank you, Lamont. I'm okay. Call you later, okay?" The phone disconnected.

Monique was upset but she remembered her promise to God. She would have to deal with the situation the best way she knew how, even if meant some people had to lose their jobs. As the saying went, "Self-preservation is the first rule of man" and Monique was about to base her life on that one statement.

Chapter Twenty-four

LAMONT

Lamont stared at his phone. Monique was upset; he could tell. He had promised himself that he wasn't going to pry, but for some reason, he had taken an interest in the woman. He would have to admit that he no longer felt a sexual attraction to Monique. It was more like a brother-sister kind of feeling and he couldn't understand why he suddenly felt that way. For the first time in his life, he could honestly say that he could look at a woman as something other than a sexual object.

Lamont pulled up in his father's driveway. They always had a weekly visit with each other, providing their scheduling wasn't too hectic. Lamont's father, who everyone called Pops, was a reformed player. A handsome man with distinguished features and salt-and-pepper hair, young women still found Pops very attractive. Lamont always teased him, saying that Pops gave him a run for his money. Lamont didn't share his true feelings with anyone about anything except his father. They were super-tight especially after Lamont's mother practically abandoned them.

It was 1975. Lamont was asleep in his bed. His father awakened him after he had just come home from a night of boozing and partying. Pops sat sleepy Lamont up on his bed and asked him if he knew where his mother was.

"She in da bed, Pops," Lamont answered groggily, as Pops watched him fall back on his pillow. By this time, Lamont was able to regain his senses and climbed out bed, trying to find out why Pops was cussing like a sailor. He got up and entered his parents' bedroom, where he saw Pops on his knees with tears in his eyes. Pops was kneeling in front of the closet that belonged to his mother, Linda. It was empty. There were no more beautiful dresses that Lamont used to love to smell when he played hide-and-seek with his cousins. All he saw was the bare wall. His mother had left them. Lamont began to cry as well.

"Pops, where's Mommy?" Lamont asked, with all the innocence of a six-year-old child.

Pops grabbed Lamont, hugged him real hard, and cried like a baby. Lamont didn't understand at the time but Pops was the reason his mother left. She found out that he had an infant daughter by another woman. As he grew up, he couldn't say that he blamed his mother for leaving but he just couldn't figure out why his mother never found the strength to continue to have a relationship with her only son.

Lamont used his spare key and walked in his father's house. Pops was in the bathroom, on the toilet and reading the newspaper.

"Boy, ya tryin' ta scare da shit outta me!" Pops exclaimed as Lamont appeared in the doorway of the small bathroom.

"Well, Pops, you already on da toilet, so it shouldn't matter if I scared da shit outta you!" Lamont joked. Pops laughed loudly.

"You somethin' else, boy! Now go in da livin' room while I take care o' my business!"

Lamont continued to laugh as he lay on the couch and turned on the television. He heard the toilet flush and Pops washing his hands. Pops walked in the living room and sat in his favorite recliner chair.

"What da hell you want, boy? Poppin' up at my damn house like you ain't got nowhere else ta go!"

"I came to see my father, man. Can I come see my Pops? I had ta ask you somethin' anyways."

Pops smiled. He loved when Lamont came to see him. "What's on ya mind, youngblood?"

Lamont sat up. It was about to get serious. "Pops, I know we never talked about dis but I been thinkin' about it lately. I had Ma on my mind fuh a minute now and even though I don't speak ta her dat much, I thought I would go 'head and ask you."

Pops eyebrow shot up. "What you tryin' ta ask, boy? Get ta da point."

Lamont took a deep breath. "Pops, I wanna find my sister."

Pops cleared his throat and cleaned out his ears. "You wanna do what? Find who?" Pops exclaimed.

"I wanna find my sister, man. I been thinkin' bout it fuh a long time. Shoot, as many women I done laid, I would be fucked up if I find out dat one of them chicks was my sister. Man, I would be fucked up!"

"You got a point. But Lamont, I thought you never liked bringin' dat shit up. I wanted ta tell you but I didn't wanna hurt you any more than you already been hurt."

"Well, I need ta know, Pops. I need ta know." Pops walked out of the living room and went into his bedroom. He came out with a large envelope full of pictures. He put the envelope in Lamont's hands. Lamont's hands were shaking as he looked at the pictures, one by one. Pops began his story.

"Well, son, I met my daughter's mother at a party I went to wit' a few of da boys. Ya know, I was young, dumb, and full of cum and even though I was married to Linda, I wasn't ready ta settle down. Anyway, on dis particular night, me and da woman got a lil' tipsy, 'cause you know ya Pops love liquor and women, and we carried on a lil' bit. We carried on wit' da affair fuh a year or so and she ended up pregnant. I couldn't get mad at her fuh wantin' ta keep it 'cause it was partly my fault too. So I agreed ta help her as much as I could. One day, ya mother found out about it and she cussed me out somethin' terrible. We tried ta work through da affair but when she found out who da woman was and that she had my baby girl, dat was it fuh me. She wanted ta hurt me real bad by not only leavin' but leave wit' no ties ta either one of us!"

Lamont continued to look through the pictures in silence. The little girl was pretty, with her pigtails and toothless grins. But there was something about her eyes that were familiar to Lamont but he just couldn't put his finger on it.

"What's da names, Pops? Where they live? Tell me, Pops."

Pops rubbed his head. "I haven't been in contact since da lil' girl turned eighteen and I had no more financial obligation to her. Dat was our agreement. But her mother's name was Ann. Ann Phillips. Da girl's name is Monique. Monique Phillips."

Lamont stood up. He wanted to vomit. "Whhhhhaaaat!" he screamed. "Monique Phillips? Pops, I knew dis shit was gonna happen! I know dat fuckin' girl!"

"What you mean, Monty?! How well do you know dis girl?"

Lamont fell back on the couch and began to hit his head. "I had sex wit' her. I had sex wit' my own gotdamn sister, man!"

Pops tried to comfort Lamont but he pulled away from him. Lamont was devastated and he needed some air. Pops tried to stop the upset Lamont from getting behind the wheel of his truck but it was too late. Lamont had taken off and sped down Francis Lewis Boulevard.

Chapter Twenty-Five

SIERRA

Sierra walked on her post and was surprised to see Monique at work. She had heard about her visit to the inspector general's officer but refused to participate in the endless gossip mill. They talk *to* you today and then talk *about* you tomorrow was what she always said. As she prepared to enter 5 North, Monique got her attention and called her into the small control room. Monique hugged Sierra.

"I just wanted ta thank you fuh helpin' me dat day. I felt like I was about ta lose my mind!" Monique stated.

Sierra shook her head. "It was nothin', Phillips, fuh real. You okay?" she asked.

Monique busied herself with paperwork while she talked. "Yeah, girl, I'm ah-ight, I guess. I'm just tryin' ta hol' it together."

Sierra looked at Monique, who had a sad look on her face. She wasn't going to pry because she would be overstepping her boundaries.

"Look, Monique, I know we haven't been da best o' friends but if you need ta talk ta me, you can, okay?"

Monique nodded her head but didn't respond. Sierra knew

when it was time for her to leave things alone. She walked out of the control room into the housing area. Inmates were locking out for breakfast. She sat at her desk and completed her routine tasks for the morning. It didn't seem the same since Rasheed left. As Sierra reminisced, she made sure that breakfast ran smoothly without any incident. Several inmates attempted to strike up a conversation with her but she didn't pay them any mind. *One inmate is enough*, she thought.

As she attended to her duties, she looked over to see Monique standing in the control-room window, apparently observing the feeding. As Sierra stood up, she observed Monique standing there and writing something on a pen and pad. Sierra frowned, wondering to herself what was the pen and pad about. Monique was acting strangely. Sierra had heard stories about IG using correction officers that were in trouble to give them information. The officers did this in an effort to save their own jobs. Sierra glanced at the inmates coming in and out of the pantry. She had heard about a cigarette operation going on between a few officers and inmates in 5 North but so far there was no physical evidence. Maybe Monique was helping her observe the feeding. Sierra walked over to the window.

"What up, Phillips? Is everything okay?" Sierra asked.

Monique quickly put down the pen and pad. "Yeah, I'm good, just countin' da inmates," she replied.

Sierra looked at Monique suspiciously. "Okay, I was just askin'," as she watched Monique walk away from the window.

Sierra went back to her seat and contemplated for a moment. She didn't know what was going on but she wasn't stupid. Something was up with Monique Phillips but she just couldn't put her finger on it. Whatever was going on with her, she was just happy that Rasheed was out of 5 North.

When Sierra arrived home later that evening, she hopped in the shower, lathering up with some body wash. She wanted to smell good for Rasheed when he arrived. She was nervous.

She threw on some Victoria's Secret PINK sweats and a matching T-shirt. She didn't want it be too obvious that she was ready for some hot lovemaking.

The doorbell rang and Sierra let Rasheed in. For one awkward moment, they just stood there and looked at each other, not knowing what move they were supposed to make. Rasheed finally stepped inside and broke the silence.

"You gotta nice crib, baby girl," he said. "I like the decor. It looks just like I expected it to, real girlie."

Sierra looked around her place like it was the first time she had noticed it. "Oh really? Thanks, Rah."

Rasheed gazed at Sierra and gave her a peck on the lips. "And, of course, you look good as hell, baby girl. You a lil' nervous, ain't you?"

Sierra sat on the couch. "Yeah, I am. I woulda never imagined you'll be standin' in my house."

Rasheed sat on the couch beside her. "Yeah, I know, right? I mean, if you feel like dat, imagine how I feel!"

Sierra shook her head. "I feel like a high school girl right now. I'm kinda shy so you gotta excuse me."

Rasheed began kissing her and she returned the kisses as well. He ran his hands all over her, causing a tingling sensation throughout her body. She had waited for this day and now it was finally about to go down!

Rasheed picked up Sierra and walked into her bedroom. He placed her on the bed and stood over her, like he was trying to figure out what to do next. He removed her sweatpants and submerged his face between her legs. He licked and sucked until Sierra was nice and moist. She held onto his long locks while he pleasured her with his lengthy tongue. Not wanting to reach an orgasm yet, Sierra helped him get undressed and took him into her mouth. Rasheed stared at Sierra, who was in a squatting position, as she slowly ran her tongue up and down his hard penis. She gently sucked on his testicles and stuck her tongue in the small hole at the head of his rod. Rasheed moaned in ecstasy. He scooped up the petite Sierra and they fell backwards on the bed. When Rasheed entered her, she had doubts about having unprotected sex with a man she knew nothing about. But it was in the heat of the moment and Sierra made most of her fucked-up decisions during this time. Sierra let out a small shriek, unaware of how abnormally big Rasheed really was. They made love several times that night and fell asleep in each other's arms, totally satisfied.

Sierra was awakened at 3:00 AM by her vibrating phone. Without looking at the caller ID, she answered.

"I know you in there wit' dat nigga! Tell his bitch ass I'm gonna kill him and I'm gonna see ya ass in da streets!"

Sierra sat up. "Tyke, you—"

"Shut up, bitch. You a fuckin' slut, you know dat? You fuckin' everybody, ain't you?"

By this time, Rasheed was awake. He grabbed the phone from Sierra but it was too late, Tyke had hung up.

Sierra was visibly upset. Rasheed comforted her. "I heard what dat nigga said." Rasheed announced. "I'm gonna push his wig back dis time!"

"Rah, I'm scared! Tyke is a fuckin' nutcase! I seen him in action before and, shit, I'm just scared!"

Rasheed jumped up and got dressed. He made sure that he had his gun, his .357 Magnum, cocked and ready.

"Look, ma, I'm gonna go and see what's really good. If dat nigga know I'm here, he probably stalkin' ya crib. I want you ta stay here, don't answer da phone unless you recognize da number, ya hear me? And don't even answer da door!"

Sierra shook her head in agreement. Rasheed walked out the door and she immediately shut her door and locked it. She knew it was about to be on now.

Chapter Twenty-six

TYKE

Tyke pulled off in his car after hanging up on Sierra. He beat his steering wheel, all the while wishing it was Sierra's head. *How could she fuck wit' dis nigga!* Tyke screamed to himself. He thought about their previous conversation, how she said she needed to deal with other people. Tyke would have never imagined it would be a former inmate and especially Rasheed, a nigga he despised. This was one of the reasons why he could never trust women. In his opinion, they were all sluts and whores and Sierra proved that theory to be true.

Tyke had come over earlier that night to try to talk to Sierra. He missed her company and he felt that once he got to her door, she would not be able to resist letting him in her apartment. As he was about to park his car, he noticed a black Range Rover parked on Sierra's block. At first, he thought it might just be a coincidence and didn't really sweat it; that is, until he happened to take the staircase up and actually saw Rasheed entering Sierra's crib. Tyke was brokenhearted! As he sat in the staircase, shedding a few tears and feeling sorry for himself, he mustered up the strength to finally leave. He continued to wait around in his car, hoping to see Rasheed exit the building but when that didn't happen, he became more and more agitated. It was then that Tyke knew they were definitely sleeping together. The thought of the two having sex with each other made Tyke sick to his stomach.

Tyke drove off and shortly after, pulled over and parked on a dark residential street. He placed the Baby Eagle 9mm on his lap, after making sure he had one bullet in the chamber. He opened his glove compartment and pulled out a cellophane packet, sniffing what was left of the powdery substance inside of it. He leaned all the way back in his seat, waiting for the heroin to take effect. Tyke had acquired the habit during his last prison bid, thinking he could chill out when he came home. After experiencing joint pain and waves of nausea, he had no other choice but to get a fix. Some minutes passed and Tyke began to feel real good. He nodded off, totally oblivious to what was going on around him. He was in his own world, needing to forget about Sierra and Rasheed, if only for a brief moment.

Chapter Twenty-seven

RASHEED

Rasheed walked to his truck and inspected it carefully. He looked for bullet holes, broken glass, and other damage. After scanning the area and seeing that the coast was clear, Rasheed hopped in his truck and pulled off. He didn't want to drive too erratically and risk being pulled over by the cops. He had a gun on him and couldn't afford to go back to jail. Rasheed tried to calm down by taking deep breaths. He thought that tonight was one of the reasons he needed to move to Atlanta. He wanted to kill Tyke, to take him out of his misery once and for all.

Rasheed picked up his phone and called Kemp, who answered the phone on the first ring.

"What up, nephew? What you gettin' into?" Kemp asked.

"Yo, Unc, it's ya man, I done tol' you 'bout ya man!" Rasheed yelled into the phone.

"Hey, calm down, nephew. Talk ta me. What happened?"

"Dis lame-ass nigga called baby girl, callin' her all out name and threatenin' us! Talkin' 'bout he gon' kill me and he knew I was at da crib!"

"*Whhhaat?*" Kemp yelled. "Fuck you mean, threatenin' you?!"

"He told her dat he was gonna kill me! I heard him, Unc!"

"I know dis nigga done lost his mind. Threatenin' my fuckin' family? He goin' too far wit' dat shit! What up wit' shorty, is she ah-ight?"

"Damn, Unc, I left her there but—"

"Look, Rah, just come get me. You tol' her not ta answer da phone or da door if she thinks it's him, right? Tyke would definitely try ta take her out because of dis!"

"Unc, between me and you, Sierra was still messin' wit' him. I know she was. But she got da bomb-ass pussy so I could see why da nigga is flippin'!"

Kemp laughed. "Rah, you ain't shit, man. You gettin' ready ta straight smoke dis dude and talkin' 'bout some pussy! You crazy, man!"

"Hey, Unc, I'm just tryin' ta make light of a bad situation. Dis nigga Tyke done blew my high and killed my hard-on. Damn, I'm feelin' dat girl, though. And now all these years, I wanted dis nigga ta gimme a reason ta do him and he never did 'till now. He wanna get all tender over shorty!"

Kemp agreed. "Yeah, Rah, I ain't mad at you. You said he was a bird but I never paid attention to dat side of Tyke. And ya know what? You don't need ta get ya hands dirty wit' dis. We got too many lil' niggas we could get ta get at dis dude."

"I ain't tryin' ta get no lil' niggas, Kemp. Hell no! First o' all, they ain't gonna do it right. Then, they might hit dis dude but not kill 'im. Then after all dat, these lil' niggas'll be tellin' po-po on all o' us! I wanna see dis cat die slow cause fuh some reason, I think da nigga about ta be outta control!"

"Why you hate Tyke so much, son? You never gave me a concrete reason," Kemp asked.

Rasheed pulled up in front of the house. "I'm outside, Unc. When you get in da truck, I'll tell you." Kemp hurriedly ran down the steps to their house and hopped in Rasheed's Range. As they pulled off, Rasheed began to run down the story. He kept the secret imbedded in him for so long and it was a relief to finally reveal what he knew to be true.

"Unc, I know Tyke was ya peeps. Yeah, he held you down in a lotta ways and you did da same fuh him. Y'all was like brothers. Anyway, da reason I don't like da dude is dis. Tyke robbed these Dominican cats from East New York, right before he had got locked up ta do his last bid. I know dis 'cause somebody approached me ta do da job and I turned it down. The shit was too dangerous 'cause da Dominican cats had their shit together and they was pushing dat dope, dat herron, heavy. It was big money involved and Tyke and his niggas hit up like two o' their spots. They came off wit' like a couple o' hundred thousands, which they split four ways. I knew dat his boy, Mel, was there but I can't tell you who else participated. Now mind you, they got away wit' it fuh a minute but da Dominicans ended up findin' out dat some niggas from da Stuy had did it and Tyke's name was mentioned. While Tyke was locked up, he ended up runnin' into one of the cats who was cool wit' da Dominicans. Tyke tol' da dude dat Uncle Pep was da one who did the jobs and was da mastermind behind everything. He basically convinced da dude dat he wasn't there and they didn't even know anything about his man, Mel, at all. The Dominicans didn't know who was who 'cause they all had on masks when they did it, they just heard da crew was from Bed-Stuy. They heard about Peppy's reputation and they also knew dat Pep was gettin' crazy paper. They then found out dat Pep be in da East, checkin'on his baby mother and lil' Peppy. Them Dominicans laid low, waited in da cut 'till they caught Pep off guard goin' ta see his son and they killed him, yo, in cold blood cause o' ya bitch-ass man!"

Kemp was silent. Rasheed was quiet too, waiting for the story to register. It was hard for Rasheed to tell anyone the real story but he felt right then was a better time than any.

"But, Rah, why you ain't never said nuthin' ta nobody? Dis

nigga was smilin' in my face, then was actin' like he felt all bad when I tol' him about us findin' out who killed my brother."

"The reason I never said anything was 'cause we needed ta keep dat nigga close ta us. Eventually, he was goin' ta get smoked whether I was fuckin' wit' shorty or not! But he was locked up when Pep got killed. I heard about all dis shit while he was incarcerated. I knew dat when he got home, I was gonna light his ass up. I just had ta rock his dumb ass ta sleep, ya know? Make him think everything was all good, then get 'im!" Rasheed continued. "Plus, our family done been through enough. Peppy's death hit us hard and I didn't want ta be da bearer of bad news. We cried enough, nah mean? Nana was fucked up, Sharee, Carrie, it was too much. Then before all dat, Mommy was killed so we needed a fresh beginning."

Kemp shook his head. "Yeah, you right, nephew. It musta been hard fuh you ta keep dat ta ya self. But let's just keep dis between us. Shaka and Nayshawn will go apeshit if they heard dat story."

Rasheed already knew that his uncles were wild. Now that everyone was established and had their own legal businesses going, he didn't want to come to any other family members with the mystery behind their brother's death. It would cause nothing but chaos and unrest throughout his extended family.

As they drove down Nostrand Avenue, they still didn't have a visual of Tyke. Kemp spoke first after a brief moment of silence.

"Yo, Rah, call Sierra and tell her ta pack a few things. We gon' go back and get her, bring her back ta our crib, she need ta stay at our crib fuh a while. I don't trust dat nigga. After we pick her up, we could call it a night."

Rasheed called Sierra, who picked up on the first ring.

"Hey, Rah," she said in a barely audible voice. "Where you at?"

"Me and Kemp is headin' over that way ta get you. Pack up a few things, you gon' stay wit' me fuh a few days."

"Okay."

Rasheed was concerned about Sierra. He knew that she had anticipated the drama and he felt bad that it looked like her worst nightmare was about to come true.

"Si, look, I feel bad dat you got caught up in dis bullshit but I am promisin' you, I'm gonna put a cease ta dis shit. I'm gonna make sure dis dude won't give nobody a problem again!"

Sierra began to cry. "I'm scared, Rah. Just come and get me!"

Rasheed hung up the phone and stepped on the accelerator. He had to take accountability for everything that was happening. He realized that if he would have killed Tyke sooner like he originally planned to, none of this would have gone down.

Chapter Twenty-eight

LAMONT

Lamont worked through his shifts at work for the next couple of days in a complete blur. He was so disgusted with himself, he wished he could have crawled in a hole. How was he going to tell a woman that he had sex with that she was really his long-lost sister? It sounded like something straight off *The Jerry Springer Show*. The challenge was not only telling Monique but he would have to live with their encounters running through his mind for the rest of his life. He knew that there was something that made him want to call her and express his concerns about her mental state.

Lamont hadn't spoken to Pops since that day. He was still disappointed in his father for not sharing the pertinent information with him sooner. Lamont felt that after all the years had passed, he deserved to know, without asking. At the same time, who would have thought that two half-siblings would end up working in the same profession, in the same facility? It was amazing, even by Lamont's standards. At first, he decided not to tell her but after considering the situation, he felt that she had a right to know. Pops should have at least attempted to reach out to Monique, especially after his marriage was ruined. As a man, he could see what type of effect his father's absence had had on Monique.

So now that he found out that Monique was his sister, he could no longer allow her to run around and make a complete fool of herself. The one stipulation would be that no one could know that they were really related to each other, especially their coworkers. He saw her at work in passing but they hadn't been able to speak with each other. Lamont decided to make an appointment with her after he called Deja. He hadn't seen his son in a minute and he missed him terribly. Deja had been giving him a hard time for the past couple of weeks and he needed to know the deal.

"What, Lamont?" Deja answered, sounding annoyed. "I'm busy."

Lamont tried to not lose his temper. "Yeah, anyway, when I can come get Trey? I haven't seen in at least three weeks, I mean, what's goin' on?"

Deja laughed. "Maybe you need ta tell me, Lamont!"

Lamont was puzzled. "What da hell are you talkin' about now, Deja? Everything wit' you is a fuckin' problem!"

"Oh, I see. I'm a problem. Was I problem when you was fuckin' a bitch in my damn house?" she announced.

"What?" Lamont shouted as his heart began to palpitate. "What bitch in your house? Like, what are you talkin' about?"

"Yeah, muthafucka, you think I'm stupid, huh? You thought you was bein' cute when you fucked another woman in my damn house wit' my son in da next room sleepin'? You a low-down dirty dog, Lamont, and da next time you gon' see ya son is in child-support court!"

"I didn't fuck nobody in ya house, girl!" Lamont lied. "You buggin' out!"

"You just don't get it, do ya, stupid? You are about da stupidest man I know. I shoulda known better than ta lay up wit' you let alone birth a child fuh you!" Deja paused. "Lamont, I videotaped you screwin' some skank in my livin' room. Yeah dat's right, a video, and I am surprised I held it in fuh dis long! So see ya in court and I want my damn arrears too!"

Lamont was livid. Not only was Deja taking him to court, she was keeping his son away from him. "Whateva, Deja. I'm sick o' ya crazy ass, anyway. Do what you wanna do!"

"Oh, yeah, by da way, you can tell da lil' porn star dat I know who da fuck she is and I am da one dat made da call to IG! I hope her lil' trip ta Sixty Hudson Street taught her a lesson cause da next time she won't have a fuckin' job and yo ass won't neither. And if ya fuck wit' me, I will give away a copy of da damn tape ta everybody dat walks on Rikers Island, inmates included, ya hear me?" The phone went dead.

Lamont fell back onto his bed. He couldn't even be upset at Deja anymore. She was more than a woman scorned; she was a head case. Ever since the day his mother left, his relationships with women had been fucked-up. He messed up a perfectly solid relationship with a woman he claimed to be in love with, to screw around with another one who got pregnant, and then ended up having sex with a woman who turned out to be his half-sister. He had to be cursed. Now he was about to lose the one person besides Pops that he loved more than life itself, and that was his son. Karma was a motherfucker.

Chapter Twenty-nine

MONIQUE

Monique looked at her cell phone and instantly recognized the 212 area code. It was from 60 Hudson Street, the inspector general's office. She wiped the sweat from her brow and breathed a sigh of relief as the phone finally stopped ringing. This whole operation was harder than she thought it would be. She could remember the times she would have jumped at the opportunity to bring down an officer, especially one she didn't like. Was she getting soft?

As Monique drove through the streets of Brooklyn, she decided to cut down Halsey Street to get to Bedford Avenue. She was on her way to Harlem to see her aunt, wanting to take the scenic route instead of the Grand Central Parkway. She glanced at the beautiful brownstones, secretly wishing she had the money to purchase one of the homes. She was amazed at one brownstone on Halsey that caught her eye, looking similar to a mini-mansion. She was equally amazed at the two people standing in front of the house, embracing each other. "Oh, shit, that's Rasheed Gordon and Sierra! What da fuck are they doin' together?" Monique said aloud. She quickly pulled over a couple of yards away from the unsuspecting couple and parked. She got out of her car and hid behind a huge oak tree, just to get a second look. She watched as they kissed each other, which confirmed that they had probably been intimate with each other. Refusing to see any more, Monique climbed back into her vehicle and took off.

Monique grappled with the personal and professional decision she had to make after what she had just observed. She knew that she and Sierra were not bosom buddies, but after they briefly spoke with each other, Monique decided to lay off of Sierra. They had been going through the bullshit for longer than Monique cared to remember, and she had too much other shit going on in her life to concern herself with trying to make Sierra miserable. She wondered how long Sierra and Rasheed were involved with each other. Maybe Sierra knew him before he was locked up in 5 North. Monique tried to convince herself that the relationship between Sierra and a former inmate did not exist.

Monique sighed as she heard her phone ringing again. She looked at the caller ID and it was Lamont. She hadn't talked to him in a minute so she answered his call.

"Monique, we have ta talk—it's, uh, important!" Lamont announced, without so much as a hello.

"Hello ta you too, Mr. Simmons!" Monique replied. "What's da urgency?"

"Can we meet somewhere? I mean, like right now?"

Monique felt butterflies in her stomach. "Well, I was on my way to Harl—"

"Look, you could do dat later. It's just dat I need ta speak wit' you. My heart can't hol' dis shit much longer. Where you at right now?"

"Um, I'm in Brooklyn, by, um, Halsey and Bedford Avenue."

"Oh, good, I'm on Atlantic and Franklin. Stay where you at." Monique stared at the phone after Lamont hung up on her. She pulled her Benz over on the corner and turned off her ignition. She felt her chest tightening from anxiety and looked in the rearview mirror to check her makeup and hair. If he was telling her some bad news, the least she could do was look presentable before she lost her mind. After waiting for ten minutes, Lamont pulled up behind her and hopped in her car. He seemed to be breathing heavily.

"Damn, what's wrong? You look like you runnin' from da law." Monique laughed nervously.

Lamont grabbed her hand. "First of all, I just wanna apologize to you. I am so sorry fuh da way I treated you all these years and especially, these past few months."

Monique looked confused. "Lamont, what da hell are you talkin' about?"

He looked away from her for a few seconds. "Listen, I know who ya father is, Monique."

Monique frowned. "What da hell you mean, you know who my fuckin' father is? Who da fuck is pryin' in my business, my mama's business?"

"Monique, please, listen to me. When I was a lil' boy, my pops was havin' an affair and my mother found out about it. The shit hit da fan when my moms found out dat da woman he was havin' da affair wit' was pregnant by Pops. It was too much for her ta handle so she left Pops and me too. I didn't realize it at da time, of course, I was too young ta understand. But I was fucked up after Pops tol' me dat I may have a lil' sister. I was in denial about it but lately I just kept thinkin' about my mother and how things would have been different if we were a family."

Monique was in no mood to hear about Lamont's life and his trials and tribulations. "Lamont, I don't get what—"

"Lemme finish. I gotta tell it da way it's comfortable fuh me. Anyway, da other day, me and Pops got ta talkin' and I asked him about da baby he fathered. He came out wit' some pictures and I wanted you ta see them."

Lamont removed the pictures from the large manila envelope. Monique was in total shock when she realized that the pictures were of her!

"Monique Nichelle Phillips, you're my sister."

Monique stared at the picture of her as an infant, a toddler and then as a young girl. There had to be at least fifteen pictures of her as a little girl and some pictures she had taken with her mother. Lamont pulled out a copy of Monique's birth certificate and a DNA test that she obviously did not know that she had taken that said that Pops was 99.9 percent her father. It was apparent that Monique's mother had sent Pops all that stuff. She couldn't believe it. Suddenly, she became overcome with emotion. Lamont grabbed her and held her tightly as Monique cried and cried. He could only imagine what she had been through, knowing that she was the product of an adulterous affair.

Finally, when Monique was able to compose herself, Lamont continued to tell her about Pops.

"I know he hurt you, but would you wanna meet him?" Lamont asked.

Monique was uncertain. "I don't know. Do he wanna meet me? He probably ain't ever laid eyes on me except da pictures. Plus, I would have ta talk ta my mama about it."

Lamont opened the car door. "Well, let me know. I really want us all ta get together, even ya moms if you could talk her into it."

"Okay," Monique managed to reply, meekly. Her father was a topic that Monique and her mother rarely discussed. He had become somewhat of an enigma and when the checks stopped coming, he might as well have been an open-and-shut case.

Lamont rubbed Monique's arm. "We had sex wit' each other and we can't take it back. It was unfortunate but we didn't know that this would come out." He paused. "Now dat we know, let's start buildin' a relationship, okay? Everyone makes mistakes."

Monique shook her head. "Yeah, you right. I thought about dat. We could let bygones be bygones, okay, big brother?"

Lamont kissed Monique on the cheek and got out of her car. She waited until he pulled off to cuss and yell. Out of all the motherfuckers in the world, she ended up screwing her half-brother! She turned around and headed back to Queens. Suddenly, she wasn't in the mood to take the long drive to Harlem anymore. She had some final decisions to make, decisions that would possibly change her life forever.

Chapter Thirty

TAMIR

Tamir drove her car through Rasheed's block. Every now and again, she would pass through the block, hoping to catch him entering or leaving his house. She was disappointed upon discovering his truck was nowhere on his block. She had time to reflect on their relationship and was upset that she had thrown away four years with Rasheed. Tamir felt she didn't deserve to be treated the way he had been treating her and she needed answers from him. She had to make him remember that she was the one who use to run up to the jails visiting his ass and keeping his commissary stacked. She was the one who accepted all of his collect phone calls, making sure that she was home in time to receive them. Overall, she was the one who was there, through thick and thin, now he was pushing her to the side like a paper food stamp.

Tamir wanted to do a complete and thorough investigation of the new female everyone seemed to be saying was his new woman. She would have to ask the right people in the hood, who probably had all kind of info on the new chick and might have the Social Security number too. The only major problem was a lot of people were very loyal to Rasheed and they probably would fill him in on Tamir's snooping. The twins, who were officially known as the "Wendy Williams" duo, for always sticking their nose in other people's affairs, would probably know what was going on. She just didn't want them to think it was all right to be in her business. They would try to throw the fact that Rasheed had a new girlfriend in her face every chance they got. They did this because they knew that Tamir would never throw her hands up to them.

She hadn't seen Rasheed since his party, which she found quite strange. At one time or another, Rasheed frequented the hood with somebody always spotting him, riding up and down the streets of Bed-Stuy, with a passenger or two in his expensive rides. Being somewhat of a "ghetto celebrity," it wasn't uncommon that Rasheed's name was mentioned in conversation with an old-timer or two, who had made the front of some bodegas or pool hall their permanent hangout spots. They would say things like, "Oh, it looks like it's gonna rain and, oh yeah, I saw Rasheed today in a cool ride" or "I like dat Rasheed. He bought me a beer today!" That type of popularity is what Tamir missed the most about Rasheed. She frowned at the thought of another woman getting some shine.

Tamir turned the corner and lit up when she saw Rasheed's truck parked in front of his aunt's beauty salon. She parked up the block and casually strolled inside. Rasheed was sitting in one of the chairs, getting his locks re-twisted. The salon, which was usually bustling with conversation, was suddenly silent as Tamir walked over to Rasheed.

"What up, Rah?' Tamir asked with a self-righteous look on her face.

"What up," he replied nonchalantly. "Ya gettin' hair done or somethin'?"

Tamir smiled. "Nah, I just seen ya truck parked out front

and thought I would drop in ta say hello. Ain't seen you in a minute."

Rasheed sighed. "Okay, I'm gettin' my hair done so do what you do. I can't talk to you right now."

Tamir was getting a little irritated. "Rasheed, why are you brushin' me off? I been tryin' ta call you and you ain't been answerin' my calls or nuthin'. What is da deal wit' you?" she whined.

"Tamir," Rasheed responded, through gritted teeth. "Don't do it ta ya self, okay? My aunt ain't here but respect her shop and just leave, man. We gon' talk about it later."

Tamir was about to leave until she caught a glimpse of Sierra coming out of the bathroom in the back. Tamir felt herself getting hot under the collar as she stared at the petite woman. Sierra, who was unaware of Tamir's presence, walked over to Rasheed and kissed him on the cheek. All of a sudden, Tamir rushed Sierra, knocking her off balance. Sierra bumped her head and seemed dazed but was able to punch Tamir in the mouth. Tamir's lip blew up instantly. She grabbed Sierra's long hair, as Sierra knocked her to the ground. Sierra threw jabs at Tamir's arm, trying to free her hair from her grasps. Tamir let go of the hair, rolled on top of Sierra, and began to choke her. Sierra punched Tamir in her eye and she let go of her neck. Rasheed and the other stylists attempted to break it up but to no avail. Sierra dug her long nails into Tamir's face, as the both of them continued to roll all over the floor of the salon. As the fight ensued for a few more seconds, Rasheed and his aunt, Sharee, jumped in and managed to finally yank them apart. The four were breathing heavily, with Sierra and Tamir mean-mugging each other.

"You fuckin' stank bitch! How dare you jump on me, bitch. You don't know me!" Sierra screamed.

"Bitch, I know you fuckin' my man! Stay da fuck out his

life!" Tamir yelled back. She attempted to break away from Sharee's tight grip around her waist.

"Fuck you, you slut! I'm fuckin' him now! Dat's why I whupped ya ass, dummy!" Sierra sneered. "And he ain't even ya gotdamn man no more!"

Sharee dragged the screaming Tamir out of her sister's shop. Sharee was short and stocky, with the boyish haircut, the boyish clothes, and a faint mustache. She also had the strength of five men so Tamir was no competition for her and she stopped resisting. Sharee's girlfriend followed them outside as well. Sharee walked Tamir to her car. When she got inside, Tamir instantly began inspecting the damage Sierra did to her face in her visor mirror.

"Dat bitch scratched me da fuck up? Wait 'till I see her ass again!" Tamir yelled.

"You ain't doin' shit, Tamir," Sharee barked back. "You shoulda never jumped on dat girl. She ain't do a damn thing ta you!"

Tamir looked at Sharee. "How you takin' her side, Sharee? See, I know you ain't never like me or wanted ta see me and Rah together! It was a conspiracy!"

Sharee tried to refrain from spewing venom at Tamir but she had to speak her mind. Everything she had said was true, except for the conspiracy part. "You set ya fuckin' self up fuh dat one! You da one rollin' up in my sister shop like you own da muthafucka or somethin', checkin' fuh Rah! Do he call you?" Tamir shook her head, with tears streaming down her cheeks. "Do he check fuh you? No, he don't! You played ya self! Leave da nigga alone—damn, he don't wanna be wit' you no more! You said you didn't wanna be wit' him after he tol' you he was finish wit' da streets. Shiiit, I don't even fuck wit' dudes, period, but even I know when ta leave a muthafucka alone!"

Tamir closed her driver's door as she watched Sharee and

her girlfriend walk away. She nursed her swollen lip and face as she drove toward her house. She was sick as she realized she was just beat up by Rasheed's new mystery woman. She calmed down after she came to the conclusion that Sierra's identity would be revealed after the local gossip mill got wind of their altercation. "Then I'm gonna destroy dat bitch!" Tamir screamed aloud.

Chapter Thirty-one

RASHEED

Sierra pulled her hair back into a loose ponytail, as the other stylists and Rasheed attempted to get the shop back in order. Luckily, Carrie was out of town and she wouldn't be back for a day or so. Rasheed tended to Sierra, inspecting her face and arms for scratches and bruises. Sierra shook her head and was visibly upset.

"Is this is what I have ta go through, Rasheed, ta be wit' you? Fightin' bitches and havin' ta watch my damn back every fuckin' minute?" she shouted, as Rasheed pulled her into the small bathroom and locked the door behind them.

"Ssssh," Rasheed hushed her. "Calm down, ma! I didn't know dat girl was gonna walk in here like dat! I don't fuck wit' her at all."

Sierra paced back and forth. "Well, I'm pissed, Rasheed. I can't go on wit' da drama and da bullshit! As if I don't say it all da time, my job, my job, my job, remember?"

Rasheed grabbed Sierra and comforted her in his big arms. She immediately submitted to him because she needed a hug. He pulled her face to his as he backed her up against the wall. Rasheed pushed Sierra's skirt up and moved her panties to one side, immediately thrusting his enlarged penis inside of her. The fight between the two women had turned Rasheed on. He fantasized about to having the both of them in bed with him. As he sexed Sierra on the bathroom wall, he imagined the two women licking his dick together, swapping his semen in and out of each other's mouths as they kissed. He pulled her closer and closer to him and watched her facial expressions change. He knew she was about to climax real soon, and so was he. They were extremely quiet, not wanting anyone on the outside to know what they were doing, which made their tryst even more exciting. Sierra came first, with Rasheed exploding inside of her, almost collapsing on the floor.

As they freshened up, Sierra agreed to continue their conversation after they left the shop. Rasheed sat back in the stylist's chair and continued to get his hair done while Sierra sat around waiting and reading an *Essence* magazine. Sharee made her way over to her nephew with a grin on her face.

"Well, Rah-Rah, it looks like you gotta fighter on ya hands," Sharee whispered to him. "She tried to take Tamir's head off!"

"Yeah, she a fighter but I ain't feelin' what went down. Personally, I'm sick of Tamir so I didn't care who whipped her ass. I just wanna chill wit' baby girl and try ta get dis relationship goin'."

Sharee's left eyebrow shot up. "Wow, nigga, dat's cool. I ain't never seen you like this. I guess it is da real thing, huh?" Sharee glanced at Sierra, who didn't notice that she was being checked out. She was engrossed in the magazine. "She look good as hell, though. Maybe dat's why my boo keep followin' me around. She tryin' to keep me from lookin' at her!" The both laughed. "Ain't she a CO?"

Rasheed sighed. "Yeah, she remind me o' dat shit every day. Now after dis altercation wit' Tamir, it's another setback fuh us. I almost had her gettin' real comfortable wit' me."

Sharee shook her head. "It'll be ah-ight, son," Sharee responded, as she fixed her blue NY Yankee fitted. "I can understand how she feel but she gotta take responsibility too. I'm pretty sure she knows what came wit' da territory when she started fuckin' wit' you." She kissed him on the cheek and signaled for her lover. "Listen, Rah, I'm out." Sharee waved at Sierra and walked out the shop, hand in hand with her girlfriend.

Rasheed stared at Sierra in the mirror. He wondered if being with her was worth all the trouble. He had beef with Tyke and now the whole Tamir incident had taken place. Not to mention they had to duck and dodge her coworkers. It was a lot to handle to just be coming home but he couldn't deny that his feelings for her were growing stronger every day.

Chapter Thirty-two

TAMIR

The fight between Tamir and Sierra spread all throughout the neighborhood. Tamir was able to find out everything she needed to know and more about Sierra, without the help of her nosy twin friends. Everybody and their mother asked her questions about the fight, which pissed Tamir off even more. She was crafting a plan to make sure Sierra paid for trying to humiliate her inside of Cuttaz and of course, taking her man. Tamir looked through her contacts at Tyke's phone number, knowing that the number would come in handy one day.

"Hullo?" Tyke answered, with his loud music playing in the background.

"Hey, Tyke, it's me Tamir, how you doin'?" she asked. Tyke turned down the music.

"Oh, hey, shorty! You ready ta see me now? 'Cause you acted like you was on some scared shit da last time I spoke ta you!"

"Yeah, yeah, I was a lil' nervous wit' you bein' dat nigga and all dat. I mean, let's face it, I ain't on your level!"

Tyke laughed at Tamir's attempt to ego-stroke. "Oh, word, I

hear dat. I see you got a lil' game too. So when I'm gonna see ya pretty ass?"

Tamir looked at her watch. It was almost 1:00 AM. She was still sore from the fight with Sierra two days ago. "Hmm, what about now? I ain't doin' nuthin. Let's take a ride somewhere so dat we could talk and get ta know each other."

"Damn, shorty, you got me wantin' ya sexy ass, right now!"

Tamir giggled. "Tyke, you are so crazy! You know, I shoulda met you first."

"Why you say dat, ma?" Tyke already knew who she was talking about.

"Rasheed was my man a lil' too long. I shoulda ventured out a lil' bit and got at a nigga like you."

"Yeah, baby, fa sho. Listen, fuck dat dude, I'm comin' ta scoop you. Where you at?"

Tamir was in the process of putting her shoes on. "Oh, yeah, I'm on Quincy and Stuyvesant. I'll be on da corner of Stuyvesant Avenue, waitin' fuh you."

"No problem, sweetheart. I'll be there in ten minutes."

As Tamir waited on the corner, she smiled at the fact that she had found out that Sierra was Tyke's ex-girlfriend. She also happened to find out that Tyke and Rasheed had some beef going on before Sierra, escalating once Tyke found about Rasheed's dealings with her. Everything was going perfectly. She didn't know how Sierra felt about Tyquan and she didn't care. She was going to make sure she gave him the time of his life. Tamir didn't realize that she was about to regret the day she had ever laid eyes on Tyquan Williams.

Chapter Thirty-three

SIERRA

Sierra climbed in her bed, physically and mentally exhausted from her fight with Tamir two days ago. She had opted to come home after they left the salon, wanting to be in her own apartment and alone. She was none too happy with the way that things were going and felt powerless to change them. Why was she feeling so helpless?

The day after the brawl, Sierra and Rasheed had a serious argument. Their argument was reminiscent of her and Lamont's relationship, the only difference was that the previous union started out wonderfully. Everything that was happening made Sierra have serious doubts about her and Rasheed's future together. The funny thing was amidst all the drama, she felt herself falling for Rasheed more and more. She didn't know if she was a glutton for punishment or just plain stupid, not like it made much of a difference. They had their brief moment where they transferred barbs with each other but she had to admit that she was still infatuated with Rasheed.

"Rasheed, you mean ta tell me dat I'm gonna have ta go through dis shit eeeeverytime I see dis stupid lil' bitch? Is dat what you sayin'?" Sierra recalled asking him.

"Man, what da hell are you talkin' about? You act like I meant fuh it ta go down like dat! I didn't think she would walk up in my aunt's shop! If I didn't feel comfortable, I woulda never asked you ta come there wit' me!" Rasheed shouted, while they sat in his truck on a dark, quiet block.

"You know what, Rah? I shoulda just left ya ass lookin' through dat lil' ass cell window, wit' you sayin', 'If I could just sniff her panties!' I'm not up fuh dis juvenile bullshit, fightin' bitches over a man who I only been wit' fuh a second, let alone my man fuh years! I don't give a fuck if I wasn't a CO, I still ain't fightin' over one!"

Rasheed rolled his eyes in his head. "Oh, dat's how you feel, Sierra? Well, guess what? Take ya ass back ta ya lil' sorry ass popcorn cop job then, and leave me da fuck alone! I think dat dis shit was a big mistake and maybe I was thinking wit' my dick! I guess I was tired of jerkin' off on ya ass everytime I saw you wit' dem tight-ass uniform pants you love ta wear!"

Sierra was really pissed off! "What, muthafucka? You ain't nuthin' but a gotdamn jailbird, a common criminal, so if you was gettin' ya rocks off, then fine! 'Cause if I woulda known betta at da time dat woulda been da closest you would have ever got ta my pussy!"

Rasheed laughed. "Well, it's too late! I already had da pussy so da fuckin' joke's on you! Ha, ha!"

Sierra opened the door of Rasheed's truck and hopped out. She began to walk down the street toward Nostrand Avenue so that she could hail a cab. Rasheed jumped out and ran after her. He lifted her off of her feet.

"Put me down, you fuckin' bastard!" Sierra yelled. "I knew dat I should have never talked ta ya ass!"

Rasheed placed soft kisses all over Sierra's face. She felt his heart beating through his chest on her back. He turned around to face her.

"I'm sorry, baby. I really care about you and I'm tryin' ta love you. I supposed to be in ATL right now but I'm here wit' you. I didn't mean all dat shit I said. I was just mad." Sierra was silent. "Please, Si, I been waiting fuh dis oppurtunity." He hugged her gently.

Sierra collapsed in Rasheed's arms and began to cry. It seemed as if that was all she was doing these days was shedding tears. The stress of their forbidden relationship was taking a toll on her but she couldn't find it in her heart to leave him alone. There was no denying that she trusted him. Now with Tyke finding out about their affiliation with each other, she felt indebted to Rasheed, knowing that he would keep her safe from Tyquan's wrath. Little did she know that it was a part of Rasheed's plan. He took her home and made love to her all night, putting all the drama out of their minds.

Sierra's daydream was interrupted by her ringing phone. It was Sean Daniels. "What up, Sean? What you know good?"

"What up, Si? Listen, when you come ta work, you gonna have ta do some damage control!"

Sierra sat up in her bed. "Whaaat? What's goin' on, Sean?" she asked.

"Yo, I heard some niggas in da locker room talkin' about how they heard you was messin' wit' some inmate and dat if you needed some dick dat bad, you coulda got some from them, you didn't have ta fuck wit' a crook. Then da chicks, you know they extra hatin' on you 'cause you cute, and blahzay, blahzay, but you know they was feelin' Rah up in here like crazy! They sayin' dat you ain't shit and that you need ta get fired especially if you out there—get this—fightin' his baby mama over him!"

Sierra felt exasperated! She knew that this was going to happen and that was what she afraid of. Now she would have to go to work and deal with all the gossip and lies going around about her. She thanked Daniels for calling her, keeping her updated on the rumors. She was happy that she had him to hold her down on that end. The old Sierra would have lost her mind trying to keep her name out of the despicable mouths of her coworkers. She shrugged it off and figured that it was her turn to be talked about. In time, they would move on to someone else's affairs.

She was due to work tonight and she would walk inside of that facility with her head up, ready to act like she didn't know what the hell everyone was buzzing about. She was falling in love with Rasheed and she was going to protect their relationship at all costs. Sierra convinced herself that she was going to have Rasheed and her damn job too. So many other female officers had been in the predicament she was in, many still working in the jails as supervisors, who made the job their everything. Many turned their noses up at women who chose mates from the "other side of the cell door" but continued to be used and abused by their present boyfriends, husbands, and coworkers. What was the big deal as long as the man treated you with the utmost respect? What was wrong with uplifting brothers in their time of need and inspiring them with your confirmation of unconditional love?

As Sierra went through her workweek, she felt the tension from her coworkers. She knew that their whole motive was to ostracize her but she put on her million-dollar smile and bubbly attitude and threw their hypocritical asses for a loop. They were unable to read her. Usually, if a female officer is involved with an inmate, she shies away from her obligatory duties and isolates herself from her colleagues out of guilt or lack of integrity. It was a defense mechanism. Sierra didn't give a fuck. She spoke to everyone, making people think that this was the best she ever felt in her life.

While walking through the corridor toward the locker room, she ran into CO Keianna Bryant, who just happened to be a malicious gossip queen. She was the type of officer who sat on her post all day and talked about people all day, every day, even her so-called friends. Sierra felt sorry for the woman and realized that she was a miserable, insecure woman who was apparently not happy with herself. Sierra knew for a fact that Keianna was just as bad or even worse than some of the people she talked about, screwing any supervisor on the downlow that could make her job a little easier, giving her access to some of the best posts in the facility. She always made sure she didn't have any inmate contact, for some reason. Sierra figured that because of her undercover-ho status, she was probably afraid she would end up fucking one of them too. With Keianna being from the bowels of the ghetto herself, Sierra couldn't understand why Keianna acted like she was the best thing that every happened to mankind.

"Hey, Howell, how you doin'?" Keianna asked with a stupid smirk on her face.

"What's up, Keianna, how are you?" Sierra asked, although she couldn't care less.

Keianna got straight to the point. Sierra noticed that she had her faithful sidekick and flunky, CO Davis, with her. "What's dis I hear you all out in da streets fightin' over Inmate Gordon? Is dat ya man? 'Cause I hope things ain't got dat bad ta where you gotta resort ta fightin' over inmates! Dat's a shame!" Keianna looked at Davis and snickered. Davis chuckled as well.

Sierra laughed. She wanted to wipe the grin off of Keianna's face. "Chile, please! What is dis I hear 'bout you fuckin' da personnel captain fuh posts? Don't he gotta wife?"

Keianna laughed. "Girl, I was just repeatin' what I heard. You ain't gotta get all nasty wit' it!"

"No, I don't, Keianna, but it seems dat you do. I hear you get nasty on a regular, Kei-Kei; why, you lil' sanctified slut, you'll fuck just about anybody in a white shirt fuh a post, now won't you?"

"I don't appreciate you talking ta me like dat, Sierra. We used ta be cool."

"Yeah, we used ta be 'till you started doin' just what you doin' now, mindin' my damn business! Now don't you have a post you gotta tend to? Oh, wait, don't forget ta get ya knee pads and make a GYN appointment, you filthy skank!"

Keianna huffed and walked off, with her lackey following closely behind her. Sierra laughed herself all the way to the locker room.

Chapter Thirty-four

Rasheed

Rasheed had found out that on the night that Tamir had disappeared, her car had remained parked on her block and her car keys were left on top of the dresser in her bedroom. Her brother Taj told him what made him suspicious was his sister's bed was unmade and it looked like she hadn't come home that night. He said he must have called Tamir's cell phone over and over again but it just kept going into voice mail. He was worried but he didn't want to alarm his parents until he found out what was going on. Taj had heard her leaving the house that night at 1:00 in the morning but never bothered to get up and ask her where she was going. His mother asked for her daughter but Taj told her that she had spent the night at the twins' house, needing a little more time to make some phone calls. Rasheed recalled the conversation with Taj that fateful night.

"Yo, what up, Rah?" Taj asked.

"Who dis?" Rasheed asked.

"Oh, I'm sorry, man. It's me, Taj, Tamir's brother."

"Oh, what da deal, man? I didn't recognize ya number. What's good?"

"Did you see my sister, man? She ain't been home since one AM and it's now going on six PM and she ain't call or nuthin'. I tried ta call her cell phone and she ain't answerin'."

Rasheed was suddenly alert. "What? Um, maybe she wit' da twins."

"Nah, da twins ain't seen her, neither. You ain't seen her?"

"I seen her a couple o' days ago, man. We don't even deal wit' each other no more."

"I heard." Taj paused. "Yo, Rah, man, please help me find my sister. I didn't tell my parents yet 'cause I know they would lose their mind!"

"I got you, Taj. Calm down. I'll ask around and see if anybody know anything."

"Thanks, Rah. Just call me, okay?" Taj said, and his voice started cracking.

"Okay, son. It's gonna be ah-ight."

Rasheed told Taj to hang up the phone because he said he heard some voices downstairs. He looked over the banister and saw the cops talking to his mother in the foyer. He was hesitant about going downstairs but their voices were barely audible from where he was standing. When his mother screamed and fainted in the police officers' arms, that was when he knew. By the time Taj called Rasheed back, he was in tears. Tamir had been murdered.

Tamir was found dead in a grassy knoll in Long Island. She looked like she had been sexually assaulted at first but whoever she had sex with had used a condom. There were no traces of semen on her body. The cause of death was asphyxiation. Police decided that she may have had consensual sex with someone.

Homicide detectives milled around every possible location that Tamir frequented, from Cuttaz hair salon to the neighborhood Chinese restaurant. Rasheed was taken in for questioning and was released immediately after. He told them about the fight, which he had no other choice but to, and detectives swarmed to Sierra's apartment. Sierra was scared as hell but was told by the detectives that she was not a suspect and that they were just doing their investigative duties.

Homicide talked to almost everyone in the neighborhood until they got a lead on a possible killer: Tyquan Williams. Tyke was known to NYPD and tenured detectives, who were familiar with his violent history. Aside from his criminal background, he had a couple of domestic-violence arrests but the charges were always dropped. They needed to know his whereabouts during the hours that Tamir was missing, but they had to find him first to bring him in for questioning. Detectives went to his place of residence and his wife cussed them out, asking them for a search warrant. They were going to take their time with Tyquan, knowing that he would eventually fall right into their lap, either dead or alive.

When Rasheed attended Tamir's funeral it was a heartbreaking event. Her parents were emotional wrecks and so was her brother, Taj. The twins sat in the front with the family, their eyes all puffy and red from crying. Rasheed was nearby and so was his family, who felt it was their duty to pay their last respects and support him in his time of sorrow. Sierra sat in the back of the funeral home, wearing a pair of dark shades, feeling guilty about how the whole situation turned out. She shed a tear or two for Tamir and for herself. She realized that the casket that Tamir was in could have easily been hers after she heard it was a possibility that Tyke was her killer. After Tamir's death, Sierra immediately packed some of her things and went to Rasheed's house. He wasn't comfortable with her staying at her apartment alone.

The reverend gave the eulogy and Taj spoke briefly about his sister. He was so overcome with grief that he had to eventually be escorted from the pulpit. The casket was then moved out to be transported to the graveyard for burial. Rasheed and Sierra got in the truck with Kemp and the funeral procession began. After Tamir's casket was lowered in the ground, everyone filed out and went home with nothing but memories of Tamir's short life.

Chapter Thirty-five

TYKE

Tyke decided to lay low at Melvin's crib until everything died down. He lied to Mel, telling him that his wife had thrown him out of the house and that he needed a place to crash for a little while.

Melvin walked into the living room with a *Daily News* in his hands, fuming. "Yo, son, what da fuck? Ain't dis shorty you was tellin' me about? Rasheed's ex?" he asked.

Tyke snatched the paper. *Oh, shit,* he thought to himself. "Yeah, dat's her. Damn, shorty got killed?" Tyke responded.

Mel snatched the paper back. "Yo, Tyke, man, I hope ta God, you ain't had nuthin' to da wit' dis, man, 'cause if you did, you gotta go, son!"

Tyke looked at Mel. He couldn't get mad at him for not wanting him in his crib. Mel was doing good for himself and he didn't want Tyke or no one else to ruin it for him.

"Yo, Mel, I ain't do dat, kid," Tyke said. "I ain't gettin' down like dat."

Mel looked at Tyke suspiciously. Tyke was emotional when it came to women. Tyke was like that with women because of the issues stemming from his mother abandoning him as a child for the crack pipe. Since Tyke had been home, he noticed that Mel had distanced himself. Little did Melvin know that Tyke's strange behavior was associated with his heroin addiction.

Melvin went into the kitchen and grabbed a Corona from the fridge. He sat at the table and read about Tamir. Tyke sat on the couch and watched Mel's facial expression while he read the article. Then Mel noticed Tyke scratching like a maniac.

"Man, what da fuck is wrong wit' you? You got fuckin' fleas or somethin'?"

Tyke laughed. "Nah, man, why you askin' me dat?"

Mel stood up. "Cause, nigga, you on my gotdamncouch scratching ya self like a damn dope fiend! You messin' wit' dat shit, ain't you?"

Tyke stood up too. "Hell no!" He gathered up his things. "Yo, man, I'm outta here. You ain't gonna be callin' me no dope fiend and no murderer—I'm outta here!"

Tyke drove around in his car with no place to go. He couldn't go home because he knew that detectives would be all over the place. Sierra wasn't around because he had driven through her block, called her phone, and knocked on her apartment door and there was no answer. His boy, Mel, practically called him a liar when he asked about Tamir. He didn't know what to do. Tyke had absolutely no family he could turn to and for the first time in his criminal history, he didn't know what to do. He punched the steering wheel and pulled out the cellophane packet again. He thought about Tamir and how he meant to kill her.

As they drove on the Southern State Parkway, smoking weed, Tyke decided to get off at the Eagle Avenue exit so that they could get to know each other a little better. Tyke and Tamir had a brief conversation; she talked about Rasheed and he talked about Sierra.

"Yeah, man, I didn't appreciate you callin' me after you had a fight wit' homegirl. I'm thinking' you was tryin' ta get at me ta make both of them jealous."

Tamir snickered. "Nah, I just like ya style. You seem mad cool and you got da gangsta appeal, I like dat."

Tyke huffed. "Yeah, right. Anyway, what's good? Ain't nobody around so you gon' bless me or what?"

"Bless you like what, Tyke?" He pulled his penis out of his jeans. "Suck you off? Is dat what you mean?"

"Yeah, dat's what I mean," Tyke replied, imitating Tamir's voice.

"I dunno," Tamir replied nervously. "I thought me and you was just comin' out here ta talk and dat shit would come later."

Tyke pulled out the Baby Eagle and pointed it at Tamir's head. "Yo, shorty, get da fuck out my car." Tamir hopped out the car, with the warning from Tyke that if she tried to run he was going to shoot her in her head. They walked a couple feet away to a grassy area. There, Tyke made Tamir give him oral sex with the gun still pointing to her head. Tyke then made her take her jeans off, while he stood there with an erection, making her put a condom on him. Tamir layed on her back, spread eagle, as Tyke forced himself inside her. As Tyke was having sex with her, he purposely pressed his muscular forearm across her neck. Tamir struggled but he was feeling good and didn't mind if she resisted a little. It only turned him on more. When Tyke finished his dirty deed, he looked at Tamir and realized that she wasn't moving. He smiled to himself, took the condom off, and put it inside a tissue in his pocket.

"Yeah, bitch, you got what da fuck you deserve. Thought I didn't know you was tryin' ta use me ta get back at dat muthafuckin' Rah!" Tyke said to Tamir's lifeless body. He got in his car and left to go back to Brooklyn, ending up in Williamsburg. Tyke sniffed his heroin and kept his gun cocked as he leaned back in car seat, drifting in and out of sleep. Sierra and Rasheed were going to be his next victims.

Chapter Thirty-six

LAMONT

"Lamont," Monique asked. "Tell me what da fuck ta do! I can't just blow Sierra's spot up like dat!"

"Damn, IG got you workin' fuh dem? Damn, I don't know whut ta say!" Lamont replied. "Are you sure you seen Sierra wit' a inmate?" Lamont felt his chest tighten.

"Yeah, I'm sure. Da nigga's from five North. Rasheed Gordon. You know him?"

Lamont couldn't recall the name. "I can't remember da name or da face, Monique. But I don't think you should say nuthin' to IG about Sierra."

Monique sucked her teeth. "I ain't thinkin' about IG, I'm thinkin' about what I saw. I gotta tell her before one of these other fucked-up officers see her wit' him. You know how these people talk!" Monique looked around the control room to see if anyone was trying to eavesdrop on their conversation. Everyone was on task, as usual.

Lamont looked at Monique. She had a look of desperation on her face. "Do you know any information about anyone besides Sierra? I need some leads by tomorrow afternoon."

Lamont thought long and hard. He had hired a private investigator to check out Deja, his son's mother. He was supposed to meet with him when he got off of work to see what was really up with her. She had been calling him and harassing lately, threatening to blackmail him with the videotape of him and Monique, which also contained images of him grabbing her that night. If he was a ruthless person, Deja would have been on Monique's list but he was not too happy with the fact that his son was involved in their mess.

"I'm sick o' dis shit, Deja!" Lamont recalled their last conversation. "Stop callin' me wit' da fuckin' threats, okay? Court is a couple of weeks from now and I'm goin' fuh full custody of my baby!"

"Full custody . . . full, what? Nigga, are you crazy? There's no fuckin' way the courts gonna let a ho like you have custody of a beautiful baby like my son—"

"Your son? You act like you made him by ya self! Remember I got da DNA test ta prove Trey is mine, don't get it twisted, ah-ight? You wanna keep harassin' me, I'm gonna make you realize dat you ain't gonna scare me outta his life!"

Deja laughed. "Okay, Mr. Simmons. We could play hardball but ya grimy ass ain't gonna win. I got you beat on dis right here so try me if you want to!"

Lamont shook his head, waking himself up from his silent nightmare. He regretted the day he ejaculated his precious load inside of Deja, thinking he should have shot it in her mouth instead.

"Mo, I think I might have somethin' fuh you. Just sit tight. In da meantime, ya need ta step ta Sierra, on some real shit. It's about time y'all let all da drama stay in da past. Shit, we grown and in these last couple o' months, you must admit dat da three of us ain't been in no bullshit wit' each other. We just tryin' ta move on wit' our lives."

Monique agreed with Lamont. "Yeah, you right. I'm gonna do dat. But I'm scared she might tell me ta mind my business! Then what?"

Lamont waved his hand. "She ain't gonna tell you shit.

Sierra loves dis job. She loves da benefits it has ta offer so she ain't gonna say nothin' but listen ta you. After you tell her, everything else she do after dat is on her. At least, you woulda cleared ya conscience."

Lamont watched as Monique walked back toward the equipment. Everyone in the control room was busy and he was glad—he needed a moment to get his head together. He looked at the tattered calendar on the wall, past the circled paydays, and looked at the date that he and Pops were going to have dinner at Monique's house. Monique had finally told her mother about Pops and she was overjoyed, if not for herself, for her daughter. Lamont found out that Monique had some emotional problems throughout her childhood, not to mention she had given birth to a daughter at the age of fifteen. Lamont felt guilty for not having it as rough as Monique, even without a mother in the household. He realized what a big impact fathers made on their families, which was one of the main reasons he was going for full custody of his own son.

As the clock ticked on, Lamont did roll call for the 5:00 to 1:00 officers, a roll call in which Sierra stood at attention. He couldn't deny that he thought about her from time to time and lately, he had been wishing they were still together. She always made all his problems seem less complicated. After roll call, he watched her from the corner of his eye and noticed that she looked tired and had a worried look on her face.

"Hey, Si," Lamont asked cautiously. "You ah-ight?"

Sierra looked up at Lamont. "Yeah, Lamont. I'm ah-ight. Just a lil tired, I guess."

He pulled her to the side. "I'm concerned about you. You don't look like ya self. You wanna chill out post instead of goin' Five North tonight? I could change it fuh ya. . . ."

Sierra put up her hand. "Nah, Lamont, dat's okay. I know a lot of officers don't like ta work up there and I don't wanna stick you wit' tryin' ta get somebody ta cover fuh me so I'll go to Five North, but thanks anyway."

Suddenly, Monique came out of the control-room door. Lamont gave her the okay to take Sierra somewhere private so that they could talk. As Lamont watched the two women walk away, he knew then that he wanted Sierra back whether she was involved with an inmate or not. He was still in love with her.

Chapter Thirty-seven

MONIQUE

Monique and Sierra walked inside of the empty locker room. They both checked the area before they started talking to make sure that no one was there to overhear their personal conversation. They both sat on the long bench in front of the metal lockers and they faced each other.

"What's up, Monique? 'Cause I gotta go ta post," Sierra stated.

"I just wanted ta thank you again fuh helpin' me dat day. I really appreciated it," Monique said.

"Okay, you're welcome but I have a feelin' dat's not what you bought me in da locker room for."

Monique sighed. "Si, I know it's been rumors goin' around about me, about you, and it's da same thing, dat we fuck wit' inmates. I don't like ta believe da bullshit 'cause people gossip so much and a lot of times, it ain't even true. When I heard da new gossip about you, I didn't even entertain it, I swear. Dat is, until I saw you."

Sierra sat straight up. "Saw me? Saw me—what, Monique?!"

Monique swallowed hard. "Saw you huggin' and kissin' wit' Rasheed Gordon. Not dat's it any o' my business but I just happened ta be passin' through the 'Stuy, drivin' down Halsey Street goin' toward Bedford Avenue when I seen y'all two together, huggin' and kissin' in front o' dis big-ass brownstone!"

Sierra gulped. She was speechless. "Who was you wit'?"

"I was by myself, Si. I didn't tell nobody else except fuh one person. . . ."

Sierra stood up. "Who da fuck did you tell?"

"Lamont." Sierra began to hit some lockers. "He not—"

"Lamont? Why da fuck would you tell Lamont? I see, you ain't changed, Monique. I tol' you if you want dat nigga, you can have 'im—"

"Wait, Sierra, calm down, it's not what you think. Your secret is safe wit' me, if my secret is safe wit' you."

"How da fuck is my secret safe when you tol' my ex-man about dis nigga?"

"Sierra, Lamont is my half-brother. His father is my father. I finally found my father, Sierra."

Sierra fell against the lockers and slid to the floor. "Lamont is ya what?"

"He's my brother. I just found out a week or two ago. As a matter o' fact, I found out da day I seen you and Rasheed together."

Sierra was stunned. Monique sat around and waited for the news to sink in. She was still amazed herself, considering all the things that happened between him and her.

"Oh, my goodness, Monique! Does Miss Ann know?" Sierra asked.

"Yeah, she know. We all supposed ta be meetin' dis weekend at my house fuh dinner."

"I'm happy fuh you, Mo. I swear I am. Now can I ask you a question?" Monique shook her head. "Are you working for IG?"

Monique held her head down. Sierra knew what the answer was when she did that. "Sierra, I'm not gonna tell on you. We knew each other from kids and even though I have been a real fucked-up individual in da past, I ain't like dat now. I wouldn't do dat ta you and I really don't wanna do it ta another officer but I'm just ready ta say fuck them. I just wanted ta tell you what I saw and ta watch ya back."

"Mo, I care about Rasheed. I'm too into my feelings to stop now. I think what makes me hang on is I am curious ta see how dis is gonna turn out. Not to mention, it feels good ta be desired."

Monique placed her hands on Sierra's shoulders. "Sierra, I'm not judgin' you. You are a smart woman and only you know what's best fuh you. But as da old sayin' goes, 'Be careful what you ask for, you just might get it!' Monique hugged Sierra and walked out of the locker room, leaving Sierra to think about those words of wisdom.

Chapter Thirty-eight

RASHEED

Rasheed left his house and walked to his vehicle with caution. He was afraid that Tyke would be hiding somewhere nearby and he wanted to be on point. Kemp came out shortly afterward and climbed into the Range with his nephew. They made a pact that one wouldn't be without the other until Tyke was completely out of the picture.

"Unc, I ain't seen dis nigga around in a minute, yo. Where you think he could be?" Rasheed asked, as he scanned around the neighborhood while driving.

"I don't know. I ain't heard shit about him, nothin'. All I know is when we catch dis nigga, he gon' die a quick death!"

"Shit, I wanted a slow one. He killed my peoples, man. He killed her, I know he did."

"How you figure? Cause da cops said it?" Kemp asked.

"Nah, man, cause dat nigga hates my fuckin' guts. And he knows dat I fucks wit' Sierra. He just a hatin' ass, and he's a piece o' shit, son. He don't deserve ta live. He wants it all. He's a greedy, fucked-up dude, man."

Kemp nodded his head in agreement. "Man, I see what you

was talkin' about all dem years. Dat dude got some real jealousy issues. It's sad."

Suddenly, Rasheed saw Tyke's cream Chrysler driving down Ralph Avenue toward Broadway. "Oh, shit, Unc, dat's dat nigga!"

They trailed him for at least five blocks before he made a turn. He must have seen the truck in his rearview mirror because Tyke began to speed up. Rasheed and Kemp were on his bumper, trying to avoid hitting anyone. Tyke knew what he was doing. He was trying to get attention so that somebody could call the cops. With the sounds of sirens, Tyke could make a quick escape and Rasheed would fall off his ass.

"Yo, get dat nigga, Rah, he tryin' ta shake us," Kemp said.

Tyke pulled his car over, unexpectedly causing Rasheed to fly right by him. He was pissed. Tyke was now behind the truck and chasing them.

"Damn, Unc, I'm gonna kill dis muthafucka! He played us!" Rasheed exclaimed.

As they crossed Bushwick Avenue, they ran a red light. A truck broadsided their vehicle and the Range flipped over once. Tyke swerved around the truck, laughing, getting away unscathed. A crowd gathered around the truck and somebody yelled out to call an ambulance. A group of old-timers inspected Rasheed and Kemp to make sure that they were clean before the cops came, removing guns and ammunition, also helping them out of the totaled truck. They layed them on the ground until the paramedics came, who treated them at the scene. Fortunately for them, they weren't hurt too badly. Phone calls were made to their family members, who immediately came to pick them up. As Rasheed rested in his bed with a banged-up body and pride, he was even more intent on killing Tyke. He had to get to him before he tried to get to Sierra.

Sierra busted in the bedroom and slid on the bed next to

Rasheed. She was crying hysterically as she hugged him tightly. Rasheed loosened her grip, still sore from the fender bender.

"Rah, you ah-ight, baby? Are you okay?" she asked between tears.

He kissed her on the forehead. "Yeah, I'm okay, ma-ma. Don't worry about me, I'm a big boy."

"Sharee tol' me what happened. Let's just call da cops and get Tyke back in jail. He not worth all o' dis."

"Yes, he is! He killed 'Mir. He gonna try to take you out. I already know he wanna put a cap in my ass and I ain't about ta let dat shit go down."

Sierra sat up on the bed. "Rah, I don't want nothin' ta happen ta you. I'm callin' da cops!" She picked up her cell and Rasheed snatched it from her.

"Si, leave onetime outta dis shit! I ain't playin'! Dis is some street beef and I can't call da cops on dat nigga! I ain't no fuckin' snitch!"

"Well, wit' my job, you can—"

"*Fuck ya job*!" Rasheed yelled. "You runnin' round here wit' me and you actin' like you so worried 'bout dat job! I don't give a fuck about dat damn job and they don't give a fuck about you! So just stop it wit' da job shit, ah-ight?"

Sierra looked at Rasheed and her lips began to quiver. Looking at her face, he instantly regretted what he said.

Chapter Thirty-nine

SIERRA

Sierra packed her things that day and reluctantly went back home. Rasheed hurt her feelings with the statements he made earlier. She knew that everything he said was true but she just wasn't ready to hear it from him. He unsuccessfully tried to talk her out of going back home, to at least wait until the beef with Tyke was over, but she had to get out. She had come to the conclusion that if Tyke was going to get her, he might as well try now so that she could call the fucking cops or kill his ass and get it over with.

Sierra thought about going to her mother's house, but Marjorie Howell, who she talked to almost every day, would have too many questions to ask. Sierra didn't want her mother to worry about her only child and there were a lot of things that Sierra had neglected to tell her lately.

As she unpacked her belongings, she recalled the conversation she had with Monique. She was happy that she had finally found her father and was a little envious that she was related to Lamont. She'd been thinking about him a lot and realized that in comparison to the drama that she and Rasheed seemed to be having, the relationship with Lamont didn't seem so bad after all. Rasheed seemed loyal and caring but the negatives were outweighing his positives right now. Should she take a chance on him and was it worth it? Risking her job was one hurdle, but now that she was risking her life, it was a whole different ball game. Sierra wondered how many other dudes hated Rasheed; that he had beef with. Was Tyke just one of many? She secretly wished that Rah would go ahead and move to Atlanta with his brother. At first, she didn't want him to leave but considering all the things that they had to endure within these few weeks, it would be much easier for her to sever the ties that way.

Sierra climbed on a chair in her bedroom to look inside of the small lockbox that was bolted on a shelf in her closet. She removed her Glock from the shelf, along with a magazine clip. She hadn't carried her personal firearm in a long time but with all the beefing that was going on around her, it seemed as if she was going to need it. Tyke had become someone who she didn't know. She tried to tell herself that the Tyke she had once loved didn't kill that girl. She didn't want to admit that she was dealing with a man who was capable of committing such a heinous act. She had come to the conclusion that it was not who these men were, it was what she had become. Sierra was looking for a protector. Since she could remember she had equated "thugs" as having that character trait. They were tough, street-smart, and instilled fear in people. She searched for that at one time in her life, but at what costs? Rasheed was ready to kill Tyke to protect himself and her. *What if Rasheed kills Tyke and goes to jail for murder?* She would feel obligated to do his bid with him. *What if Tyke kills Rasheed?* Then she would feel somewhat responsible for his death and his family probably would look at her sideways. She had to try to persuade Rasheed to leave town for Atlanta. He had to go. She would take care of Tyke by herself. She owed it to her sanity, which she was starting to question.

Sierra stared at Lamont's phone number in her phone. She came to the realization that impregnating another woman wasn't that bad compared to her falling in love with an inmate. If she had to do it all over again, she would love his son like he was her own. She would love Lamont like he needed to be loved. Right now, Lamont would tell her what to do. He wasn't into the streets but he was street-smart. More importantly, she had been too quick to judge him. What was she thinking when she let him go?

Sierra put on her fuzzy slippers and walked around her apartment, tidying up and keeping busy. She wanted to keep her mind off of the fact that Tyke could knock on her door at any minute. With every noise she heard, it scared her half to death. She needed to disappear for a while, somewhere that was a safe haven, a comfort zone. Somewhere neutral where Tyke or Rasheed wouldn't be able to locate her.

Sierra picked up the phone and dialed the phone number, real slow. As the phone rang, she contemplated on hanging up but it was too late.

"Hello?" yelled the voice into the phone. Sierra closed her eyes and breathed deeply.

"Lamont?" she replied. "It's me, Sierra." There was complete silence on the other end.

"Hey, you ah-ight? I didn't think dat I would see dis number again," he said softly.

"I know." Sierra began to sob silently while on the phone.

"Hello? Si, are you there?" Sierra tried to get herself together. "You know what? I'm coming over there—"

Sierra stopped him. "No, no, don't come over here. I called ta ask if I could come over for a few days, I really need somewhere ta stay right now. I can't stay here."

"Do you need me ta come get you, Sierra? You know I will!" Lamont paused. "Are you in some kind of danger?" Sierra began to cry. "Pack ya shit, Si, I'm on my way!"

Sierra hung up the phone and began repacking her clothes. Suddenly, her doorbell rang. She instantly grabbed her 9 mm and cocked it back so that one bullet was in the chamber. She carefully went to her door and looked through the peephole. It was Rasheed. She rolled her eyes and opened the door, quickly.

As Rasheed entered, he looked at Sierra, standing there with the gun in her hand. He snickered, which pissed Sierra off.

"What was you gon' do wit' dat?" he asked, while limping over to her couch to sit down. He must have thought he was staying.

"Rasheed, what da hell are you doin' out da hospital? You just had a car accident!" She wanted him to leave before Lamont got over there.

He made himself comfortable on the sofa by putting his bad leg up. "I came over here ta get my girl. Ya need ta come back home wit' me, Sierra. I ain't lettin' you stay here by ya self. Dat nigga could be somewhere around here waitin' fuh you!"

"You know what, Rah?" Sierra yelled from her bedroom. "Fuck Tyke! I'm tired o' dis bullshit, of everything. I don't appreciate y'all puttin' me and Tamir in middle o' y'all beef wit' each other, neither. Now a girl is fuckin' dead and you get into car chases wit' dis nigga, riskin' ya freedom, riskin' other peoples' lives and ya own! I tol' ya ass ta call da the cops if you seen him but no, you wanna be a fuckin' vigilante!"

Rasheed was annoyed. "Well, Sierra, if you wasn't still fuckin' da nigga, a lot o' shit wouldn't be goin' down right now!"

Sierra came out the bedroom. "Well, if you woulda tol' me you fuckin' knew Tyke and knew dat I used ta talk ta him instead o' tryin' to be sneaky about it just ta get some pussy then maybe, maybe we wouldn't be goin' through dis, now would we?"

Rasheed shook his head. "Yeah, I didn't tell you I knew him 'cause I figured you wouldn't have talked ta me!"

"Because you was bein' fuckin' selfish! You think about ya self and only ya self. I tol' you, we had a lot at stake here and ta just call da fuckin' cops and get dis deranged muthafucka locked up, but no! You gotta keep it real, you a gangsta, you gotta take dis nigga out ya self, Mr. Captain Save-a Ho! When you was in Five North, you tol' me dat you was a changed man. You tol' me when you come home dat you was gonna be better, all dat street shit was a wrap and you know what, Rasheed? I believed you! Do you think I need you to kill Tyquan? No! He ain't worth it. He took a woman's life over some bullshit and you out here almost killin' ya self and your uncle tryin' ta get at him! Leave it alone, Rasheed, or leave me alone!"

Rasheed got up and limped over to Sierra. "Si, I love you but—"

"But you love da streets even more. Good-bye, Rasheed. I'm goin' ta stay wit' a friend fuh a lil' while, so don't call me, I'll call you."

She kissed him on the lips and opened the door for him to leave. Rasheed limped down the long corridor, looking back at Sierra. When he disappeared in the elevator, Sierra locked her door and waited for Lamont to pick her up.

Red called and Sierra answered quickly. "Hey, girl! I'm on my way out da—"

"Si, you okay? You know dat Tyke tried ta stay at Mel house and Mel threw dat ass out, right?" Red volunteered.

"Get outta here! Did Mel find out about da girl?" Sierra asked.

"Yeah, it was in da paper dat day and Mel read the article. Apparently, Tyke had tol' Mel about da girl when he met her and how he was gon' get wit' her 'cause she was Rasheed's ex since Rah was talkin' ta you. You know, some tit-for-tat bullshit. Anyway, my boo, who by no means is a stupid man, remembered her, and questioned ya boy about it."

"Word, Red? What did Tyke say?" Sierra inquired.

"Tyke said he didn't do nuthin' to da girl. He don't get down like dat, blah, blah, blah. Tyke had originally tol' Mel he needed ta stay there 'cause him and his wife had some problems. You know Tyke ain't never lied ta Mel about shit! Come ta find out Tyke is sniffin' that heroin too!"

Sierra instantly felt dirty. "He what?" she yelled.

"He on dat heroin. Mel caught him usin' it a couple o' times. Dat's why he had ta leave Tyke alone. Tyke is grimy, man. Oh, I was callin' ta see if you was ah-ight."

"Yeah, girl, I'm good. Lamont is about ta come pick me up. I'm gonna stay at his house fuh a couple o' days."

Red was excited. "Good, Si. You need a guy like Lamont. Rasheed seems okay. I never met him, but it sound like he still in da streets and we don't need dat no more."

"You right, girl. You right. I'ma chill wit' Lamont for a few days and whateva happens, happens. I ain't gon' try ta stop it," Sierra responded, annoyed that Red knew anything about Rasheed.

Red sighed. "Well, think about it. You been on my mind lately and I don't never be home 'cause I'm always wit' Melvin. You welcome to stay at my house."

"Red, I'm okay. You a lil' too close fuh comfort and besides my crib, dat'll be da first place Tyke'll come lookin'. I'm goin' ta Queens right now but thanks. I'll call you later."

They said their good-byes and hung up the phone. Lamont's number came up and when Sierra answered, he told her he was waiting downstairs.

Chapter Forty

LAMONT

Lamont was still reeling from Sierra's phone call. He had replayed over and over in his head how he would react if she ever called him again. When he saw her phone number on the caller ID, it was unexpected but he was ecstatic nonetheless. He must have run around his house like a chicken with his head cut off, trying to clean up and make sure his home was presentable. It had been a while since Sierra had been over so he wanted to make sure she was comfortable.

As he drove on the Conduit Parkway en route to Sierra's house, he wondered what was going on with her. He wasn't going to let on that he knew anything about her dealings with the inmate. Lamont decided that he was going to let her talk and he was going to be attentive and of course, nonjudgemental. He was going to do whatever it took to get her back, whether she was messing with the inmate or not.

When he arrived at Sierra's building and she came downstairs, he looked at her. He had forgotten how attractive she was. He hadn't seen her in anything except her uniform since they had broke up. He was speechless as she climbed into the passenger seat of his truck.

"Hey, Lamont, I appreciate you . . ." Sierra started but Lamont couldn't hear the rest of what she was saying. Her presence was distracting. "Hello, Lamont? Did you hear me?" she asked.

"Oh, yeah, no doubt," Lamont replied. "I know you appreciate what I'm doin' and it's not a problem. Now, are you okay?"

"Nah, I'm not. I just got myself caught up in some unnecessary drama and I regret it," Sierra replied.

"Well, you could talk about it, if you wanna. I'm all ears."

She looked at him. "First, let me start by sayin' dis." Lamont looked lost. "You have a son now. A child is a blessing, something beautiful and at the time, you felt that you needed to hide it from me. You did what you did, and even though I was angry about you havin' a fling wit' Deja behind my back, I was more upset at da fact you tried ta hide da baby."

"Well, ta be honest. Deja was a jump-off and I wasn't in love wit' her. I loved you and still do. I mean, I don't regret my son but I wished I woulda done things differently. I know it may sound like a lame excuse but it was just history repeatin' itself. Pops gotta woman pregnant while he was married ta my mother and here I am doin' da exact same thing to a woman I claimed to be in love wit'. I shoulda known better, but I was thinking wit' my dick and not wit' my head."

"So why did you do it?" Sierra asked.

"No reason. Because I could at da time. What I did, though, ain't had shit ta do wit' you! I was just accustomed ta havin' women flock to me and I just took advantage of it, dat's all."

"Well, I just want us ta be friends, Lamont, and just let da chips fall where they may. Is dat cool?" She kissed Lamont on the check and he blushed.

"Damn, girl, you gotta brother blushin' over here," Lamont gushed. "Da bottom line is we have a lot ta talk about. Da both of us."

Sierra shook her head. "Yeah, we do." She looked out the window. "Lamont, you know what? I think I need ta move outta Brooklyn. Maybe Queens or Long Island. I need some peace, you know what I'm sayin'?"

"Yeah, dat's why I'm in Queens now. Try it, you'll like livin' out there." Lamont put on his signature smirk. "Queens is reeeeaaal nice!"

Sierra glanced over at Lamont. "You are so crazy! I'm catchin' on ta what you sayin'!"

After Sierra was settled in, they both sat on Lamont's couch for their talk. Lamont listened intently as she described her attraction to Rasheed Gordon.

"Fuh one, I never entertained inmates," Sierra stated. "Dudes tried ta get their holla on but I don't pay it any attention, dat is, until I met Rasheed."

"What was it about Rasheed dat was different?" Lamont asked.

"Rasheed was persistent. He was persistent in a smooth, convincin' kind o' way. He wasn't disrespectful in his approach and he was extremely patient."

"But didn't you think it was game? You know them cats got some of da best game in da world!"

Sierra sighed. "You right. Rasheed shot some game. I can't say if it was intentional or not 'cause I must admit, he got swagger."

Lamont looked at Sierra, eye to eye. "Why did you do it? Did I play a part in you makin' the decision to deal wit' Rasheed?"

"I'm gonna be completely honest, Lamont. You did play a part. I was brokenhearted when we broke up. I think I got to da point where I was lonely, miserable, and desperate. I just wanted a man in my area, good guy or bad guy. Sometimes da good guy treats you fucked-up and the bad guy treats you like a queen."

"What you mean by dat?" Lamont inquired. "I'm da good guy dat treats women fucked-up, huh?"

"Nah, I'm speakin' in general." She paused. "Any more questions?"

"Yeah, what's goin' on in ya life, Sierra? What made you end up callin' me?"

Sierra told Lamont about all the drama that occurred in the past months or so. Lamont listened intently. By the time Sierra had gotten to the end of the story, Lamont was emotionally exhausted.

"Damn, Sierra, what da hell have you gotten ya self into? You rollin' wit' some straight hood niggas! Dat murder story was just in da paper like two weeks ago!"

"Yeah, in da meantime, Tyke is on a fuckin' rampage. I just needed ta chill somewhere and da safest spot is yours."

Lamont frowned. "You usin' me, girl? Wit' all ya drama, it don't seem like I fit on any page in dat script!"

"Hell, no, I ain't usin' you. You owe me dis favor after all you put me through! What's up wit' ya baby mama, anyway?"

"Yeah, she takin' me back ta court. She wants more money and I want full custody. She ain't let me see my son in weeks."

"You ain't seen ya son? Wow, she's buggin'! Do you need me to whip her ass, Lamont?"

Lamont laughed. "Nah. We gonna do dis da right way. I got a lawyer and I got a private investigator, lookin' into some things fuh me. A couple of weeks ago, I got dis threatening letter from somebody and I'm figurin' it was her ass. Then she claim she gotta videotape of me and another woman havin' sex wit' each other."

"How did she get dat? A videotape?"

"I'm gonna be real. I was at her house watchin' Trey while she went out. I invited some company over fuh a hour or so and things just happened."

"Lamont, no you didn't do dat! Why did you invite another woman over her house?"

"I dunno. I tol' you dat I just do some dumb shit sometimes wit' out even thinkin' about da consequences 'till later. Anyway, dis nutcase had a hidden camera in her livin' room, taped da whole thing."

Sierra's mouth was opened. "Oh, shoot! Who was da woman on the tape? A female dat you're involved wit' now?"

Lamont hesitated. "No, not really."

"Okay, who was it? Don't tell half of da story. I didn't hol' back so now you gotta be real wit it!"

"Da other person on da tape was Monique." There was complete silence as Lamont watched Sierra's jaw drop. He didn't like where the conversation was heading.

"Monique? You fucked her, Lamont? In ya baby mama's house? I don't believe it!"

Lamont stood up. "Well, it's more. Monique turned out ta be my half-sister from my father so it's punishment enough fuh me, knowin' dat I slept with my sister!"

Sierra began to laugh. "Now I guess you finally learned ya lesson!"

"Yeah, and I had ta ask Pops if he had any more daughters out here dat I needed ta know about!"

Chapter Forty-one

TYKE

Tyke was exhausted. His money was about to dry up and he had nowhere to go. Bed-Stuy was swarming with police officers so he had to make sure he watched his back at all times. He already knew that Rasheed and Kemp had an APB out on his black ass. He couldn't believe that he went from having it made to having absolutely nothing at all but his Chrysler 300. He didn't even have the urge to pick up any women; he even had to admit that he was afraid that he would kill another one. He was having urges to kill lately and he was doing everything in his power to resist them.

Tyke pulled up on Dean Street, where he observed the two-story stash house. It was his dream hit. Being that he had fallen on hard times, he didn't have any other choice but to hit the house. Tyke drove around the neighborhood, looking for a couple of up-and-coming thugs to assist him with his plan.

Tyke eased down the block toward Kingsborough Projects. He knew a couple of young cats over there that were into getting some quick money and he needed some hungry dudes on his team. Tyke ended up on Bergen Street, seeing two young dealers that were selling crack hand to hand on a bench in front of the brick buildings. They instantly came over to greet Tyke.

"What up,Tyke?" said a slim, brownskin man with braids. "What's poppin', nigga?"

"Yo, what up, Quan? What up, 'Teef?" Tyke replied, greeting the young men with a pound and hugs.

Lateef checked out Tyke's car. "Son, you doin' it well. Ya car is hot, nigga!"

Tyke glanced at the Chrysler. "Yeah, it's straight. I call it my 'ghetto Phantom' since I can't afford da real thing. But fuck it, dat's a small thing ta a giant!"

Quan laughed. "Ya still doin' it, nigga. A lot of these cats aroun' here ain't got shit so they can't talk about nobody, ya heard?"

Tyke smiled. He liked Quan and Lateef. They were some loyal young soldiers and Tyke admired them for that. He saw a lot of himself in the both of them.

Tyke got to the point of his visit. "Yo, who stash house is dat on Dean Street?"

Quan smirked. "Yo, it's dis dude from Bushwick, son. I forgot his name but I heard dat duke is a straight lame-o. Me and 'Teef been wantin' ta hit dat shit fuh months now but we didn't want ta involve none o' these sucka-ass niggas."

Tyke spoke in a low voice. "Yo, I wanna hit dat shit dis week, kid! All y'all need is ta get me some ammo and we could start plannin' dis shit right now."

The men sat on the bench and talked about robbing the stash house. Tyke learned that the house contained mostly women and at least four bodyguards that manned the doors to the place. No one knew who the guys were because they were from the other side of town, which made it even better for the trio. Tyke told the young thugs that he needed the money and that was why he was pushing for the end of the week.

"So, son, let's meet here Friday night. Have the artillery ready and I'm gonna come pick y'all up in a hoopty, a gray Honda Civic," Tyke stated.

The men said their good-byes and quickly dispersed into the projects. Tyke hopped back into his vehicle and took off down the block. He needed to get some rest and decided that after he copped his "medicine," he was going to check into the Surf Inn in Howard Beach to get some sleep. He wished that he could be in Sierra's bed with her, while she slept with her ass on his dick. Every time he thought about her, Rasheed's face appeared in his mind. He wanted to wring her neck for dealing with a buster like Rasheed. *It's ah-ight* Tyke thought to himself, *'cause after I'm through wit' Sierra, she ain't gonna be no good ta no other man!*

Chapter Forty-two

RASHEED

Rasheed tossed and turned in the bed for the last two nights. He hadn't heard from Sierra and she hadn't even tried to call him. He was beside himself. Rasheed did not like to put his hand on women but the way he had been feeling, he felt like slapping the hell out of Sierra the next time he saw her! He was upset and worried that Tyke had gotten ahold of her. He didn't know what to do.

Rasheed's phone rang and he saw Sierra's phone number. As soon as he picked up the phone, he instantly began his tirade.

"Yo, what da fuck is wrong wit' you, Sierra? You had me worried about ya ass and you ain't even tried ta call or nuthin'! Is dat's what dis is about? Huh?" Rasheed waited for her to respond but she was quiet.

"Do you hear me, Sierra? What is wrong wit' you?" he asked.

"Rah, I tol' you dat I needed a minute, dat I would call you. Why are you breakin' when I gave you specific instructions ta—"

"Wait a minute! I'm tired o' dis shit! I'm not ya fuckin' flunky! Don't tell me about some muthafuckin' instructions when we got a killer on da loose out here! A muthafucka dat wanna kill me and probably you! You can run dat cutesy shit wit' dem cornball-ass niggas you used ta fuck wit' but I ain't da one, man. Da problem wit' you, Sierra, is dat you know how I feel about you and you playin' wit' me! You been playin' a lot!"

Sierra was surprised. Rasheed sounded real angry, angrier that what she was accustomed to him being.

"Rasheed, I just needed ta get—"

"Get what, Sierra? What is goin' on wit' you? You got me on a wild-goose chase and dat ain't me. I fell in love wit' you, man, can't you see dat? You got my heart and you always talkin' about dis job shit, what people think. I don't give a fuck about other people! People is what got me on da phone screamin' on you right now. You need ta have ya ass here wit' me, right now, 'cause when dat nigga Tyke come through and try ta hurt you, my baby girl, I'ma blow dat nigga head clean off his shoulders! Get ya ass ta dis house in a half hour, man! No bullshittin'!"

Rasheed threw his cell phone across his bedroom. He had been in that room for two days, wondering if Sierra had given up on him, on them. He knew that he was overly aggressive with her but he needed to her to understand how he felt. He was stressed-out from the moment she had walked in his coming-home party because he knew once he had her, ATL was gonna be wiped off of his to-do list. His brother, Karim, called him everything but the child of God because of his refusal to leave New York.

"Rah, what up wit' you? You just got home, you supposed to be here wit' me, you crash da truck I got you and you done hooked up wit' dis broad, now ya pussy-whipped ass don't wanna come down here right now? You losin' ya mind, nigga!" Karim exclaimed.

"Karim, man, I love dis girl. I would like ta try ta convince her ta come wit' me," Rasheed replied.

"What?" Karim screamed. "She need ta stay her ass right there on Rikers Island. Atlanta ain't payin' what they payin' in

New York for jobs. You can't ask dat woman ta give up her career to bounce outta New York wit' you!"

"You did it. You did it with Aaliyah. So why can't I do it?"

" 'Cause Aaliyah didn't have a bangin'-ass job like ya shorty. I was takin' care of Aaliyah's ass and when I stopped, you see what da bitch did? She ended up workin' in Magic City, strippin'! Is dat what you want, damn, what da fuck is her name again?"

Rasheed told him Sierra's name. "Yeah, Sierra gonna be swingin' from a pole too, ya fuck aroun'! Bring her ass down here if you want to!"

Rasheed laughed hysterically. "'Rim, you crazy, man. She good peoples, though. I'm feelin' her."

"No, hell no! You ain't only feelin' her, ya ass is whipped. She put dat thang-thang on you and dat was it. Oh, by da way, sorry ta hear about Tamir. Did y'all see dat nigga, Tyke, yet?"

"Nah, not since da accident. He gotta die, 'Rim."

Karim sighed. "Rah, don't get ya hands dirty. Me and Kemp got you on dat one, son. Kemp tol' me you finally tol' him about Tyke and da Uncle Pep situation."

"Yeah, I tol' him. Tol' Kemp dat Tyke is a rotten creature, man. Had ta make him a believer!"

"Yo, I'm out but I notified insurance and you should be gettin' a new truck in a week or so. I'm havin' it imported from here ta New York so I'll call you in a day or so. Love you, man, and be careful, ya hear me?"

"Yeah, love you too, 'Rim. Later."

Rasheed snuggled under the covers and waited for Sierra to arrive on his doorstep.

Chapter Forty-three

SIERRA

Sierra had almost given Lamont some sex that night. A part of her wanted to because she knew what he was capable of. He never failed to disappoint in the sex department and he had made her appreciate his loving in every stroke. But this time it was different. They kissed and messed around a little but from some reason, it didn't feel the same to Sierra. She knew that it wasn't Lamont, it was her. She politely asked him to stop and he obliged, not wanting to make her feel uncomfortable. Sierra gained even more respect for Lamont when he did that.

"I apologize, Si, for makin' you feel uncomfortable," Lamont stated.

"Nah, Lamont, it ain't you. It's me. I can't do dis. Somethin' is keeping me from doin' dis," she answered.

Lamont turned around on his back. "I know what it is, Si. I'm a man."

Sierra was confused. "What is it, then?"

"It's dat nigga, Rasheed. You're really feelin' him." Sierra tried to contest the statement but Lamont stopped her. "It's okay, baby. I know dat you still love me. I know dat you will probably always love me and the same here. You keep tryin' ta fight it, but I see it. You are fallin' in love wit' him."

Sierra was quiet. She had been trying to fight her feelings but even she had to admit it, it was hard to not be in love with Rasheed Gordon. Aside from his past mistakes, he was what she wanted or so she thought. She didn't know if it was a temporary or permanent feeling, but all she knew that it was a feeling that made her feel like she was a part of a relationship once again.

"I'm sorry, Lamont," Sierra managed to say.

"Don't apologize. Look, if he makes you happy then go ta him. But I know dat if da nigga fucks up, I'm right there, man, I promise you. I fucked up so I can't even get mad if you found someone dat you feel makes you happy. I shoulda been on my job and we wouldn't have to be havin' a conversation about da next man tryin' ta get wit'you!"

Sierra smiled. She happened to like Lamont's new attitude. She guessed the chain of events in Lamont's life had made him do some self-reflection. She laughed at herself as she thought about Sean Daniels knocking Lamont out. *Maybe Sean knockin' him on his ass dat one good time did him some good,* Sierra thought as she laughed to herself.

When she finally spoke to Rasheed, he let her have it! She didn't blame him, considering Tyke probably running around the five boroughs like a drug-crazed maniac. All that Sierra knew was when Rasheed told her she better have her ass over his house in thirty minutes, she felt compelled to get there and fast.

Sierra thanked Lamont for dropping her off by her house and she immediately ran to her parked truck, throwing her parking ticket in the glove compartment and sped off. She had fifteen minutes to get across town to Rasheed's house and she was wasting no time in doing it.

When she rang the doorbell to Rasheed's, his grandmother, who was a vision of loveliness in her Sunday clothes, welcomed her inside with a warm hug.

Sierra kissed the woman on her cheek. "Hey, Miss Carrie, how are you?" she asked.

Miss Carrie hugged Sierra. "I'm fine, baby. I know how you doin' too," Miss Carrie replied with a smile on her face. Sierra had seen pictures of Rasheed's mother, Lavon, who Sierra thought was absolutely gorgeous. When Miss Carrie smiled, she saw that Lavon Gordon had been the exact replica of her mother.

"Huh? What you mean, Miss Carrie?" Sierra asked.

"Baby, you pregnant. I see it all over your face. Your face is fillin' out and you got da pregnant woman glow."

Sierra looked in the large mirror in the living room. "I'm pregnant?"

"Honey," Miss Carrie began, while putting on her hat. "I was a registered nurse fuh thirty-five years. I worked in da maternity ward and ob-gyn and done seen women come and go. Wit' me, they don't even need to take a test except ta find out how far along they are and like I said, you pregnant!" Miss Carrie opened the front door. "My grandson upstairs waitin'. Dat boy got on my nerve runnin' up and down these stairs lookin' fuh you. See ya later, baby."

Sierra walked up the stairs to Rasheed's bedroom. He was sitting on the edge of his bed, with his hands folded under his chin.

"Sierra, where you been?" he asked. "I been worried 'bout ya ass, man."

Sierra was surprised by his calmness. "I was at a friend's house, Rasheed. I tol' you dat I needed a break from all da drama," she replied.

He stood up. "You know, Sierra, you had me so damn mad, dat you actually had me contemplatin' ringin' ya pretty-ass neck. But dat ain't da way ta solve dis right here."

Sierra was instantly annoyed. "Solve what, Rasheed? We—"

"Lemme finish." He paused. "You was at a friend's house, huh? You know why dis shit is so crazy, Sierra? I realize dat I don't know none of ya damn friends. Dat's messed up when I did nuthin' but gave you all of me. You done been aroun' my family, I mean, look how you walk up in my fuckin' house wit' no problem! Lemme ask you somethin'—are we in a relationship, Sierra?"

Sierra was stuck on stupid. "Yeah, we, um, are, you know—"

Rasheed stood face-to-face with her. "Are you my girl and am I ya man or what, Sierra?"

Sierra began to cry. Rasheed continued. "Dat's what I thought. You don't wanna put a label on dis. If you do, dat would mean dat you would have ta be responsible fuh da consequences. You would have ta introduce me ta ya family members, ya friends. Dis shit ain't nuthin' but ya fuckin' secret!"

Sierra tried to hug Rasheed. "Rah, don't do dis. I don't know if we ready—"

"Ready?" Rasheed yelled. "Ready? Do you know what da fuck I went through ta get wit' ya ass? I broke up wit' a female who had been there fuh me through hell and back. She wasn't perfect, but you know what? Dat girl was there durin' da hardest of times. Now she dead, fuh some stupid reason, cause dat jealous nigga you was fuckin' wanted ta get back at me and you."

"What? Rasheed, you can't blame dat on me 'cause Tyke never liked you anyway!"

"Sierra, Tyke could have killed me a long time ago, if he wanted to. I even saw da nigga a few weeks before he even found out I knew a Sierra Howell. He coulda killed me, then. But he didn't, did he? Oh, yeah, I ain't finished. Five North. I'm da one dat got Scooter set up. I tol' dudes to give him da buck twenty stitches he wearin' across his face right now! You know why, Sierra? I found out dat he was talkin' ta IG about ya girl, Miss Phillips and about us possibly havin' dealings wit' each other! I did dat, Sierra, fuh us ta be together. Oh, and our boy, Sean Daniels? Yeah, he was in on it too. He knocked out ya lil' boyfriend, Captain Simmons! Oh yeah, Sean held me down on dat one. I'm da one dat tol' him da first opportunity dat he got ta put dat lame-ass nigga on his ass, do it and it was done! I heard about how he hurt you by gettin' his side bitch pregnant while you was still his woman. Ask me how I know dat, Sierra? Huh? Da baby mama fucks wit' one of my homies, right now! He was locked up in her jail when they met and he's still fuckin' wit' her ta dis day. She was over there spillin' da guts ta my nigga about you and Captain Simmons's relationship! I tol' him ta push up on dat silly chick, to get her open and do her ass dirty but even he had a heart and realized dat she has a child she had ta take care of. I was doin' dat fuh you. Now here I am, once again tryin' ta keep you safe, worried about your whereabouts, tryin' ta keep dis muthafucka from killin' you and me, and you don't even appreciate it!"

Sierra was extremely quiet. What could she say after Rasheed told her all of the things he had done to be with her? She didn't know whether to feel flattered or to argue him down because she hated to be in the wrong. But she realized that he was right, even she had to admit, that she hadn't been putting her all into their relationship like he surely was. That was because she figured that the relationship wasn't going to last very long, regardless of how they felt about each other. There were too many obstacles for their new relationship to withstand. Now that Rasheed had shared with her all of the difficulties he had to deal with to get with her, she kinda felt bad about her behavior.

"Sierra, I am fallin' more and more in love wit' you. I couldn't wait to get out of dat stink-ass jail cell fuh a chance to get wit' da female dat I thought was da closest thing ta da woman of my dreams. I ain't da best nigga in da world but I respect da hell outta you and always have since da first day I laid eyes on you. Y'all females always complainin' about how y'all need a good dude, then when you finally got a nigga dat loves you, he gets shitted on!"

"Rah," Sierra exclaimed. "I care about you so much! I can't believe dat you feel like I don't care about you, dat I ain't fallin' fuh you too. I can't—"

"Sierra, I don't wanna hear no more! I'm worn-out. Dat nigga, Tyke, is gonna be taken care of but I don't even want his blood nowhere on my body! As far as you concerned, do what you want! I thought maybe, maybe we could have somethin', you know, go against da grain and you could help me grow, be my partner in life, yo. But you can't 'cause you ain't even admitted dat, hey, maybe you got da problem! Maybe you push niggas away! Well, I'm here ta tell you, Sierra, dat ya shit stinks just like everybody else's!"

"Rasheed, don't act like dat. I just don't wanna get—"

"And I don't wanna hear about dat job. You act like dem muthafuckas go home at night, thinkin' like 'Damn, I wonder what dat Sierra Howell is doin' right now?' Baby girl, you give ya self tooo muuuch credit! You ain't dat fuckin' serious! We ain't dat serious!"

Sierra watched as Rasheed pulled out some suitcases and began to pack some of his belongings. She was crushed when she realized that this may very well be the end of the road for them, after all.

"Rah, where are you goin'? Why you packin' clothes?" she screamed at him.

"I gotta get outta here fuh a minute! I'm leavin' New York today. I already made my reservations and my flight to ATL. Da plane leaves in two hours."

Sierra felt her pressure go up. She hadn't wanted to run him out of town on a bad note. She was obviously getting what she asked for and she didn't want him to leave anymore. She couldn't change overnight but she knew that she had better think of something before Rasheed walked out of her life for good.

She stood in front of him. "Rah, I'm sorry, I'll do better. Please, I don't want you ta go!"

Rasheed walked around Sierra and continued to pack his things. "I gotta go, Sierra. Why don't you go back ta ya cornball Captain Simmons where it's safe? Dat way, you ain't gotta worry about gettin' fired fuh fuckin' wit' him!"

Sierra was confused and her chest began to hurt. She felt like she couldn't breathe. Right before her eyes, a man who she would have never guessed would be someone that she would grow to love was about to leave her. She had never been "left" by any man before and with Rasheed leaving for Atlanta, he seemed as if he was about to break that record.

She looked at his suitcase and saw that he had packed enough clothes that would last him for a week or so. Rasheed dragged the large suitcase out of his bedroom and called out for Kemp, who was in his own bedroom at the other end of the long hallway. Kemp emerged from his bedroom, followed by a bootylicious babe with a short, spiked hairstyle. He immediately smiled when he saw Sierra, standing by the banister of the staircase.

"Hey, Si Si!" he said. "Oh, yeah, meet my boo, Yasmin. Yasmin, dis is Sierra, my nephew's girlfriend." The ladies politely smiled at each other and said hello. Kemp finally noticed that Sierra and Rasheed were extremely quiet.

"What's up, y'all mad or somethin'? I don't hear nuthin' but crickets right now!" he exclaimed. Kemp observed the luggage Rasheed put outside his room. "Rah, where you goin', man?"

Rasheed exited his bedroom and closed the door. "I'm goin' ta stay wit' Karim fuh a lil' while. Can you take me ta da airport?"

Kemp looked at Sierra. "Si, why don't you take ya man ta da airport? Me and Yasmin about ta go somewhere right now."

Rasheed was not amused. "Nah, son, she good. She was just leavin'!" Rasheed looked at Sierra. "As a matter o' fact, why you still here?"

Sierra twisted up her face, catching a glance of Yasmin, who looked like she felt sorry for her. "You right, Rah. I'ma leave." She started down the staircase. " 'Bye, Kemp. Nice meetin' you, Yasmin." They all watched Sierra go down the stairs until they heard the door slam.

Sierra climbed in her truck and pulled off. She was too heated to cry, especially after Rasheed embarrassed her in front of Kemp and Yasmin. She couldn't really say that she blamed him for being upset, being that she had him worried about her for the last couple of days. She felt guilty about even thinking about having sex with Lamont while Rasheed sat at home, blowing up her voice mail and wondering if she was dead or alive. Sierra heard a plane in the distance, which made her think about the comment Miss Carrie had made about her being pregnant. What if she was pregnant? Who would be the father, Tyquan or Rasheed? There had been so much going on that she couldn't remember if she had gotten her period for the month. Sierra pulled over to run inside of a CVS drugstore on the way home. She purchased a pregnancy test to take as soon as she arrived home.

Chapter Forty-four

MONIQUE

Monique nervously opened the front door. She stood there tongue-tied for a minute as Lamont and Pops, her biological father, stood on her front porch, waiting to be invited in. She instantly snapped herself out of her daze and watched as they slowly walked in the living room of the quaint home. Monique suggested the men have a seat on the overstuffed sofa and make themselves comfortable. Everyone was quiet until Lamont finally broke the silence.

"So, Pops, this is Monique Phillips, your daughter, and Monique, this is Charles Simmons, your father and mine, of course, but you gotta call him Pops. Not Dad or Daddy or even Ol' Man—I still call him dat sometimes—but fuh real, just call him Pops!"

They all laughed as Pops stood up and hugged Monique. As soon as he did this, Monique was overcome with emotion and the waterworks began. How could she have a negative reaction toward the man whose love she had been yearning for all of her life? After regaining her composure, she hugged Lamont too, and thanked him. He had given her one of the best gifts that she had ever received in her life. As they talked, Monique's teenage daughter, Destiny, came downstairs and the two men stood up at the same time. Destiny was a pretty young lady and that's when Monique noticed that her daughter, who she originally felt looked like her father, Ali, actually bore an uncanny resemblance to Pops. They were amazed as the teenager came over and politely spoke to the men. Pops encouraged Destiny to give him a hug and he gave her a hearty embrace, overjoyed that he had been blessed with a beautiful granddaughter. Monique's brother, Timothy, emerged from his downstairs bedroom with his son, TJ, in tow. TJ looked adorable in his Jordan outfit with a pair of sneakers to match. Lamont's heart sank when he saw the baby boy, making him think about Trey.

Making a grand entrance, Monique's mother, Ann, finally walked downstairs, looking sophisticated and fit in her jeans with a short-sleeve shirt. Lamont embraced Miss Ann first, with Pops standing in the background like he had just seen a ghost from his past. Everyone stood around to see who would make the first move.

"Hello, Ann. You look fabulous! I mean, look at you. You ain't changed much since we last seen each other!" Pops stated.

"Why, thank you, Charles! You haven't changed, neither! You been workin' out or somethin'?"

Pops pushed out his chest. "Yeah, you know, I gotta get my workout on, right boy?" Pops replied while nudging Lamont.

"Miss Ann, if it wasn't fuh me gettin' him in dat gym wit' me sometimes, da only excercisin' Pops would be doin' is liftin' da fork ta his mouth!" Everyone laughed.

They all filed in the dining room and took their respective seats, while Monique and her mother brought out the food. Lamont's and Pops's mouth watered and they couldn't wait to get their taste buds going with the home-cooked meal. Miss Ann made everyone bow their heads and hold hands for the grace.

"Father God, I thank you fuh allowin' us ta be able ta come together today to share dis wonderful meal, Lord. Father God, you have answered my prayers and bought dis family together wit' da person dat we needed ta make it complete and dat was my daughter's father. Amen."

They all said their amens and commenced to helping themselves to fried chicken, macaroni and cheese, candied yams, collard greens, sweet corn, and other delicacies that Miss Ann had prepared for Pops's visit. Monique watched Pops and Lamont interact with her family and decided that this was just what she needed all along. Pops was the final ingredient.

After dinner, Lamont and Timothy went downstairs to the basement for a game of Madden football on PlayStation, while Destiny and Miss Ann were in the kitchen cleaning up and tending to TJ. Monique and Pops walked in the backyard for a much-needed talk with each other.

"Monique, I sincerely regret dat I wasn't a part of ya life all o' these years. I don't want you ta think dat you was a mistake—a lil' unplanned—but not a mistake. I really cared about ya mother. We was young and carefree, maybe too carefree, when we got involved wit' each other. I was a young married fool and ya mother was a sensual young lady, who I was extremely attracted to and things happened."

Monique looked at the stars. "She tol' me da story about how y'all met and how y'all carried on this affair wit' one another. She tried ta make me feel special but she couldn't make me feel special without my help. It felt like a part o' me was missin'."

Pops shook his head. "Lamont tol' me dat you and him were, well, intimate wit' each other. I mean, how do you feel about dat now dat you found out dat he's ya half-brother?"

She held her head down. "Pops, dat was a whole different Monique at dat time so I don't even acknowledge what happened between us. I'm not goin' ta even acknowledge dat woman. What's done is done. I have closed da chapter ta dat ol' Monique and started anew, tryin' ta put my mistakes behind me and move on. I had some very low self-esteem at dat time and I was lookin' fuh love, a father's love."

"Well, you know what, baby? I'm here now and you don't have ta look no more. I always wanted ta be wit' you but I must admit, I was a big punk. I thought dat you would hate me 'cause of da circumstances, you know wit' me havin another family and all. Can you forgive me?"

Monique gave Pops a hug. From that moment on, she felt complete. It took some struggling to get where she was and she promised herself to never look back. Monique realized that she was on her way to finally start loving herself. Every occurrence leading up to her meeting with Pops had humbled her and she was glad of it because she might not have been alive to see that special day.

After Monique and Pops had their talk, Pops was able to chat with Miss Ann. They agreed that any old torch that they carried for each other wouldn't be rekindled. They were going to remain good friends because the meeting wasn't about them, it was about Monique.

Monique listened by the back door to see what her parents were going to say. She never understood why her mother chose to have a baby with a married man.

"Ann, I must say dat Monique turned out to be a very lovely young lady. You did a great job. I know dat I haven't been there fuh you and her all of this time but I hope dat da money I sent was helpful," Pops said.

Monique heard Ann sigh. "Well, Charles, I can't really be mad at you. I was just as much ta blame. I knew what I was getting into when we started dealin' wit' each other. I also knew dat I could find you but wit' you bein' a married man and all, I didn't want to cause any more problems than what I already caused. I knew dat Linda had left you but I wasn't sure if she had decided ta come back or what," she stated.

"Oh, no, Ann, Linda left me fuh good. She left Monty wit'

me too. I was happy about dat because ta be perfectly honest, if she had taken him wit' her, I probably would have never seen my boy again and dat would have killed me. Da one thing dat did disappoint da most about her leavin', she never tried to reestablish a mother-son relationship wit' Monty. She rarely called and I would always find myself gettin' in her ass about makin' and breakin' promises ta him. He didn't have anything ta do wit' our mistakes and I didn't appreciate her punishing him fuh them. After a while, me and my boy just gave up on her."

"Where is she now, Charles?" Ann asked.

"Please, dat woman is probably on da other side of da earth somewhere. I don't try ta contact her, her family members or nothin'. Shit, they didn't like me anyway. Me and Lamont talked about it recently and we both came ta da conclusion dat she really didn't want ta be there in da first place. I never tol' Monty dis, but she was da first one ta cheat on me in our marriage and I gave her another chance like a damn fool."

Ann patted Pops's back. "She did you a favor, Charles. I knew Linda fuh a long time and she was somethin' else. I'm glad you spared Lamont da details about her life, he's been hurt enough."

"Yeah, me too. Linda had her own problems wit' drugs and mental illness. She couldn't have done Lamont and me a bigger favor. I just didn't know it at da time. Anyway, back to my daughter. Tell me about some o' da things I missed out on."

Miss Ann gave Pops the intricate details on how it was to raise Monique Phillips. She started from her early childhood and how she was very jealous of the relationship between her and Timothy's father. She also shared how Monique falsely accused him of touching her, as she discovered later, but Monique's allegations prompted Ann to sever the relationship anyway. She didn't want to take any chances with her daughter. There were tales of boys and sex, and she told Pops about the pregnancy Monique managed to hide from her and the death of

Destiny's father, Ali. Throughout the story, Pops felt even guiltier for not trying to be a part of Monique's life sooner.

"Well, Charles, dat's da story of my daughter's life in a nutshell. She tries ta come off as some hard-ass but she is not as strong as she looks. At one time, wit' all da promiscuity, I thought that she may have been addicted to sex but I realized dat it was somethin' deeper. Dat's why I sent you da pictures and was so glad dat you agreed to take da DNA test. But seriously, I went through all dat trouble because my daughter needed her father. "

Pops looked down as a tear fell from his eye. "You know what, Ann? She ain't gotta look no more 'cause I'm here. I'm here and I'm not goin' anywhere."

Chapter Forty-five

TYKE

It was 2:00 AM. Tyke, Quan, and Lateef sat in the Honda Civic, which was parked on the block where the stash house was located. Tyke and Lateef were going to go inside, while Quan stayed in the car with the motor running. The plan was to meet up with a female who worked inside of the house. She was going to knock on the door, as usual, with a password that had to be used to gain access. When someone inside the house saw the familiar face in the peephole, the door would be opened. At that point, Lateef and Tyke were going to rush inside. The female was promised a small cut for her services, but Tyke had already planned to kill her during the robbery.

While waiting in the car with the sawed-off and black hoodies, the female accessory walked by the car, thereby giving the crew the signal. Tyke and Lateef hopped out, following the female to the door of the house. They exited the car and hid in the bushes next to the house. She knocked on the door and gave the secret password. When the door was opened, Tyke and Lateef jumped out of the bushes from opposite ends of the doorway. They pushed the female in the house, blindfolded and tied everyone up, and Tyke immediately shot the female accessory in the head. After hearing what happened to the unfortunate young woman, everyone in the house was at a standstill. Tyke grabbed a slim, pimply-faced man, sticking the large sawed-off in his face.

"Where da fuck is da money?!" Tyke asked in a gruff voice.

Warm pee flowed down the man's pants leg. "Umm, umm, I don't know . . ." Tyke shot the man in the chest. This was dead body number two. He walked over to a petite woman with expensive jewelry on and a nice ass to match. Tyke licked his lips and the woman began to cry.

"Sweetie, I ain't tryin' ta hurt ya pretty ass," Tyke said as he used his gun to play with her hair. Lateef stood by the door, becoming impatient with the hotheaded Tyke. He was holding the others hostage and it was about to get real old in a minute.

"Yo, son, fuck dat bitch! Let's get da shit and be up outta here!" Lateef stated.

"Where da cash at? Where da stash at?" Tyke asked the woman, quoting a verse from one of Biggie's infamous songs, "Gimme the Loot." Lateef rolled his eyes in the back of his head, not in the mood for Tyke's untimely wittiness. The woman led Tyke to a large closet with a metal door with a bolt. She pointed to it and he pushed her into the door, ordering her to open it. She quickly obliged. Once the door was opened, Tyke's eyes bulged out of his head, as he observed the stacks of money and drugs inside of the closet. He then forced the woman to put some of the large stacks of money inside of a tremendous duffel bag that was nearby.

"Put about five keys in there, ma. I ain't tryin' ta be greedy—I just want a piece o' da pie!" he exclaimed.

He made the female drag the bag, depositing it at Lateef's feet. Tyke told Lateef to check upstairs to see if the coast was clear, meaning the closets, bedrooms, and bathrooms would not go unnoticed. Those were common hiding spots.

When Lateef came back downstairs, he grimaced as he watched Tyke rape the woman. He banged the woman like there was no tomorrow while her body writhed with pain. Lateef turned his head, unable to watch Tyke do his dirty deed.

"Yo, what da fuck are you doin, nigga?" Lateef screamed, with his face turned the other way. "You just givin' these muthafuckas DNA, huh?"

Tyke had not heard anything Lateef said. "Oh, baby, dis pussy is so good. I ain't had none in a while. Damn, girl!" was all that Tyke managed to say. He was caught up in the moment. Tyke grabbed her hair and ejaculated all over the woman's back. After regaining his senses, he fixed himself up and shot the female he raped, as well. The three remaining people were on their knees with their hands behind their heads and facing the wall.

"Yo, man, let's go!" Lateef yelled.

Tyke was on some madman shit; it was almost like he had a death wish. They both finally ran outside with the huge bag in tow. As soon as they hopped in the car, Quan pulled off before they could even shut the doors all the way. They rode up Atlantic Avenue en route to Queens to Quan and Lateef's hideout to count the large sums of money.

"Tyke, man, you a wild dude!" Lateef called out from the passenger seat. "I didn't know you was like dat, nigga!"

"No doubt. I go in when I do my thing! Dat lil' bitch was fine as hell, though, I couldn't resist, I just had ta get me some!" he replied, proudly.

Quan shook his head and looked at Lateef on the sly. They were much younger than Tyke but they came to the conclusion they weren't as dumb as he was. When they finally counted the money, they had come off with $250,000. Tyke got $100,000 and one kilo for setting everything up. Quan and Lateef got $75,000 and two kilos apiece. Everyone was fine with their cut, even though Tyke had murdered three people to get it. Quan and Lateef smiled at each other as Tyke excused himself to go to the bathroom.

* * *

As the men proceeded to drive back to Brooklyn, Tyke pulled out his faithful cellophane packet and began to snort it in the backseat of the car. He didn't care that Lateef turned around, shaking his head in disgust, as he watched Tyke nod off right before his light brown eyes.

Pathetic, Lateef said to himself. He and Quan watched as Tyke continued to nod off from the effects of the dope. Quan got off on the Rockaway Boulevard exit and drove toward the airport. He continued down the desolate road toward Five Towns and made a left turn on Brookville Boulevard. They pulled over near some shrubbery and trees on the side of the dark road, pulling a doped-up Tyke out of the backseat of the car by the hood of his black sweatshirt.

"What da fuck?" Tyke mumbled, unable to resist the two young men, who were completely sober. They knew what they had to do and they had to do it quickly before they were spotted. Lateef put on a pair of black leather gloves, while looking at Tyke on the ground. He slowly removed the beloved Baby Eagle from Tyke's front pocket, putting the gun in Tyke's hand. Lateef slowly placed Tyke's finger on the trigger of the gun, with his gloved finger putting pressure on Tyke's finger as well. Lateef pointed the Baby Eagle to Tyke's temple and looked at Quan. Quan gave him the signal to go ahead with the plan. Tyke was so high he didn't know what was going on.

"Yeah, muthafucka, you wanted ta kill my fuckin' cousin, right?" Lateef shouted. "Well, this is fuh Tamir, nigga, and my boy, Rah! One, ya self!" At that moment, Lateef helped Tyke pull the trigger, with one shot to his temple. Lateef removed his gloved hand from the gun and left it alongside Tyke's lifeless body. "It's about time somebody took you outta ya misery," Lateef stated. "I did ta you what you been wantin' ta do ta ya self all these years!"

Quan and Lateef then sped off with the money and drugs, leaving Tyke's pitiful body in the shrubbery. Lateef called Rasheed on his cell phone.

Chapter Forty-six

RASHEED

"Hey, my man, waddup!" Lateef announced. "Dat nigga is outta here! Now I hope my cousin can rest in peace!"

Rasheed smirked. "No doubt, 'Teef. Good lookin' out! Tell Quan I said what up. Thanks fuh everything."

"Man, it was not a problem. Dat dude was a menace ta da hood and after everybody find out he been terminated, they'll probably have a ticker-tape parade!"

Lateef continued. "Listen, we came off wit' some flow. I wanna drop somethin' off wit' you. . . ."

"Nah, kid. I'm good. Go take care o' ya family wit' dat money. I'm outta town anyway."

"Ah-ight, son. Love is love. Take care, Rah."

"You too, 'Teef. Oh, by da way, you know I loved ya cousin, right?"

"Yeah, I know, son, I know." They both hung up.

Rasheed turned over in the king-size bed and looked at the clock. It was 5:00 AM and he was wide awake. He slipped on his Nike slippers and made his way downstairs to the kitchen for something to drink. As he stood against the island in the middle of the huge kitchen, drinking his orange juice, his mind drifted off. He thought that he would get gratification from Tyke's death, but it just left him feeling empty and unfulfilled. He assumed it was because Sierra was all in his head. Even as he lay in bed that night with a beautiful stripper, he couldn't find the guts to have sex with her. She ended up going to sleep on him, disappointed.

Suddenly, Karim walked into the kitchen, half-asleep and opened the refrigerator, unaware of Rasheed's presence. As he closed the door, scratching his butt, he jumped when he realized that Rasheed was standing there in the dark.

"Damn, Rah, you scared da shit outta me!" Karim said. "Man, what da hell are you doin' outta bed, anyway?"

Rasheed put his empty glass in the sink. "I can't sleep."

"What happened? Shorty put it on you like dat?" he asked.

Rasheed sucked his teeth. "Hell no. I didn't even have sex wit' dat girl!"

Karim slapped his own face. "You what? Son, come on! You know dat chick cost me like five hundred dollars, man, and you didn't slay dat? Are you losin' ya mind?"

Rasheed stretched his long arms. "Man, fuck her! I don't know dat trick and I ain't into no damn strippers anyway!"

"Rah, dat girl's ass was bananas. I mean, she's a woman before she's a damn stripper." Karim looked at his brother. "Oooh, I know why! You thinkin' about what's-her-name. Aww, shit, you in love."

Rasheed was silent. He thought he could come to ATL and forget about Sierra. He was wrong. He had been there for three days, met all kinds of different women, but Sierra stayed on his brain.

"Check dis out, Rah," Karim began. "Give her a shout-out, man. You miss her and I didn't meet her yet but if she got my baby brother thinkin' 'bout her so much 'till he can't get it up fuh dat bad muthafucka in the bedroom, she must be da shit!"

Rasheed laughed. " 'Rim, come on, man! I could get it up, trust me. I just want what I want and dat's baby girl. I left NY on some mad shit, and now dat my slate is clean, I can go back."

Karim took a sip of his juice. "Oh, 'Teef took care o' dat fuh you, huh?"

"Yeah. I'm sure he did it right too. 'Teef is one o' da best hit men out there in BK. 'Mir introduced me ta da nigga a while back and it's been on ever since. He is official in dat department."

Karim put up his glass fuh a toast. "No doubt. Dat one was fuh Uncle Pep and Tamir. May they rest in peace." Karim paused. "Now go call ya baby girl, Rah."

Rasheed called Sierra's home phone. It just kept ringing and ringing. He hoped that Tyke hadn't got to her after all.

"Hello?" she answered. "Who is this? It's like five in the morning!"

"Hey, ma. It's me, Rasheed.You on ya way ta work?" There was silence on Sierra's end.

"Rah? Hey, what's up? I'm off tonight. Are you home?" she asked, suddenly wide-awake.

"Oh, nah, I'm still in da ATL. You ah-ight, though?"

"Yeah, I'm cool," Sierra replied with a hint of disappointment in her voice.

"I been thinkin' about you," Rasheed said.

"So why did you leave, Rah? You left unexpectedly . . ."

"Sierra, we not talkin' about dat right now. I'm tellin' you dat I miss you."

"I miss you too. I swear I do. Come back, please. I'll try harder. I won't get on ya nerves wit' talks about da job and—"

He laughed. "No, boo, you can talk about da job all you want. Just don't put me and da job in da same sentence."

Sierra laughed too. "Okay, okay. I won't. So how's ATL?"

Rasheed sighed. "Oh, it's straight. I'm outta here, though. I'm comin' home."

After talking to Sierra for a few more minutes and with her

agreeing to pick him up from the airport, Rasheed returned to his bedroom. He stared at the stripper chick who was in his bed and shook her until she was awake.

"Yo, go in Karim's room," Rasheed ordered. "Get da fuck outta my bed."

Chapter Forty-seven

SIERRA

Sierra was awakened again later on that morning. It was Red, who sounded frantic.

"Si," Red screamed into the phone. "Tyke is missin'."

Sierra was unmoved as she made her way to the bathroom to pee. All the drama with Tyke had made her cringe every time she heard his name.

"Okay, like I give a fuck. Tell Melvin ta call Tyke's gotdamn wife!" Sierra snapped.

"I know, I know but it's just crazy because Melvin called me, buggin' out. NeeNee called him and tol' him first."

Sierra was annoyed. "Okay, ah-ight! What da fuck y'all want me ta do? The muthafucka ain't over here!"

"Wow, missy! Who pissed in your Cheerios dis mornin'? What is wrong wit' you?"

Sierra wouldn't dare tell Red about her positive pregnancy test. "I'm fine. I guess I'm just tired."

"Did you hear from Rah? Is he still in Atlanta?" Red asked. Sierra knew Red was being nosy and probably trying to get information for her man, Mel. They wanted to see if Rasheed had anything to do with Tyke's disappearance.

"Yes, he is and he's been there fuh da last couple o' days. Why, who wants ta know?"

"Sierra, what is wrong wit' you? Why are you so bitchy?"

"What is it, Red? Is it because you're usually da bitch? I just woke up on da wrong side o' da bed, I guess."

"Dat was mean, Sierra, but I'm gonna let it slide." Her phone beeped. "Oh, dat's Melvin. 'Bye!"

Sierra sucked her teeth. She knew that Red was calling for Melvin. Mel still kept in contact with Tyke's wife. She figured that he had probably put Red up to asking her the twenty questions, if she didn't volunteer to do it.

Sierra reluctantly got up, dragging herself into the shower. She got dressed shortly afterward, not wanting to do anything but sleep all day. Rasheed's flight was due to arrive in JFK that afternoon and she told him that she would pick him up. Sierra opened her door to retrieve the *Daily News* while she ate a bowl of Honeycomb cereal. As she skimmed through the articles, she stopped as one caught her eye.

MAN FOUND DEAD IN QUEENS WITH NO SUICIDE NOTE

The body of a 34-year-old man was found in a desolate area in Queens. Detectives identified the male as Tyquan Williams, of Bedford-Stuyvesant, Brooklyn. A 9 mm was found near Williams, who suffered one gunshot wound to the temple. Williams, a known felon, who was still on parole after several stints in state prison, was a key suspect in the murder of Tamir Armstrong, 25, whose body was found in Hempstead last month. Cops also said that Williams was a suspect in the drug-related rape and murder case that occured a short time ago. No further information was provided.

Sierra put her hand to her mouth and ran to the toilet. She threw up all her breakfast.

* * *

Sierra drove through the airport and managed to smile as she spotted Rasheed waiting curbside with his luggage. Sierra jumped out her truck and ran to hug him. They kissed until a Port Authority officer instructed her to move her truck.

On the way home, Rasheed kissed Sierra's hand and face. "Look at you, Si. You glowin' and everything."

She laughed off Rasheed's comment and quickly changed the subject. "Oh, yeah, I don't know if you heard about it, but Tyke was found dead in Queens," she volunteered.

"Oh, word?" Rasheed said. He seemed uninterested.

Sierra looked at him strangely. "Da *Daily News* said dat he committed suicide. Personally, I don't think he would have killed himself."

Rasheed was visibly annoyed. "Da man probably did kill himself! He was a damn dope fiend and he was on da run from everybody. The only place left fuh him ta go was hell!"

"Okay, Rah, calm down. I was just wonderin' if—"

"Man, who are you, Inspector Gadget? Fuck Tyke! Dat nigga was gonna kill me and you whenever da opportunity presented itself. He flipped on you, remember?" Rasheed yelled.

Sierra sighed. She wasn't going to argue about Tyke. Rasheed seemed agitated by the mention of his name.

While Rasheed sat in the passenger seat of her truck, sulking, Sierra thought about the old Tyquan, the man she used to love. She knew that Tyke had an attachment to her, and though he was married, she secretly felt as if she had let him down in some way. Tyke had never had a real family upbringing, growing up going home to home. He would visit her mother on a regular basis and Marjorie Howell always welcomed him with open arms, good conversation, and a hearty meal. Sierra and Tyke shared a lot together and their relationship was even more special than anyone would ever know. Sierra would have loved to pay her last respects to Tyke but it would have been a conflict of interest. She just chose to remember the good times, trying to remove any negative images of Tyke out of her mind.

"Sierra! Sierra!" Rasheed called out, snapping her out of her daydream. "What you thinkin' about? I know you ain't thinkin' about dat nigga, Tyke!"

Sierra sucked her teeth. "Please, Rasheed. I ain't thinkin' about him so just drop it. Okay?"

Rasheed stared at her. "Ah-ight. Ah-ight. You don't have ta get a attitude."

She rolled her eyes at Rasheed, who had succeeded in irritating her that quickly. Sierra cautiously rubbed her pregnant belly, as she thought about her appointment at the clinic the next day. Once she had the abortion, she knew she would always wonder what her baby would have looked like.

Chapter Forty-eight

LAMONT

Lamont was on the phone, speaking to the private investigator he hired. Howard "Slim" Taylor had been a licensed private investigator for ten years after retiring from the Corrections Department. He was worked with the department for twenty-five years in many different facilities. Slim was referred to Lamont by one of his buddies and he was supposed to be the best in the business. He specialized in investigating correction officers, even working for the inspector general's office sometimes. Slim's customers consisted of wives, mistresses, boy-friends, husbands, boy toys, gay lovers, etc.—the list was endless. Lamont came to him the month before asking for him to find out anything about his son's mother that he could get ahold of and he was ready to spill the beans.

"Hey, Slim, what you got good?" Lamont asked. "Court is the following week and I need as much scoop as possible."

"Lamont," Slim began, speaking with a deep baritone. "It's not good but that may be exactly what you wanted to hear. Deja Sutton, let's see—okay, here we are. She resides at this address in Hollis, Queens. Correct?"

Lamont anxiously confirmed the address. He was nervous as hell and his palms were sweaty.

"Okay, Miss Sutton is apparently living with a man or vice versa. We took a few pictures of the duo coming in and out of her home, with a small child in tow, approximate age two years old. The man was holding the male child in his arms, with Miss Sutton walking a short distance behind them. They were seen entering a late-model Nissan Altima, registered to Miss Sutton, and took off. Upon return, the adult male was seen parking the car, without the woman and child and entering the house with a key, only to shortly return to the vehicle and taking off. We tailed the young man for a short distance and he was seen hugging and kissing another female, who was not Miss Sutton, helping her into the passenger side of the Altima, thereby taking off once again."

Lamont was stunned. "Oh, wow. Who is da guy?"

Slim cleared his throat. "This is the good part. The guy is Anwar Jones, thirty-five years old, hailing from Brevoort Projects in Brooklyn, paroled felon, career criminal, and drug dealer. Mr. Jones was apparently released from Rikers Island three months ago, after completing ninety days for a parole violation. He has a rap sheet that dates back to 1985 and he is a very dangerous man. Apparently, Miss Sutton doesn't know who this guy really is."

"Who is he, Slim? Dis idiot is aroun' my son?" Lamont yelled.

"Well, Lamont, I wouldn't try to approach this man. He doesn't have any domestic or child abuse, or any sexual offenses on his rap sheet, but he is a very volatile person according to some of the people I interviewed about him. They were afraid to talk to me at first but after I told them it was strictly confidential, they spoke freely, almost happily, if I must say so myself." Slim continued. "Mr. Jones was arrested for two separate murders but was not convicted for any of them because of insufficient evidence and witnesses that refused to cooperate.

He has done at least two eight-year bids in prison, with various jail infractions on Rikers Island alone, including breaking a captain's nose in C-seventy-four in 1991. According to the Eighty-first precinct, he was also suspected in several different drug-related murders but it couldn't be actually proven."

Lamont sighed in frustration. "Was dis guy locked up in her facility? She worked in C-ninety-five."

"Let's see, here." Slim paused, while Lamont listened to him shuffle through papers. "Oh, okay, here it is. Yeah, he was in C-ninety-five and was just released—yeah, three months ago!"

"Slim, thanks, man. You a lifesaver. You think she was hollerin' at dis man while he was in her jail?"

"I was waitin' for that question. She sure was. I gotta couple of folks I still deal with that are on the job or know someone that works in the various facilities. They keep me up to date about the happenings and Miss Sutton's name came up in the conversation with tales of sex with inmates and obviously, this isn't her first relationship with a former crook. Her character is known for dealing with inmates and local street hoods."

"Why does she still have her job?" Lamont asked.

"She covers her tracks. I must admit, she's a good one. No phone records and no connection. For the job to investigate her, they would actually have to be in her home to catch her doing anything. I'm surprised I caught her. She must be slipping. Anyway, Lamont, whenever you're ready, I have all the information in a large, manila envelope for you to pick up. I will leave it with my secretary, Eva, if I'm not in the office."

"Thanks, Slim. If you not there, I'll leave the rest o' da money with her as well, okay?"

"That's fine, Lamont. Good luck on your case and I hope you get custody of your son. He's a handsome little boy."

Lamont hung up the phone and immediately began pacing the room and punching the air. He felt his salty tears run down his cheeks as he thought about his baby boy and how he would have to strangle Deja! Why would she put their son and herself in jeopardy by dealing with this Anwar guy? What was wrong with these CO hoes, risking their jobs and—possibly—their lives for these fools? First, Monique, then Sierra, and now Deja. Was there really a shortage of men? Then Lamont thought about it. All three of the women had one man in common and that was him. Was he the one with the problem?

He pushed the women out of his mind. The most important topic on his mind was his son. He wanted custody of Trey, even more than ever now.

The judge presiding over Lamont and Deja's case sat at his bench with a blank look on his face. He was a tenured judge and had seen just about every case known to man thrown on his desk. Being a criminal court judge for years, he thought he heard it all until he came to family court. He looked at Deja and Lamont.

"Miss Sutton, you are here today because you would like to receive child support on behalf of your son, Lamont Terell Simmons the second? I have looked over these W-four statements and I see that you have a considerable amount of income yourself, is that right, Miss Sutton?"

Deja's lawyer spoke first. "Yes, she does, Your Honor, and Miss Sutton is also seeking full custody of their son, along with supervised visitation for the child's father."

The judge looked up, taking off his glasses. "On what grounds, Counselor?"

Deja's lawyer spoke again. "Your Honor, my client states that Mr. Simmons has proven over and over again to be irresponsible and unreliable. He is extremely disrespectful. Also, she fears for the safety of her and her son. She is very fearful of Mr. Simmons. He also has had numerous female companions in the company of her son and my client has requested several times for the defendant to discontinue this reckless behavior, but he has refused to comply. He even disrespected her home and their son by having intimate encounters with an unknown female in her home and—"

Lamont's lawyer interrupted. "I object, Your Honor," he stated. The judge let him proceed. "My client has proof receipts of items he purchased for his child from birth, times and dates he had his son in his care, along with photos on these dates and further evidence of the note and the brick that was thrown through his car windshield, along with the note."

Deja's lawyer objected but the judge insisted Lamont's lawyer continue. "As I was saying, Your Honor, Mr. Simmons has receipts from a glass shop to support his claim of property damage to his vehicle. On that day, Miss Sutton just happened to be off from work. Also, Mr. Simmons has neighbors that witnessed a man throwing the brick through—"

"You lyin' muthafu—" Deja screamed out, suddenly.

The judge banged his gavel. "Order in the court!" he screamed. "Miss Sutton, one more outburst like that, I will hold you in contempt of court! Is that understood? Counselor, talk to your client! As a matter of fact, I have something to say. This case is not about Miss Sutton or Mr. Simmons. We are here for the child's interest. This is turning into a sideshow and I will not have it in my courtroom!"

Deja's lawyer spoke up. "We apologize, Your Honor," she said, as she gave Deja the evil eye. "It will not happen again."

The judge continued. "Now, if we have any evidence to support claims of inappropriate behavior and neglect, please come forward with it. I will dismiss this session for lunch while I retire to quarters with the counsel of both parties to go over everything. Court is dismissed. Return in one hour." The judge banged the gavel once again and Deja and Lamont filed out of the courtroom.

Lamont turned the corner to walk toward the elevator when Deja approached him. He was trying to avoid a scene and decided to take the stairs when she ran in front of him.

"Muthafucka, how dare you try ta put me on blast!" she hissed. "You ain't know shit about me! You musta hired som—"

Lamont cut her off, trying to keep his composure. "Stay da fuck away from me, you crazy bitch! You goin' around fuckin' inmates then you have da nerve ta try ta keep me from my son? Not ta mention, you had da nerve ta call IG on da next woman? I tol' ya ass not ta fuck wit' me and ya insisted on doin' just dat. You lucky I ain't send them gotdamn flicks I got o' you wit' Anwar ta IG!"

Deja simmered. He watched as tears of frustration filled her eyes. "Oh, so dat's what da judge is lookin' at in there? Pictures o' me and Anwar? How da hell you know about Anwar, Lamont?"

Lamont pointed his finger at Deja. "Deja, I don't give a shit who you lay up wit'. You can fuck da whole Five block fuh all I care. Da one thing I do care about is Trey and I want my baby. You denied me da right as a father ta see my child but you rather have him aroun' some gun-clappin', crack-dealin' thug, then wanna come at me like I'm da deadbeat. You know, I'm a good-ass father. I made a lot o' mistakes, like fuckin' you, but you can't say dat I don't love my son!"

Deja looked around and observed a few stragglers in the corridor, looking their way. She felt her face flush. "Lamont, I—I know you a good father but I wanted us ta be a family and you never wanted it wit' me. I spent every day since I had my son, wonderin' why you never wanted to be wit' me. I needed you to be a good father but a good man, also!"

Lamont turned up his lip. "Deja, from da day you ended up pregnant, you tried ta convince me dat we were meant ta be together. No, we weren't! It was sex, Deja. Nothin' but lust! You was a jump-off, I had a girl at da time and it served me right fuh getting all of dis 'cause I did her dirty." Lamont turned to walk away when Deja called his name.

"Lamont," she sighed. "I—I can't take our son from you. Let's make a deal."

He looked at her suspiciously. "Deal? What kind o' deal?"

"You can have full custody o' da baby," she replied. Lamont looked shocked. "I know it's crazy but I'm sorry, Lamont. I'm in love wit' Anwar. I need him and I'm not gonna give him up, fuh—fuh motherhood."

Lamont shook his head. He realized Deja never really wanted to be a mother unless he was included in the package. Now she was about to give up her parental rights for the sake of a man.

"When we go back inside, I'm gonna tell them ta reverse everything. I want you ta have full custody. Just don't make me lose my job, Lamont. If I don't have dat job, Anwar will leave me!"

Lamont watched Deja walk away. She looked almost childlike as she shuffled down the hallway with hunched shoulders. He felt like it was history repeating itself. Pops had finally revealed some more truth behind Lamont's mother, Linda, leaving. He discovered that she was waiting for the right moment to leave Pops for another man when she found out that Pops got Miss Ann pregnant. That was all she needed. Apparently, the man Linda had fallen in love with was not happy about being a ready-made father to young Lamont and he was left behind with Pops. It was as simple as that.

When they returned to the courtroom, it was agreed that Lamont would obtain full custody of Trey. Deja was told to surrender the child to Lamont in forty-eight hours or risk being arrested for obstruction of justice. Lamont was smiling ear to ear as he walked out, thanking the counselor and the judge.

While walking to their respective cars, Deja walked over to Lamont again and shook his hand.

"I'm sorry, Lamont. I hope dat you can forgive me fuh everything," she said.

"Yeah, I'm cool. Just bring my baby ta me. He don't need nothin', I got everything he need right at my house." Lamont got into his truck and sped off before Deja was able to see him crying like a baby. He needed his mother.

Chapter Forty-nine

MONIQUE

Monique walked into 60 Hudson Street with some information. She had thought long and hard about what she was about to do, just wanting to get it over with so that she could get on with her life. She had finally learned from her mistakes and promised herself and God that she would not ever put herself in a position like that again. She must have prayed all night long for this day to be over.

She sat in the waiting area to be called in to the chief investigator's office. She dreaded the sight of the man and felt nauseous as she thought about meeting with him. She looked at the clock, wishing she could just blink her eyes and it be 9:00 AM the next day. The secretary finally called her name and Monique nervously walked inside a large conference room. Investigator Holden, a Latino woman, and the departmental lawyer were sitting there at a long conference table, looking at her.

"Have a seat, Miss Phillips" Mr. Holden said with a smile. He looked fake as hell.

"Miss Phillips, this is Mrs. Rosa Torres, who is also an investigator and Peter Marin, departmental attorney. He represents us. You are not on trial or anything. They are just here to ensure that all the information that you are about to give me is commendable enough for you to keep your job as a correction officer. This is a closed meeting and it is just between us three. The information you give us will also ensure us our positions next year and I hope that you will not disappoint."

Monique opened her Coach briefcase and began to remove typewritten notes. They were various statements from inmates and recorded tapes to support her findings. Refusing to give up the various females that she knew were having rendezvous with various inmates, she opted to give up information about a huge cigarette ring that was operating throughout Rikers Island in different facilities. In the city jails, cigarettes were like money but cigarettes were strictly prohibited, a law enforced under the new regime. Although smoking was not allowed, inmates and officers always found the time to take a pull. Cigarettes in a correctional facility were welcomed because the smoking calmed a lot of inmates down, making a workday easy as hell for the staff that worked amongst them. But if an inmate was caught with a pack of cigarettes on a search, it was guaranteed that they were smuggled into the facility.

Monique had used her rapport with the detainees to obtain as much information about the ring as possible, knowing full well that inmates talk and dry snitch on officers and each other all the time. She had the names of the officers and other staff members, with their dates of appointment and facilities, neatly typed with the times and dates of their offenses. She watched and took notes carefully, not wanting her cover to be blown, which could have been detrimental to her career—or even worse, her life.

After she ran down everything she knew to the three, Holden looked over her notes. He seemed satisfied. After a brief consultation, Monique was happy to hear that she was in the clear. Aside from her tarnished reputation, she was glad that assorted deputy wardens and wardens had commended her on her work ethic. She knew then that her prayers did not go unanswered. As she gathered her belongings to leave, Holden approached her. She held her breath, wondering why he couldn't just let her go.

"Miss Phillips, I was very pleased with the information that you gave. We had a lead on it for months but you actually closed the case for us. You understand that corruption is abhorrent and definitely not tolerated. You, of all people should know this, am I correct?" Monique nodded her head in silence, as he continued. "Don't feel like you're alone, Miss Phillips. Hundreds of correction officers are accused of corruption all the time and many of them have been in the same position as you were. To be honest, without black female officers like you—you know, the ones that can't keep themselves from screwing inmates—our jobs would only be harder. Snitches like you make it possible for us to keep the Department of Corrections running smoothly and actually keep my job! So now you are free to go, Miss Phillips. Your job is done here but we will have our eye on you. Next 'mistake,' Miss Phillips, and you will be out on your fat, black ass! Have a good day and good luck on your promotion!"

Monique quickly exited the conference room and headed straight for the bathroom. She threw her belongings on the sink and ran in the stall, only to vomit in the toilet. When she finished, she threw cold water on her face. She had never been so insulted. Holden had talked to her like a second-class citizen and degraded her in a way that no man had ever come close to doing in her life. Monique recognized that although she was doing something that was beneficial, she was still considered a snitch to the department and that she was always going to be under constant scrutiny. She thought that she would at least receive praise for what she did, but she figured her reward was keeping her job. She couldn't help but wonder what was the next task they had in store for her.

She exited the gloomy building without looking back. Her

heels clicked on the sidewalk as she walked briskly to her vehicle, where she instantaneously began dialing a number on her cell phone. She couldn't cry anymore; there were no more tears left. She needed that important someone in her life to make her feel like everything was going to be okay.

"Hello?" the male voice answered. "Hello?"

"Hey, Pops, it's me, Monique," she said. "Can I come over?"

"Sure, baby," Pops replied. "Anytime. I'll be right here waiting for you."

When Monique hung up the phone after speaking to Pops, everything that was said in 60 Hudson Street suddenly didn't matter to her anymore. She would no longer allow her actions to define who she was. She turned her car around and headed toward Queens to see her father.

Chapter Fifty

RASHEED

Rasheed called Sierra's phone over and over again and there was still no answer. *Here we go again*, Rasheed thought to himself. He wasn't going to let the unavailable Sierra put a damper on his mood, especially after picking up his new Range Rover from the dealership on Northern Boulevard in Manhasset, Long Island. He had plans to take Sierra out for a nice dinner, which was something they hadn't done in a while but he wasn't going to chase her down to do it.

Now that Tyke was out of the picture, Rasheed was unsure of how their relationship was going to end up. There was no more drama with Tamir, no threats on their lives, and all the rumors swirling around about their union were subsiding. But for more reasons than one, he still was not convinced that Sierra was ready to be with him. Although he was still smitten with her, he came to the conclusion that it may not be her that was afraid. It was him. He had been home for a few short months and it seemed as if he had been through so much. He hadn't been able to find his niche, only concentrating on the needs and wants of Sierra, making sure that she was safe from harm and that she was happy. He was still apprehensive of her, of the way she felt about him, and the possibility that would she decide to just up and leave him one day. At times, he thought, *Fuck Dat! I'm A Gangsta!* but he certainly had feelings too and being a gangsta twenty-four hours a day and seven days a week takes a toll on a brother. Bad boys needed love, too, but the other person would have to be willing to give it in return as well.

Karim was blowing his phone up, trying to convince the stubborn Rasheed to hightail it back to Atlanta. There was nothing in NY for him and he knew it. All that NY had to offer was struggle and strife for Rasheed. The proof was the deaths of his mother, Peppy, and Tamir. It was only a matter of time before he would have to meet his maker but he wasn't trying to rush it. He felt that he owed it to the legacy of Lavon Gordon to make her proud of him, to be the man that his father could be had he tried. He wanted his much-loved grandmother to spend the rest of her days in pure bliss instead of just being happy that he was alive. He went to Atlanta and still was thinking about Sierra, forgetting that he was still young and virile. After living the fast life for so long, he had never been able to fully enjoy life to its fullest. He had spent so much time in the streets that he had allowed to the streets to steal most of his youth, always living on the edge and suspicious of everyone and everything. There was more to life than just surviving, there was living. Right now, he was merely existing, like a Social Security number was just being wasted.

As he rode through Queens, he just happened to catch a glimpse of Captain Simmons exiting his truck. He purposely drove through Lamont's block, half hoping that he would catch Sierra with the handsome captain. Rasheed laughed at out loud as he thought about the note and brick he threw through Lamont's windshield. No one ever suspected it was him, which made it even funnier. He was secretly envious of Lamont, who had a good job, position of power, and most of all, he had total control of Sierra's mind, body, and soul at one time. If he could, he would trade in his life for Lamont's any day. Then maybe he wouldn't have to deal with his subconscious telling him that he was unworthy of being with a woman like Sierra. Rasheed knew that he had connived his way into the Sierra's life, only to have it backfire. When he finally opened his eyes, he realized that he was more in love with her than she was with him. In the beginning, trying to capture Sierra's heart was a game to him. His plans were to get revenge on Tyke for the death of Peppy. He held Tyke fully responsible for the death of his uncle. Becoming somewhat obsessed with the revenge plot, Rasheed found out through the grapevine that Sierra was Tyke's former sweetheart. While he was still locked up in 5 North, he made it his business to get in Sierra's head, knowing that it would strike a chord with the now deceased Tyke when he found out. He shook his head as he thought about how he was going to use Sierra to bring Tyke to his deathbed. He hated to classify himself as just another grimy street nigga, but he was more than that. He was a master manipulator, but for some reason Sierra wouldn't allow him to get into her head, which frustrated him and turned him on at the same time. When Sean Daniels finally agreed to bring her to his party, that was the final chapter to the scheme. Now after all of his hard work and methodical planning, Rasheed was enamored with the beautiful CO Howell, making his life more complicated than he would ever have imagined it to be.

Chapter Fifty-one

SIERRA

Sierra walked out of the abortion clinic, happy with her choice. She was a little groggy so she turned her cell phone off for the day, not wanting to be bothered with a soul. Not even Rasheed.

She smiled as she thought about having babies. She wasn't sure that it would be in a better place with her as a mother because she was no stranger to confusion and dilemma. Sierra pulled into a parking space in front of her apartment building, walking very slowly. She looked around her, half expecting to see Rasheed pulled up somewhere and watching her. She knew that was only her guilty conscience talking to her. Why she felt guilty about it, she didn't know. She was grown and she didn't owe anyone any explanation. At least, she tried to convince herself that she didn't.

Finally able to climb into her bed to get some much-needed rest, she remembered to cut off her home phone. She needed a break from everyone. She realized that the honeymoon with Rasheed was about to be over, considering Tyke was out of the picture. She never expected to feel the way she felt about him. After all, he was a former inmate. Rasheed was a street dude and he was always thinking of ways to get over on someone. That was going to be one trait that wasn't going to be easy to get rid of; it was ingrained in him from a child. Sierra knew that she was no different. If Rasheed could get over on her, he would do it. Sierra wasn't going to let that happen.

Sierra listened to her voice mails. She hissed as she sat through Rasheed's drawn-out messages, with him talking about where was she and why wasn't she picking up the phone. The last message was from her mother, who she hadn't talked to in a couple of days. Sierra picked up her house phone and dialed her mother's number.

"Hi, Mommy," Sierra announced in a pleasant voice. "What you know good?"

"Hmmph. Apparently, not nothin' good enough dat my child don't call me as much as she used to! What is goin' on wit' you, chile?" Marjorie screamed into the phone.

Sierra rolled her eyes back in her head. "Mommy, I been real busy—"

"Girl, you up to no good. You forgot you Marjorie Howell's daughter. Shit, you ain't talkin' ta a perfect angel. What you been up to, Miss Sierra?"

Sierra swallowed. She decided to tell her mother about Tyquan's death so that the focus wouldn't be on her. "Anyway, Mommy, I got bad news. Tyke is dead."

There was silence on Marjorie's end of the phone. "Oh my goodness! What happened?"

"It's in yesterday's paper. You got da *Daily News*?"

"Yeah, I do but I didn't read it yesterday. Oh my . . . Where did they find him? What happened?"

Sierra sighed. "I don't know, Mommy. You know Tyke was in da streets, doin' all kinds of stuff and—"

"Oh shit!" Marjorie interrupted. "I'm lookin' at da article from yesterday. Wait, he was a suspect in da murder of Tamir Armstrong? Who is dat? You knew her?"

"Umm, no, Mommy. I didn't," Sierra lied. "I don't know who da female was and dat he was a suspect."

"Sierra, what kind o' people are you dealin' wit'? I always thought dat Tyke was a decent young man. He seemed respectful enough. You had him all up in my house, knowin' full well he was a gotdamn killer!"

"Ma, why you gettin' mad at me? I didn't know—"

"Sierra, you are my daughter. I know you better than anybody and you a slick one. You ain't called me as often as you used to 'cause you up ta somethin'. I just spoke ta Ann da other day and she was jus' tellin' me about Monique up in dat jail wit' some inmate and how dat department got dat girl jumpin' through fuckin' hurdles ta keep dat good-ass job! I sincerely hope dat you ain't in there doin' da same thing cause Lord knows I would whip ya ass myself, as grown as you are!"

"Ma, nobody ain't doin nothin'! Stop assumin' stuff and most of all, stop puttin' me in da same category wit' Monique!"

"No, I can't cause da chile is gettin' promoted to captain! You jus' runnin' aroun' wit' dis Tyquan maniac and Lamont Simmons, cryin' about how he had a baby on you! Whateva you doin', Miss Thing, it's gonna come to light! Because fuh some reason, I think you know more about dis Tyke thing than you lettin' on!"

Sierra frowned up her face at that statement. She wanted to hang up on her mother so bad, but wouldn't dare disrespect Marjorie like that. She couldn't argue with her mother because Marjorie knew her like a book.

"Mommy, I gotta go. I'm real tired and I gotta get some sleep."

Marjorie sucked her teeth. "Sierra, I'm not tryin' ta be hard on you but you need ta get ya self together. You spend a lot of ya time worryin' about some sorry negroes dat ain't doin' a damn thing fuh you but wastin' ya time. I know you probably got a new one right now 'cause you ain't been callin' ya mama.

You know how you do. Leave them men alone fuh a minute and focus on Sierra and take dat captain's test too. You can say all you want about Monique Phillips but dat girl came a long way. She take care of Monique's business first before she go out there and open her legs to Tom, Harry, and Dick, especially Dick!" Sierra laughed, breaking the ice between her and her mother. "Remember, baby, think about you first, okay?"

"Okay, Mommy, I will. And I will call you every day, every other day, I promise."

"Good. Now take ya behind ta sleep, girl. You sound horrible! You need somethin'?"

"Nah, I'm fine. 'Bye, Ma. I love you."

"I love you too, baby. 'Bye-'bye."

Chapter Fifty-two

LAMONT

The doorbell rang as Lamont was just getting out of the shower. He threw the towel on the floor of his bedroom and slid into some sweatpants and a T-shirt. As he ran to the door, he glanced at the clock on the wall of the foyer. He swung the door open and was greeted by Trey and Deja. Lamont smiled and removed his son from his mother's arms.

"Hey, Trey-Trey!" Lamont greeted enthusiastically. "Hi, man. I missed you!" Lamont immediately began showering the giggling baby with kisses while Deja looked on. She felt a twinge of jealousy as she saw how much love Lamont showed toward their son. She felt butterflies in her stomach.

"I know you said you had everything fuh him but I bought some of his things anyway," she said, without making eye contact with Lamont. "I have some extra bottles and Pampers, T-shirts, ya know, those types o' things."

Lamont looked at Deja. "Well, thanks, Deja. I appreciate it. Most of all, I appreciate Trey. Thank you."

Deja nodded her head. There was an awkward silence between them. Lamont spoke again.

"Deja, don't be a stranger. You can see Trey anytime you

want. Over here, dat is. I can't allow my son ta be aroun' ya boy."

Deja shed a tear. "I understand, Lamont. I'm scared ta get rid of Anwar. He might tell on me."

Lamont sighed. "Deja, I can't help you wit' dat. You chose ta get ya self involved wit' him now you gotta get ya self out of it. You a big girl and I can't tell you what ta do wit' ya life, not ta mention, I gotta protect my own shit 'cause I gotta child I have ta support."

"I feel you," Deja responded as she wiped her tears. "Uh, I love him, Lamont. I think he loves me but . . . anyway, enough about Anwar. Trey is in da right place. I'm still tryin' ta find myself, I ain't ready ta be a single mother."

Lamont hugged Deja. "You gonna be ah-ight. Jus' take care o' ya self. Trey'll be right here wit' his daddy."

Deja turned to walk to the door. She turned around to kiss Lamont square on the lips and kiss Trey as well.

"You a good man, Lamont, and an excellent father. I hope dat we can remain friends."

"Deja, we cool. You blessed me wit' a beautiful son, how could I be mad?" He watched as Deja walked down the driveway to her car. Lamont always thought that Deja was a gorgeous, independent woman who didn't need a man to hold her down. He guessed he was wrong.

Lamont put Trey down on the floor. He laughed as he watched Trey follow him all over the house, observing his father putting away his belongings in his new home. Lamont had specially painted his son's room a deep blue, getting rid of the original Mickey Mouse theme, replacing it with a sports theme. He went out and bought Trey a big-boy trundle bed along with the dresser, chest, desk, and chair. Toys were everywhere and Lamont was going to make sure that his boy had the best of everything. Monique's mother, Ann, who was retired, volunteered to babysit on the nights he had to work and Pops was to babysit on the nights he had a little company over the house, in case there was some "hanky-panky" involved. He had everything covered. He smiled as he watched Trey play with the toys and gawk at the bed. He knew that with or without Deja in his life, Trey was going to be just fine.

The bell rang again and Lamont grabbed Trey in his arms, not wanting to leave him alone for one minute. He looked out the peephole and was surprised to see Monique standing outside. Lamont quickly opened up the door and she walked right past him, snatching Trey out of his arms.

"Oh, my gosh, Lamont" she announced. "He looks jus' like you! Look at all of dis curly hair!"

Lamont gushed. "I know. He a fine young man, jus' like his daddy too!"

"Oh, puh-lease, man! You ah-ight. He a better version of you!"

"You wasn't sayin' dat when you—" Monique gave Lamont the look of death.

"My bad, we said we wasn't goin' ta bring up dat anymore."

"Yeah, I know. We both don't need ta remind each other of dat. It was da past."

Lamont cleared his throat as he watched Monique play with his son. "So, how's everything wit' da captain's class?"

Monique smiled. "Oh, Lamont, I'm doin' real good. I mean, da people in da academy are so nice. I made da right decision ta take dat test and of course, I appreciate all da support you been givin' me." Monique went in her bag and removed a gift box. Lamont was stuck. "Dis is fuh you, Lamont. You been a great friend and an even greater 'brother' these past months. I love you."

Lamont felt a lump in his throat. He opened the box and laughed as he pulled out a Gucci watch with an inscription on the back, *2 L, Luv Mo*. He was surprised.

"Aww, thanks, sweetheart!" Lamont exclaimed. He hugged Monique as Trey looked on. "It's beautiful but you didn't have to—"

Monique interrupted. “I know I didn’t. I’m just glad dat you and Pops are in my life now. I feel rejuvenated now. No more late-night creeps—shit, no more creeps in my life, period. I jus’ feel like a new woman.”

Lamont smiled. “I love you too, baby girl. I’m happy fuh you. Yo, you want somethin’ ta eat?”

“Nah, I’m good. I jus’ came over ta help you wit’ da baby fuh a lil’ while. I gotta go home and make sure Destiny finishes her homework. Speakin’ of Destiny, me and her been gettin’ along much better lately. No arguin’, no hassle. Plus, she’s been chillin’ with Pops fuh da last couple o’ days. He loves every minute of it!”

“I heard. You can tell Destiny ta bring her ass over her ta see her uncle too.”

“I will. She jus’ thinks you work all da time but now dat Trey is over here, she’ll really be over here wit’ no problem.”

Lamont and Monique talked as he prepared Trey for bed. When she finally was about to leave, they hugged again and Lamont, from his front door, watched her drive off. He closed the door and went into his son’s room, watching him while he was asleep.

Chapter Fifty-three

RASHEED

"I can't take dis shit!" Rasheed yelled while driving with Kemp and his other uncles, Nayshawn and Shaka. They were trying to convince Rasheed to go to Atlanta with his brother for a while until everything died down. The cops had called Rasheed in for questioning about Tyke's "suicide."

"I can't leave town now, man!" Rasheed screamed at his uncle Shaka. "Da police'll be all over me fuh some shit I didn't do. I ain't tryin' ta go back ta jail fuh dat dead nigga, Tyke!"

"Rah, da cops just asked you a few questions. You don't know shit. They just called you in 'cause they heard through da grapevine dat Tamir was ya girl. Dat's da hood talkin'. Dat's why you gotta go," Shaka replied. Shaka scratched his full beard, like he always did when he was aggravated. At that moment, his nephew was aggravating him!

"You know what, Rah and I ain't afraid ta say it. Ya hard-headed and ya stubborn!" Nayshawn shouted from the back-seat of Kemp's truck. "You rather sit here in New York where you ain't doin' shit but worryin' ya nana wit' all ya bullshit and problems instead of goin' ta ATL wit' Karim. What is ya fuckin' problem?"

"Oh, he in love," Kemp stated matter-of-factly. "Yeah, he in love with a CO chick."

"Whuuut?" Shaka yelled. "You still in New York over some broad? Are you stupid?"

"A CO? Man, you crazy! Dat chick is gonna drop ya ass like a bad habit. She ain't fuckin' wit' you like dat. You a piece o' dick ta her and dat's it. I had a few and them bitches is jus' as bad as a man. They'll fuck and suck you dry, then leave ya ass. You jus' a experiment ta them," Nayshawn laughed.

Rasheed looked at Kemp, who shrugged his shoulders. "Yo, she different, man. She not like dat."

The brothers laughed at Rasheed. They had all been with correction-officer women before and it was the same thing—sex, sex, and more sex. They couldn't believe that Rasheed thought it would be any different for him. Few women would risk their jobs to have a "relationship" with a former inmate unless they just didn't give a shit, but it was hard to not give a shit, about $70,000 plus a year.

"Nah, but fuh real, Rah, move on, man. Dis female dat got ya balls in her mouth is not givin' a fuck about you right now. She ain't tryin' ta risk her job fuh a nigga dat ain't got shit. I mean, ya lil' chips ain't gonna suffice her yearly income, nigga. So you better start makin' some serious decisions!" Shaka said.

Rasheed stared out the window while his uncles clowned him for the rest of the ride. He knew that they were right but he didn't want to believe that Sierra thought of him as an experiment or a piece of dick. What started out as a game turned into a crush and ended up with him having intense feelings for Sierra. He had been trying to get in touch with her for the last day or so and she wasn't answering his phone calls. He was getting tired of her playing him for a sucker and now that his uncles were getting in his ass about it, he was really pissed.

Rasheed called Sierra's phone again while standing outside Kemp's truck, waiting for his uncles to take care of their business. She finally decided to pick up.

"Hey, Sierra, you forgot about me or somethin'?" he asked.

"What's up, Rah?" Sierra replied. "What's good?"

Rasheed cringed. He looked at the phone. "Yo, you ah-ight? I ain't heard from you. You got somethin' on ya mind?"

Sierra sighed. "No, Rah, I'm okay. Why? 'Cause I ain't talk ta you? I'm okay."

Rasheed couldn't take Sierra's nonchalant attitude anymore. "Yo, ma, check dis out, it's over. I ain't tryin' ta be ya fuckin' experiment no more so I'm gonna fall back!"

"My experiment? Where dat come from? What are you talkin' about?"

"Don't call me no fuckin' more and I ain't callin you. I ain't shit ta you and you ain't shit ta me."

"What? Who da fuck you think you talkin' to?" she yelled.

"You! You can have ya job and ya life back too. Trust me, I never wanted to cause any problems in ya life. I know it's a big headache dealin' wit' me and I'm about ta solve it. Don't worry about me no more."

Rasheed listened as she sniffled in the background. "You do what you wanna do. I ain't gonna beg you ta be wit' me, Rasheed. I have feelings fuh you but if you wanna go 'head, then you gotta do what you gotta do."

As Rasheed continued to converse with Sierra on his cell phone, he didn't notice the stocky dark-skinned man walk by him and do a double take. Lenox Avenue in Harlem was bustling with people in the middle of the afternoon and Rasheed was too preoccupied to notice. The man hurriedly rushed to retrieve a gun that belonged to him that was stashed inside of a hole in an abandoned tenement building. That was his throwaway in case he needed to bust a cap in someone's ass within that vicinity, which was just what he was going to do now. He watched as Rasheed got real animated with the phone conversation. He pulled his Yankee fitted down over his eyes and slowly walked by Rasheed to get a good shot. Suddenly, *bam!* The man shot Rasheed one time and managed to get away as people screamed and pointed to him running down the block. Rasheed fell to the ground holding his chest, with Sierra screaming on his phone. His uncles ran outside and immediately began to yell and scream at passersby to call the police and ambulance. Someone managed to do just that and almost like clockwork the paramedics and a few police cruisers arrived on the scene. Some patrol cops moved the crowd, making sure they were under control. The paramedics attempted to put Rasheed on the stretcher and his uncles hopped in the truck to follow the ambulance to the nearest emergency room.

Kemp paced around the waiting room, while Nayshawn and Shaka were slumped in the chairs, exhausted from all the excitement. They were waiting on the diagnosis from the doctor and were nervous as hell. Kemp kept blaming himself for bringing Rasheed to Harlem.

"Damn, if it wasn't fuh me, Rah wouldn'ta been shot, man!" Kemp cried. His brothers got up to comfort him. "Dat's my nigga. He can't die, man!"

"It ain't ya fault, Kemp. Dat coulda happened anywhere. Just be glad we was there. He coulda been somewhere by himself and bled to death!" Shaka replied.

Kemp wiped his tears. "First, Tyke, now dis. Man, Rah jus' need ta go to Atlanta. All da signs is pointing in dat direction, man."

Nayshawn sat back down. "Rah is here on da strength of dat CO bitch, man. Where she at, anyway? I wanna see her!"

Kemp looked at Nayshawn. "Don't blame her, Nay. Rah care about dat girl but she ain't keepin' him here. Trust me, I know her."

The doctor came out to the waiting room and they all stood up. He had a smile on his face.

"Well, gentlemen," the doctor began. "Rasheed is going to be just fine. He suffered a small wound to the right shoulder and we removed some fragments. There was a lot of bleeding but it wasn't anything life-threatening. He is in stable condition and he needs to spend a day here with us so that he can rest and change his bandages. Also, we need to make sure that he doesn't get any infections so we can send him home to his family. Are you related to this young man?"

Shaka spoke. "We're his uncles," he responded.

"Okay, he's in good hands, then. Rasheed was very lucky because the bullet missed his chest by a few inches. There is no telling how this would have turned out." There was a slight pause. "Well, your nephew will be ready to see you in a minute. The nurse is just making him comfortable because he just came out of the operating room. She'll come out and let you know when it's time for you to go in his room. Good luck, guys!" The brothers thanked the doctor and sat back down in the waiting room. Everyone breathed a sigh of relief. All of a sudden, two detectives walked in the waiting room.

"Good afternoon, men," the pudgy detective with a comb-over greeted them. "I'm Detective Flanory and this is my partner, Detective Hilliard. We just needed to give you some information on the shooter and we have to ask your brother some questions."

"He don't know nothin'!" Kemp volunteered. Detective Flanory looked at Kemp and smirked.

"Mr.—umm, what's ya name, son?" Flanory asked.

"Kemper. Kemper Gordon."

"Actually, no one's on trial here. I have information about the shooter and all the things I need to arrest him right here. I just needed confirmation from your—umm, brother?"

"No," Shaka responded. "Our nephew."

"Okay, ya nephew. Anyways, the guy that shot your nephew's name is Shamel Abrams. Does dat name ring a bell?"

"Hell, no!" Nayshawn said. "We don't know dat clown!"

Flanory twitched. He needed a cigarette break. "Well, he knows ya brotha. Apparently, they were locked up together on Rikers Island in the same housing area. Mr. Shamel has a long gash on his face, apparently receiving it while on Rikers. It was because of some jail beef he had with some inmates."

"What dat got ta do with my nephew?"

"Well, the streets say dat ya nephew set him up. Da guy was snitchin' so he got a stitchin'. But the day that he was attacked, Rasheed was on his way home from Rikers. There's no evidence that he even had any part in that whole fiasco."

"Well, they ain't catch dat nigga yet?" Kemp asked.

Flanory didn't flinch at the usage of the word *nigga*. He heard it from black men every day and still couldn't understand why they used it so freely, especially around white people.

"No, they didn't, but we have an all-points bulletin on his ass. This guy is a real creep and he's going to jail when I catch him for attempted murder in the first degree." Flanory looked at his partner and then looked at Rasheed's uncles. He knew that they had been in the streets and back. He needed to convince them that Shamel was going to be in jail within that week before they tried to get to him first. "Shamel, aka Scooter, is going to the pokey. So just warning you fellas, don't try to play vigilante with this. Just let the department handle everything and send this asshole to jail, okay?"

They all nodded their heads. At that moment, a young nurse walked out to the waiting room to give them the okay to see Rasheed. They all walked in and Rasheed's upper body was bandaged. He seemed coherent, even though his shoulder looked like it hurt like hell. He was happy to see his uncles and he was twice as happy to be alive.

"Hey," Rasheed managed to whisper to his uncles. "Dis shit hurt!"

"Don't try ta talk, son. Just relax," Kemp instructed. He leaned over and pointed to the door. "Look, there some DT's outside. They wanna talk ta you. Go 'head and talk but you know how we do. Don't give them mothafuckas nothin' to run wit'!"

Rasheed nodded his head. "Ah-ight. Y'all ain't leavin' me in here wit' them cats, right?"

"Hell, no, nephew!" Kemp announced in a loud whisper. "We gonna be right here."

Shaka let the detectives in to ask Rasheed a few questions. He ordered them to make it quick so that Rasheed could rest.

"Good evening, Mr. Gordon. I'm Detective Flanory and this is my partner, Detective Hilliard. We just want to ask you a few questions but before we do that, we just want you to know you are not in any trouble. We don't have to read you any rights, we just needed some information. Is that okay with you?" Rasheed said yes. "Okay. First of all, we have information on the shooter that was obtained by a few witnesses that were at the scene. Apparently, he is a resident of this area and he was obviously not very popular with the locals. They were more than happy to give him up. Now it's just a matter of catching this idiot. According to my brief investigation, you and Mr. Shamel Abrams were locked up together on Rikers Island for a short period. Is that correct?"

Rasheed nodded with a frown on his face. *Oh, so dat's da mothafucka dat shot me*! he thought to himself.

"Okay." Detective Flanory looked at Hilliard, who was scribbling on a notepad. "I checked his history and it stated that Mr. Abrams was assaulted and slashed in his face, receiving a hundred and forty-eight stitches for it. After the incident, he implicated you and two other inmates by stating that you were the mastermind behind the slashing. I went further to check your records and I see that you were actually released on the day he was assaulted. I'm not saying that you are or are not responsible for Mr. Abrams's incident, but being that you were released the day of, this clears you of any wrongdoing or further implications in this matter. Do you understand that, Mr. Gordon?" Rasheed nodded. "Anyway, I wanted to ask if you had any other affiliation with Mr. Abrams besides Rikers?"

"Nah," Rasheed whispered.

Detective Flanory smiled. "Good. Mr. Gordon, we're here to help you. I know that you spent a little time behind bars but my job is to try to keep guys like you on the street. I told you or uncles to leave this matter to the police department because Mr. Abrams is not worth you guys going to prison for. If I find out that you guys are fucking with this simpleton, understand that I will lock your asses up as well. And remember, it's not personal, it's business." He pulled out a card with his name and number on it and handed it to Kemp. "Call me if you need to know anything. You guys are law-abiding citizens now, right?" They all nodded their heads. "Good. I'll be in touch." The two detectives walked out the hospital room almost as fast as they came in.

"Dat nigga is gonna die!" Kemp said. "We need ta be on the phones now. I don't want nephew goin' ta court and testifyin' against dis nigga like he some snitch!"

Shaka rubbed his wavy head. "Man, we can't touch dat cat! You heard what dat cop said. We might as well just walk in da nearest precinct with the loaded fuckin' gun. Look, after you get outta here, Rah, you on da next thing smokin'! You goin' to Atlanta wit' Karim. What we gonna do is make some phone calls and convince dat bird-ass nigga to turn himself in and take a fuckin' plea bargain. Dat way, it's no trial, no testifyin'!"

Kemp sighed. "Damn, nephew, you outta here. I'm gonna miss you but you gotta go."

Rasheed pulled Kemp to him while Shaka and Nayshawn were engrossed in their conversation. "Call Sierra and tell her I'm ah-ight."

Chapter Fifty-four

SIERRA

Sierra sat in her house, screaming hysterically. She heard what sounded like gunshots and Rasheed's phone went dead. She attempted to call his number back several times but to no avail. She didn't have his uncle Kemp's number so that had her even more stressed-out. She sat in her bed, rocking back and forth, not able to think of a single soul to call about the situation. Sierra looked at the phone but no call came and she fell asleep.

It was 9:36 PM. Sierra had taken some aspirin for a headache and was tired as hell. Her cell phone must have rung numerous times before she heard it.

"Hello?" she answered in a barely audible whisper.

"Sierra. It's me, Kemp." She sat up immediately.

"Oh my God!" she shouted. "Kemp, is Rasheed all right? What happened? I hope he—"

"Calm down, sweetheart. Rah is fine. He got shot in da shoulder. He gonna be out in a day or two. I know you was on da phone wit' him when it happened and he wanted me ta call you back. Ta let you know he was fine."

Sierra was grateful for the phone call. "Thank you, Kemp. Thank you so much. I was worried about him." Sierra began to cry. "I really love Rah, Kemp. You know dat!"

Kemp sighed. "I know, baby, I know. You been through a lot these past months with Rah. But I'm here ta tell you, Si, ta move on. Leave my nephew alone."

Sierra was silent. "But, why, what happened?"

"You gotta think about you, baby girl. You got a good—ass job, don't ruin your career fuh no nigga out here, even my nephew. Love him ta death but he got too much drama. You don't need ta get ya self involved wit' him. Rah got a lotta shit goin' on dat I don't even know about!"

"You right, Kemp. I'ma leave him alone."

"Yeah, find you a nice correction officer, get married, and have a couple o' kids. You a beautiful young lady and dis ain't your cup o' tea. I mean, look at Tyke. Dat nigga ended up dead. Do you need dat stress?" Sierra shook her head. "Anyway, ma, Rah is goin' straight to ATL to live wit' his brother, Karim. My suggestion ta you is ta move on wit' ya life. Dis chapter is officially closed. Okay?"

Sierra continued to cry. "Okay, Kemp. Tell Rasheed I said good-bye."

"I sure will and Sierra, take care o' ya self." The phone went dead. Sierra fell back on her bed and bawled like a baby.

Sierra sat on her post in a daze the next morning. All she did was replay the conversation between her and Kemp over and over in her mind. She knew that there was nothing that she could do but fall back from Rasheed and do exactly what Kemp said to do and that was to get on with her life. She ran back all the events that had occurred and figured that Rasheed's shooting was a sign from God himself.

As she wrote in her logbook, she noticed an inmate staring at her while he was on the phone. Sierra glanced at him, noticing that he was strikingly handsome. He smiled at her and she returned it with a scowl on her face. He frowned and turned his back to her, as he continued to talk on the phone. She was sick of being in 5 North around inmates. She had to find herself another post to work with no inmate contact.

It was months later and the spring air made the trees rustle in the backyard. Sierra was laughing as she opened the presents. She was happy to have her family and close friends there with her for the joyous occasion. They were there to celebrate the birth of her first child and the gifts were in abundance. Marjorie flashed pictures of Sierra from every angle, stating that she was the most beautiful pregnant woman she had seen in her life.

"Aww, Mommy, you jus' sayin' dat 'cause I'm your daughter!" Sierra exclaimed with a bashful smile on her face.

"Girl, you are gorgeous! Claim it now 'cause dat baby gonna drive you crazy!" Marjorie replied. Everyone at the shower laughed hysterically. "Shoot, you ain't gonna be lookin' dis good in a couple o' years after dealin' wit' dat lil' rug rat!"

"I know dat's right!" Miss Ann, Monique's mother agreed. "Tell 'er, Marjorie!"

Sierra gushed as she opened a present from Monique. It was a beautiful basket with assorted designer baby clothing inside of it.

"Thanks, Mo!" she yelled. Monique came over and kissed her on the cheek. "I love it, girl!"

They continued to *ooh* and *aah* at every gift that was displayed. Sierra had received lots of love from her female friends and family. After the presents were out of the way, the backyard was opened to the guys, who were waiting in the house until the "girlie" stuff was over with. They all filed outside as the DJ played the latest hits. Sierra smiled as her fiancé walked her direction and swept her off of her feet.

"Hi, baby. You look so pretty!" he complimented her as he kissed her anxious lips.

"And you ain't lookin' so bad ya self wit' ya fine ass!" Sierra replied. She ran her hands through his hair.

"Wait until everybody leave. I'ma tear dat ass up!"

"Jus' don't hurt da baby, 'kay?"

"I promise."

"C'mon, Lamont, Sierra, y'all save dat shit fuh anotha time! Dat's how you got pregnant!" yelled Monique. "Let's partyyyy!" Lamont and Sierra laughed and rejoined the party.

While everyone partied, Sierra had no idea that Rasheed was in town. He was lurking in the dark, across the street from the house. A couple of months had passed and it would be bittersweet seeing him once again, even though she knew it was over. Little did she know Rasheed had watched her and her new family for a couple of days, as she walked in and out of the house with Trey and her big pregnant belly. The life that he chose to live eventually kept her from being with the man she fell in love with. Sierra was stunned when she saw Rasheed in the driver's seat of the Range Rover parked in front of the house. Rasheed spotted Sierra heading toward his truck but he didn't have enough time to hide. Sierra stared at the reformed thug with her beautiful brown eyes in disbelief, with her wondering how he even found her. The world stopped for that moment as she looked at him with more surprise than fear. They both searched for the words but they were never found and they remained speechless for a few moments. Rasheed seemed as if he was hesitant to exit his vehicle. She looked around and was relieved to see that no one was paying them any attention. They were still in the back, partying. He grabbed her and she immediately began to squirm.

"What are you doin', Sierra? How could you do dis ta us?" he said through clenched teeth.

Sierra frowned. "Rasheed, dis is not da time or place. You left, remember? Ya people tol' me ta leave you alone! So I did. I thought dat was what you wanted!"

Rasheed kicked the tire of his truck. "They tol' you what? They tol' me dat you said it was over, dat you never wanted ta see me again!" Rasheed rubbed his chin, while deep in thought. "Those muthafuckas!"

Sierra looked around nervously. Everyone was still in the backyard, partying. "Rah, I still love you but everything got twisted. I didn't wanna leave you. I was ready ta make an official commitment ta you. After the shootin', I just knew dat you was dead. I woulda lost my mind if anything happened ta you."

Rasheed touched Sierra's belly. "You're pregnant by dis Captain Simmons dude? Why? Why you go back ta him?"

She shrugged her shoulders. "I dunno. He was there fuh me when you left. It just kinda, ya know, happened." She looked over her shoulders again.

"Do you love him? Can you tell me dat you don't love me?" Rasheed asked with a longing in his eyes.

Sierra held her head down. "Rah, I can't . . . I love Lamont. But—"

He cut her off. "But what? If you love him, you love him. I mean, damn, you havin' his baby and all—"

"Rasheed, it's not Lamont's baby, okay? He know dat it's not his baby."

Rasheed looked at the petite Sierra with a sideways glance. "What da fuck you mean, he know dat it ain't his baby? What kind o' bullshit is dat? I left and you runnin' around layin' up wit' niggas and gettin' pregnant now?!"

Sierra swallowed. The day she went to have the abortion she realized she couldn't do it and left the clinic. She was afraid because she was unsure of who the father of her baby was. It could be Tyke's or Rasheed's—she just didn't know. The day that she was going to tell Rasheed about the pregnancy was the day he was shot, then to add insult to injury, his uncles intervened and suggested that she move on with her life. This made Sierra want to shield her unborn child, recognizing how important it was to have her child grow up in a positive family setting, something that Rasheed or Tyke—now that he was deceased—obviously could not provide. Money wasn't a contributing factor, knowing that her baby would be well taken care of if Rasheed had anything to do with it. After Tyke and Tamir's death, she felt that she needed to be with someone constructive. Lamont was the perfect candidate. They made an agreement with each other that he was going to raise Sierra's baby as his own and she was fine with that.

"Look," Sierra stopped Rasheed from ranting. "You chose ta move ta Atlanta without even a phone call to me to say goodbye. I jus' came ta da conclusion dat what we had was one big lie."

"A big lie? Sierra, you got another man actin' like dat baby you carryin' is his and you wanna talk about a big lie?" In the back of Rasheed's mind, he had a gut feeling that the baby Sierra was carrying just might be his. "Well, I want a damn blood test! I think dat's my baby!" *Why is she punishin' me?* he thought to himself.

Sierra gritted her teeth. "Rasheed, I don't wanna talk about dis shit right now!"

Suddenly, Sierra grabbed her belly and felt something warm running down her leg. She grabbed Rasheed's arm as the pain became increasingly worse.

"Oh my God, Rah," she said in a barely audible voice. "My water broke! Get outta here, I can't let nobody see me talkin' ta you!"

Rasheed held Sierra tightly, not wanting to let go. When he looked up, he saw Lamont walking from the backyard. Lamont stopped in his tracks when he saw Rasheed holding Sierra. He looked like he had seen a ghost.

"Who are you?" Lamont asked, before realizing Sierra was going into labor.

Rasheed sucked his teeth. "Man, don't worry about me. Worry about ya girl here! Her water broke!"

Lamont carefully held Sierra and helped her to his truck, while he ran inside the house to gather her suitcase.

Rasheed reluctantly climbed back into the Range Rover. Sierra sat in the truck, watching the man who she truly loved and whose baby she was carrying pull off into the night. Once she saw his rear lights fade off into the distance, she screamed as loud as she could for Lamont.

"*Lamont!*" Sierra yelled at the top of her lungs. "*I'm having da baby!*"

As several cars followed Lamont's truck with Sierra in tow to Mary Immaculate Hospital, Rasheed sat on the corner of the block in his parked truck, a sly smirk on his face. All of a sudden, he had an idea. He was going to make sure he was present for the birth of what could possibly be his firstborn child. For some strange reason, he had a gut feeling that the baby Sierra was carrying was his seed. He was going to demand a DNA test from Sierra. If he was the father, they would be one big happy family and Lamont would be a done deal. As he discreetly followed the small procession of cars to the hospital, he realized that he didn't want to miss that day for nothing in the world.

Sierra was helped into the wheelchair by a waiting attendant. She was immediately taken to a triage, where her doctor was waiting to see how many centimeters she was. Howling in pain, she looked out the corner of her eye and standing outside the room was Rasheed! She couldn't believe that he had the audacity to come to the hospital. What was wrong with him?

She pulled Lamont close to her. "Lamont," she whispered. "I know you ain't tryin' ta hear dis right now but da guy standin' outside is Rasheed."

Lamont glanced in Rasheed's direction and sighed. "So what you wanna do, Si? Do you wanna go through wit' dis DNA test or what? He ain't gonna stop botherin' us!"

Sierra shook her head as a tear dropped. "Lemme jus' talk to him, Lamont, please."

Lamont left the triage room and motioned for Rasheed to go inside. Sierra was in pain but it was now or never. She needed to let Rasheed go. Rasheed grabbed her hand as she winced from the pain of the contractions.

"Rah, you can't do dis. You can't come back and disrupt my life like dis!" she stated. "Dat's bein' selfish!"

"Sierra, I don't give a fuck about bein' selfish! I know dis is my baby! Why are you doin' dis to me? To us, man, c'mon!" he pleaded.

She felt another contraction coming. They were becoming more frequent. She was nervous as hell as she squeezed Rasheed hand. "I'm engaged ta be married, Rasheed. I wanna provide my baby's life wit' stability and consistency. I love you, I do, but dat doesn't mean dat you are da man fuh me. In another life, another time, we probably would have been good together but I can't do it wit' you. Da aggravation really isn't worth it." She squeezed his hand again.

Rasheed held his head down. "All I wanna know is the baby mine, Sierra. If it is, please, let me be a part of their life, please."

Sierra was hesitant. She was just beginning to get her life on track, thinking that she would never see Rasheed again. Everything between her and Lamont were going good and it looked as if she was going to finally have a comfortable existence. Sierra took the separation of her and Rasheed as a sign. But if the test came back positive, he still wasn't going to go away. He would be coming for her next and she didn't want that to happen. It was a lose-lose situation. She didn't know what to do.

EPILOGUE

Lamont was not too pleased with Rasheed's reappearance but he made a commitment to Sierra to be supportive of whatever she wanted to do.

"Why is dis nigga showin' his face now?" Lamont exclaimed. "Did you ever tell him about da pregnancy?"

Sierra sighed. "I didn't get a chance to, remember? His uncle called me and tol' me ta move on, ta leave Rah alone. I can't get mad at him fuh doin' dat and ta be perfectly honest, they did me a favor. I took his departure as a good thing 'cause I was unsure of who da father was. It was between him or Tyquan."

Lamont looked at Sierra and shook his head. "Damn, you scandalous! I thought I was off da chain wit' da drama!"

Sierra kissed Lamont's soft lips. "Well, dat's why I love you 'cause you ain't judgin' a sister. I needed a loyal brother like you in my life."

Lamont wrapped the petite Sierra in his arms and gave her an intimate kiss. "I love you, da future Mrs. Simmons."

"I love you too, Captain Simmons." The baby began to cry. "Today is da blood-test results. You do know dat, right?"

Lamont paused. "Si, if dis dude is da father, I'm gonna step back and let him do his fatherly duties. But I'm Daddy. I'm gonna treat Messiah like he's my own son. We a family over here and you better let dat nigga know dat, you hear me?"

Sierra shook her head. She watched as Lamont left their bedroom to check on Messiah while she finished getting dressed. Trey ran in the room and gave her a big hug. He was too young to know that the hug was what she really needed at that moment.

As Sierra waited for the test results to come back, she was a nervous wreck as her newborn son, Messiah Amir Howell, fidgeted in her arms. Rasheed sat across the waiting room, staring at her and the baby, making her feel quite uncomfortable. She had a dry mouth and her postpartum was kicking in but she knew that she needed to know the answer as well. She was actually embarrassed sitting there in that clinic. She couldn't believe that she was actually waiting for the results of a fucking paternity test. It hit her that the father of her child could possibly be Rasheed Gordon, a former inmate in her housing area with whom she had a clandestine affair with and who she still had feelings for. How could she have played herself like that? Rasheed got up and walked over to sit next to her.

"Si, I know you nervous but I need to know. I can't go back to Atlanta knowin' dat I have a seed out here. Especially a child wit' you. I don't understand why we can't be together ta raise our child."

Sierra cringed. "Rasheed, could we just see what da test results say before you start talkin' about our child!" she announced.

Rasheed looked at her. "I know what it is. You are tryin' ta erase me from your memory! You wanna forget dat you met me in Five North, fell in love wit' me and now you might be havin' my baby." Rasheed came so close to Sierra, she felt his breath across her neck.

"Listen, baby girl, if dat baby is mine, I ain't goin' nowhere. I'm gonna be in ya life forever and you are goin' ta fall in love wit' me all over again. I'm gonna do it right this time, so don't sleep, ya hear me?"

The lab technician finally called the twosome into an office for some privacy. They looked at each other as the lab tech handed them both the results. Sierra closed her eyes as she stared at the paper because it was something she had not hoped for. Rasheed Gordon was the father of her baby.

"Could I hold my baby, please?" he asked, as Sierra obliged. Rasheed looked at Messiah's toes and fingers. He kissed his face tenderly as he watched him sleep. He looked at his ears and felt the texture of his hair. Sierra watched Rasheed closely as she started to see the roughneck persona slowly fade away. Rasheed kissed Messiah and began talking to him, almost forgetting that Sierra was in the room.

"Daddy loves you. I'm gonna make sure you grow up ta be a better man than I could ever be. No jail, no guns, no drugs fuh you. I'm gonna make sure you make Mommy real proud, lil' man. And ya nana and ya grandma, Lavon, who's in heaven wit' da angels. But I can only do dis if ya mommy lets me." Rasheed looked at Sierra. "Si, I know you have ya reservations about me but can I be a part of his life? Look at him, he's beautiful. And most of all, he's my son. My firstborn child. What do you say?"

Sierra agreed, with tears in her eyes, to let Rasheed be in his son's life. It finally hit her that her son was fathered by a man who was not only a former inmate that she guarded, but a man who she realized she was still in love with.